OTHER TITLES IN THE LEONAUR
COLLECTED SCIENCE FICTION & FANTASY OF
STANLEY G. WEINBAUM SERIES

THE COLLECTED SCIENCE FICTION & FANTASY
OF STANLEY G. WEINBAUM: VOLUME 3

Strange
Genius

Classic Tales of the Human Mind at Work
Including – *The New Adam*, the Complete
"van Manderpootz" Stories and Others

Stanley G. Weinbaum

LEONAUR

Strange Genius: Classic Tales of the Human Mind at Work Including - The New Adam, the Complete "van Manderpootz" Stories and Others

by Stanley G. Weinbaum

FIRST EDITION

Published by Leonaur Ltd

Material original to this edition and this editorial selection
copyright © 2006 Leonaur Ltd

ISBN (10 digit): 1-84677-055-6 (hardcover)
ISBN (13 digit): 978-1-84677-055-5 (hardcover)

ISBN (10 digit): 1-84677-048-3 (softcover)
ISBN (13 digit): 978-1-84677-048-7 (softcover)

http://www.leonaur.com

Publisher's Notes

Contents

The New Adam

Prologue

This is a story of a superman. It details his origin, his search for happiness, his loves, and, finally, his success or failure, of which you alone can judge. It is a story perhaps fantastic, but a story based, nevertheless, on possibilities.

A superman is not a man, not a creature of the species Homo Sapiens; this is the fallacy of Nietzsche, the fallacy of H. G. Wells. These, like others who deal with the matter, have believed that a man, a human being, raised to the nth degree, represents the superman. Nietzsche picked one set of qualities —those of fitness, potency, power—Wells chose another set, the contemplative, the serene, the intellectual. So probably, a Neanderthaler in his filthy cave, using his embryonic imagination, might have pictured his superman as a giant in strength and size, a mighty hunter, one whose meat-pot and belly is never empty. Certainly he never considered a race whose very thoughts were partly beyond his conception, and he saw nothing ironical in freezing to death upon a ledge of coal. As we are to the cave man, superman must be to us. His coming is surely a possibility; perhaps it is inevitable.

For not everything in the world is subject to mathematics. Not every factor in this particular sector of the cosmic whirl can be reduced to formula, expressed in calculus, integrated, packed into nicely labeled bundles, and filed away in a book. Because one rises from the dinner table and announces his intention to go across the hall to the library, it does not inevitably follow that he will arrive there. There is a chance factor in the universe—entropy, luck, free will, or what you wish—but an x-factor that prohibits exact calculation. Nothing is ever quite certain, and behind every cause lies another more obscure. A housewife puts a kettle of water on the fire to boil; it will almost certainly boil, but there is a chance, a very slight one, that it will freeze. For even the transfer of heat is a random process, and the water may dissipate its warmth to the fire.

Mendel packed heredity in a neat mathematical box; Freud and Jung labeled and filed environment. Yet variations creep in. Sometimes an offspring possesses qualities which neither parent could possibly have transmitted; biologists call these beings "sports"; evolutionists speak of "mutations." These odd individuals are common enough in the plant kingdom and the insect world; their discovery creates not a ripple of scientific excitement, and day by day the curious natural experiments are born and work out their destinies. Sometimes, if the variants possess inherent advantages, they survive and breed true as a new species, sometimes they breed back into the mass and are lost, and sometimes they die. A commonplace of Nature among plants and insects; it is seldom that a scientist thinks of the phenomenon in terms of humanity.

Introduction

1. Dawn on Olympus

Anna Hall died as stolidly as she had lived, died unimaginatively in childbirth; and was perhaps spared some maternal pangs, for her strange son lived. Nor did grim middle-aged John Hall waste his emotional strength in either futile regrets or useless recriminations of the child. This business of living was a stern, pitiless affair; one took what befell and did not argue. He accepted the infant, and named it after his own father, old Edmond.

It must have been a rare accident of genes and determinants that produced Edmond Hall—a spindly infant, straight-legged from birth, with oddly light eyes. Yet his strangest abnormality, one that set brisk Doctor Lindquist muttering, was his hands, his tiny slim fingers, for each of these possessed an extra joint. He clenched his three-knuckled thumb against his four-knuckled fingers into a curious little fist, and stared tearlessly with yellowish gray gaze.

"She would not have a hospital," Doctor Lindquist was muttering. "This is what comes of home births." One doubted that he meant only Anna's demise; his eyes were on her son.

John Hall said nothing; there was little, indeed, that he could say. Without cavil and in grim acceptance of little Edmond, he did what was to be done; he arranged for a nurse to care for the child, and returned somberly to his law practice. John was a good lawyer, industrious, methodical, earnest, and successful.

Certainly he missed Anna. He had liked to talk to her of an evening; not that she contributed much to the conversation, but she was a quiet and attentive audience. The vocal formulating sometimes served to clarify his thoughts. There was a loneliness, too, in his solitary evenings; the baby slept or lay quiet in an upstairs room, and Magda in the kitchen made only a distant clatter. He smoked and read. For many weeks he threaded the idealistic maze of Berkeley, and turned as counter-irritant to Hume.

After a while he took to addressing the child. It was as quiet and possibly as understanding as Anna. Queer little brat! Tearless, almost voiceless, with eyes beginning to show peculiarly amber. It gurgled occasionally; he never heard it cry. So he talked to it by evenings, sending the nurse away glad enough for the moments of liberty. She was puzzled by the little whelp; abnormal hands, abnormal mind, she thought; probably imbecilic. Nevertheless, she was kind enough, in a competent, professional manner. The child began to recognize her presence; she was his refuge and source of comfort. Perhaps this thin, dark, nervous maternal substitute influenced the infant more than he was ever to realize.

John was startled when the child's eyes began to focus. He swung his watch before it; the pale eyes followed the movement with an intensity of gaze more kitten-like than human. A wide, unwinking stare. Sometimes they looked straight into John's own eyes; the little being's gaze was so curiously intent that he was a trifle startled.

Time passed quietly, uneventfully. Now little Edmond was observing his immediate world with a half purposeful expression; now he was grasping at objects with his odd hands. They were agile little hands, unusually apt at seizing what was within their reach. The fingers closed like small tentacles about John's swinging watch, and tugged it, strangely and precociously, not toward the thin-lipped mouth, but before the eyes for examination.

And time dragged on. John gave up his office in the Loop, moving it to his home on Kenmore. He installed a desk in the living room, and a wall telephone; just as good as being downtown, he thought, and it saved the street car ride. He had the house wired for electric light; everybody was abandoning the hot gas-burners. His practice was well-established, and clients quickly learned of his new business quarters. And at this time a new company was being formed to manufacture gasoline automobiles; he bought a few shares as a speculation, believing the devices due for a wave of popularity. And the "L" nosed northward block by block. This was Chicago of the first decade, sprawling in its mud and glitter. No seer nor sorcerer whispered that the young city had spawned an egg whose maturity was as yet inconceivable.

The child Edmond was speaking a few words now. "Light," he said, when the yellow carbon-filament flashed on. He toddled around the office, learned the sound of the telephone bell. His nurse dressed him in little shirted suits that went unhar-moniously with his pinched and precocious features; he looked like a waxen elf or a changeling. Yet, from a parental standpoint he was a model child; mischief seemed absent from his make-up. He was strangely content to be alone, and happily played meaningless games with himself. John still talked to him at evening. He listened owlishly solemn, and seldom questioned, and seasons came and vanished. Nothing ever disturbed his poise. John's equally grim and never friendly brother Edward (also named for that old father of both) came once or twice to call in the early years.

"The brat's lonesome," he stated baldly. "You'll bring him up queer unless you get him some friends."

The four-year-old Edmond answered for himself in a piping voice: "I'm not lonesome."

"Eh? Who do you play with?"

"I play with myself. I talk with myself. I don't need any friend."

His uncle laughed. "Queer, John, like I told you."

Queer or not, the imp developed. At six he was a silent slender child with curious amber eyes and nondescript brown hair, and a habit of spending many hours alone at the window. He betrayed none of the father-worship common to sons, but he liked the slowly aging John, and they got along well together in a distant way. His curious hands had long ago ceased to bother his father; they were at least as useful as normal members, and at times unusually apt and delicate. The child built things—tall houses of cards that John's steadiness could not duplicate, intricate bits of machinery from a mechanical building toy, and sometimes neat little sailing planes of paper, matches, and glue.

At this age Edmond's quiet way of living was rather ruthlessly upset. John chose to enter him in school.

2. Morning on Olympus

There was a public school at the time not more than a block and a half from the house on Kenmore. John placed young Edmond there, disregarding the Kindergarten and starting him in first grade. The nurse, more or less of an ornament the last two years, dropped out of the boy's sphere. His father took him the short distance to school for a week or so, and thereafter he trudged it himself, as he had often watched others do from his window.

For the first time in his short life his world impinged on that of others. He was thrust willy-nilly out of his privacy into the semi-public ordeal of grade school. His first day was something of a trial; he was stared at, and stared back, and stood for the most part quietly waiting for instructions. A few young sophisticates who had come up from Kindergarten grouped together, calling each other by name, and definitely dividing themselves from the others. However, there were many newcomers like Edmond who stood at a loss; some of them cried, and some waited aimlessly for the assignment of seats.

And that stage passed. The strange child refused association with others; he came and left alone, and spent his recesses wandering by himself about the school-yard. He did not seem unusually bright. The goad of competition simply slipped off his hide; he flatly and definitely refused to compete. Questions put by the teacher were answered with unvarying correctness, but he never volunteered. On the other hand, his memory was faultless, and his grasp of explanations rather remarkable. And so the strange child moved in a world as frictionless as he could contrive and the grades slipped by with the lengthy seasons of childhood. He seemed to learn with acceptable facility. He was never late, seldom early, and still pursued as solitary a course as conditions permitted.

In fourth grade he encountered a physical training instructress who had taken a summer course in the psychology of morbid children. She singled Edmond out; here, she thought, is both a good specimen and an opportunity to help. Introverted, repressed, feelings of inferiority—these were the tags she applied to him.

She arranged games during the gymnasium hour, and attempted to arouse Edmond to compete. She paired him with one or another of the children in races, jumping contests, competitions of various sorts. She appointed him to drop the handkerchief when that game was in progress, and in various ways tried to direct him in paths she thought proper from her three-months study of the subject.

Edmond realized the situation with some disfavor. He promptly and coolly obtained an excuse from physical training, displaying his curious hands as a reason. In some ways he paid for his privilege; the excuse drew the attention of his classmates to his manual deformity. They commented on it in the blunt manner of ten-year-olds, and were continually asking to see the questionable fingers. Edmond obligingly wriggled them for their amusement; he saw in this the easiest attainment of the privacy he desired. And after a while interest did fade; he was permitted again to come and go alone.

He was not, of course, spared entirely in the fierce savagery of childhood. Often enough he was the butt of gibes, the recipient of challenges to fight, or the bearer of a derisive, though usually short-lived, sobriquet. He faced all of these ordeals with a stony indifference. He came and went as he had always done—alone. If he held any resentment, he never showed it, with but possibly one exception.

He was in the sixth grade, and just twelve years old. In every grade, as he had noticed, there had been one leader, one boy who assumed mastery, and whom the others obeyed with a sort of loose discipline. For two years this leader had been Paul —Paul Varney, son of an English professor at nearby Northwestern University, a fine blond youngster, clean-featured, large for his age, intelligent, and imaginative. Very grown up was Paul; he dated with little Evanne Marten in the fifth grade in Platonic imitation of his elders. It was his custom and his privilege to walk home each afternoon with Vanny, who had the blackest hair in school. And it was Paul who coined the sobriquet "Snake-fingers," which pursued Edmond most of a week. At the beginning the name gave Edmond a day of torment—not that he minded the epithet, but he hated with a fierce intensity the attention it centered on him. He stalked icily out of the door that afternoon. The nick-name followed him, taken up by others in the cruel hunting-pack of children. A group trailed him, headed by Paul.

At the sidewalk he encountered little black-haired Vanny of the fifth; she took in the situation instantly, and seized his arm.

"Walk with me, Edmond."

There was a cessation of sound from behind him; this situation was up to Paul. And Paul strode up to Edmond; he was a head taller than his slight opponent.

"Vanny's walking with me!" he said.

"I'll walk with whom I please, Paul Varney!" Vanny cut in.

"This guy won't be able to walk in a minute!" He advanced toward Edmond.

"All right," said the latter coldly, with a curious intense light in his amber eyes. He doubled the troublesome fingers into curious fists.

"Sure, you're bigger'n Edmond. Bully!" Vanny taunted Paul. He stopped; whether Vanny's gibe or Edmond's defiance had halted him was not evident.

"Can't fight with girls around," was his comment, as he swung on his heel. The pack, leader-less, watched the quarry depart.

"Why do they call you Evanne?" asked Edmond as they walked.

"One grandma's name was Eva and the other's name was Anne," sang Vanny. She had answered the same question numerous times. Her mind reverted to the scene of a moment before. "Why don't you get mad at Paul once in a while? He rides you too much."

"Perhaps," said Edmond. "Sometimes." He fell silent, and they walked on until they reached Vanny's home.

"Goodbye, Edmond." She took the books he had carried for her and skipped into the house. Edmond trudged on alone.

In the morning the quarrel had been forgotten; at least, Paul did not refer to it, and Edmond saw no reason to revive it. Paul walked home with Vanny as usual that afternoon, and every afternoon following. Edmond was satisfied, he sought no further meeting with the girl, but he felt a slight thrill of pleasure to have her smile and greet him thereafter when they met in the hall or on the playground. He always smiled a thin, youthfully sardonic smile in answer. It was the friendliest grimace he could manage with what features he had available.

The years in the grades dragged on—futile, stupid years, the boy thought. For, though no one had realized it, Edmond never studied. True, he handed in the usual themes and exercises when these were required, and he purchased the usual text books, but these were never perused. The explanations of the teacher, the little drill he had in class, were all he required; his almost infallible memory served him sufficiently to render needless any further study.

In these awakening years he was beginning to appreciate something else—that there was a difference between the beings about him and himself. Not the minor physical differences that he had always known, but a mental and emotional gap that he was unable to bridge. This realization was slow in dawning. He began by recognizing a slightly superior feeling, a mild contempt, for his class-mates; they were stupid, slow, plodding; they worked over problems that yielded instantly to his perceptions. Even Paul, who was incessantly being called on for answers when others failed, and who always made the highest marks, seemed merely a less complete dullard than the rest.

But the vital difference was of another sort, a variation not of degree but of nature. This conclusion came to him as the culmination of many semesters of reprimands by his various teachers, and the accumulated repetitions of an adage that seemed meaningless to him. He was in seventh grade when the realization dawned, and it came about in this fashion.

The geography period was in session, and the teacher was expounding at some length the growing importance of South America to the United States. Edmond, who was seated near a window, was staring disinterestedly out at the street. He noticed a commotion at the corner—two automobiles had mutually dented fenders—and turned his head, focusing his eyes on the scene. His motion drew the teacher's petulant glance.

"Edmond Hall!" was her impatient exclamation. "Please forget the window and pay attention!" This she followed with the most surprising statement he had heard during his seven school years. "No one can think of two things at once!"

Edmond knew she was wrong. He had been following her. For he himself could with perfect clarity pursue two separate and distinct trains of thought at the same time.

3. Introspection

High school. A larger world wherein it was far easier to walk alone. Classes under various teachers and with various associates, and freedom from the prying glare of prolonged intimacy. Edmond was half content.

He was now a slender quiet lad of fourteen, of about average height. His features were beginning to betray a youthful ascetic saturninity and his rare smiles seemed almost sneers, foreshadowing a sort of demoniac beauty to come. Boys disliked him, and girls ignored him; he made no advances to either and quietly repulsed casual attempts at companionship.

The work itself weighed very lightly upon him; he had not lost his miraculous facility nor infallible memory. His two study periods sufficed to complete any form-work his courses required, and he disregarded the rest. He had, therefore, ample leisure for a rigid regime of introspection he was following. For more than a year the youth had been examining his own mind.

The realization of his difference had become a certainty; evidence abounded in his reading, in his associates, in the very manner of the school's teaching. He had two minds, equal and independent, capable each in itself of pursuing a train of thought.

He could read with half his being and dream idly with his other self; or on occasion, he could fuse his twin mentalities, focus both on the same point as a single unit, and reason with a lucidity and insight that might have amazed his instructors. He could read with astonishing facility, garnering the contents of half a page of print in an instant's glance, or he could deal with the simple quadratics of high school algebra without the need of chalk or pencil. Yet he never flaunted these abilities; he pursued his accustomed path, never volunteering, never correcting, watching the blond Paul perform pridefully, and holding silently a secret contempt.

In his second year, little Vanny arrived, with her glowing black braids of hair; Paul walked with her in the halls in a manner mature as befits a sophomore in high school, and she still smiled at Edmond when they met. He noted a shade of distraction in her face, and recalled that her father had died during the summer.

In the house on Kenmore, the senescent John smoked on in his library. His little block of motor shares had multiplied itself into a respectable nest-egg; he had given up his practice for a quiet existence in the shade. He refused to own an automobile, berated the rumbling of the distant "L", and read the conservative Daily News. A war in Europe was two years old, and a white-haired philanthrope had sailed to get the soldiers out of the trenches by Christmas. A president was re-elected after a race so close that victory hung in the balance for several days.

Edmond and his father got along well enough. Old John was satisfied with his son's quiet reserve and asocial bent; it seemed to him a sign of industry and serious mind. And Edmond was content to have his leisure undisturbed; the two spent their evenings reading, and seldom spoke. Berkeley and Hume were back on the shelves, and John was plodding through the great Critique, and Edmond, finding novels of little interest, was perusing page by page the volumes of the Britannica. He absorbed information with a sponge-like memory that retained everything, but as yet the influx was unclassified and random, for the practical and theoretical had no differences in his small experience. Thus the older man absorbed a flood of philosophy with no retaining walls of knowledge, and the younger accumulated loose bricks of knowledge that enclosed no philosophy.

The years rolled on tail-to-trunk like an elephant's parade. Edmond entered Northwestern University, and here found a privacy almost as profound as that of his early youth. A war had been fought and finished without disturbing the curious household other than the mild vicissitudes of meatless days, Hooverizing, and Liberty Bonds. The stormy aftermath was over the world, and the decade of Youth was in its inception.

Edmond chose a medical course, and settled into a routine of home-to-class. The campus was just beyond the city limits, and he made the trip by street-car since old John still held steadfastly to his refusal of motor cars. His first year's sojourn in the College of Medicine was but a repetition of high school. Paul was there, majoring in English; occasionally they passed on the campus with casual nods, and Edmond had his father, Professor Varney, in an English lecture course. He was not greatly interested in any of his freshman studies; they were simply requirements to be put by since his pre-medic course permitted little latitude for choice. However, he mastered French with considerable facility.

In his second year, he derived some enjoyment from an elective course in Physics under Professor Albert Stein. The brilliant little Jewish savant was already famous; his measurements of electrons were beginning to open up vistas looking to the unknown. Behind his near-sighted eyes and slightly accented speech, Edmond perceived a mind alert and intuitive, an intellect that thought in lesser degree almost as he did himself.

And that year Vanny appeared again, and that was also the year that old John died. Edmond was twenty, a slender young man with strange amber eyes. His grim Uncle Edward became his guardian for the year remaining until his majority, and managed the not-too-extensive estate with a grumbling astuteness. Edmond lived on at the house on Kenmore, and Magda, grown plump and ruddy, ran the house as she had done for twenty years.

So Edmond drifted on, a slim saturnine figure, toying with knowledge in those incredible minds he possessed. He read voluminously in every field save fiction. Learning came to him with a consummate ease. He moved through the University like a lonely, flaming-eyed spirit, coming and going in solitude and scarcely ever addressed outside the classroom. Only Evanne Marten, grown very lovely with her glistening black mop of hair, tossed him an occasional word of greeting.

He was not yet really lonely. He watched the panorama of city and college, and was fairly content with his own company. There still grew in him the sense of superiority, of contempt for these single-minded beings about him. To see only one side of anything! To be unable to toss thoughts back and forth within one's self, never to know the strange conceptions that are beyond expression in language! No wonder they herded together for company!

Then he was twenty-one, and assumed the management of his resources. His income was sufficient for comfort; he made few changes in old John's investments. However, he purchased a long grey roadster of rather expensive make; there was something about mechanical excellence that pleased his curious character. He drove the machine with almost miraculous dexterity, slipping through traffic like wind through grain. His slim, tentacular fingers seemed especially designed for the management of machinery, and the thrill of driving was as intense as if he used his own muscles. Sometimes he drove to the open country, selecting unpatrolled dirt roads, and here drove at breathtaking speed, pitting his skill against the vagaries of the terrain.

His courses neared completion. Toward the end, the queer Edmond was somewhat less content; a sense of futility oppressed him, and he perceived no outlet anywhere for his energies. The curious being was lonely.

"I am enclosed in a viscid mist," he reflected. "Knowledge is a barren thing, since I see no closer to its end than the dullest of these about me." And his other mind replied, "This conclusion is unwarranted since hitherto I have made no attempt to attain happiness, but have let my fortunes drift without plan to the beckonings of chance."

Thereafter he formed a plan. His degree was granted and he departed, making no effort to serve as an interne, since he did not wish to practice. An experiment awaited him that he relished; if happiness could be reduced to formula, he meant so to reduce it, solving at least for himself the elusive mystery.

Yet an unusual sense of sadness pursued him; he endured the graduation exercises in a sombre silence. After the return to his home, he put away his car, and wandered aimlessly westward, past the decrepit school of his early youth, past the house that had been Vanny's home, past the high school now empty for the summer's recess. The half-deserted summer streets seemed sterile and melancholy; he was lonely.

Before him spread the glass fronts of a business street. A group of half a dozen persons clustered before the window of one—a pet shop. A glance revealed the attraction—the gambols and grimaces of a small monkey. Edmond paused for a moment; an impulse stirred him. He entered the shop, emerging in a moment bearing a paper-wrapped cage. The group filtered away as the attraction vanished.

"Here is my companion," thought Edmond, "and my defense against loneliness. At least he will be as understanding as any among these who watched him."

He bore the chattering little animal to the house on Kenmore.

"Your name," he said, "shall be Homo, after the being who apes you less successfully than you him." He smiled as the creature chattered in reply. "My friend," he continued, "your sympathy and intelligence shall aid me in my appointed task."

The monkey Homo chattered and grimaced, and rattled the bars of his flimsy cage; Edmond slipped the catch, and the little being pushed open the door, bounding with tree-born agility to Edmond's knee.

There he sat in patent enjoyment of his liberty, while his strange master watched him with an expression almost of amusement, finding in his antics a momentary release from his own sombre nature. The youth toyed with his unusual emotion of pleasure, reflecting, "This creature, unthinking and happy, may direct my quest, who am thinking and therefore unhappy; let me see whether I can complete the circle, and in the pursuit of knowledge find happiness." Thus Edmond entered upon his search.

Book 1
The Pursuit of Knowledge

1. Traffic with Nature

During this epoch of his life, Edmond was not unhappy, at least until the period was approaching its end. He threw himself into a round of labors and speculations; he spent many hours in the unraveling of mysteries by processes purely rational. For a span of several months he found no need for the mechanics of experiment since the tabulations of others' results were available for his use. He absorbed the facts and rejected the speculations of science. This rejection was due in part to his distrust of the theories of these half-minded creatures about him; he was inclined to doubt the truth of any hypothesis promulgated by such beings.

He set about his own researches, therefore, working with an enthusiasm that almost deluded himself. He realized, indeed, that his purpose in these researches was artificial and sterile; he had no consuming love of knowledge, and no deep inherent desire to serve humanity; what drove him like a seven-tongued scourge was the specter of boredom standing just behind him. To a being of Edmond's nature this was sufficient incentive.

His income was ample for his immediate needs. He subsided therefore into a quiet regime of speculation, building for himself an esoteric picture of the universe to assist his purposes. In this field as well he found little meat in the hypotheses of his predecessors; excepting, and with qualification, Einstein.

"The Bohr atom, the Schrodinger atom," he reflected, "are two meaningless attempts to describe that which is forever indescribable and are worthless for my purposes. The very nature of matter is a problem not entirely physical, but partly metaphysical, and as such defies any absolute resolvence, at least by human kind with its single viewpoint.

"From my standpoint, the universe consists, not of concepts or sensations, like Berkeley's, not of matter and energy, like the scientists of the first decade, not even of mathematical quantities, like James Jeans, but purely and entirely of Laws, or perhaps a Law. This chair on which I lean is an aspect of a law; my breath, this very thought, are other phases."

His companion self, following an allied course, continued, "Einstein's little booklet, assuming of course its correctness, represents my universe, yet even this conception lacks something! One does not eat a law, live in, carve, sleep, nor reproduce with an equation. Behind these laws stands Authority; had I the necessary Authority, these dozen scraps of equation-scribbled paper would be in very truth the universe. This demiurgy is beyond even my potentiality."

His minds merged; the two thought courses were one.

"It would not astonish me to find the Authority behind all Law to be only my old acquaintance Chance. Perhaps the supreme wisdom lies in the law of averages."

Suddenly Edmond abandoned these futile speculations, perceiving that they pointed nowhere. He determined to dally for a while with experiment, and to this end moved what equipment he possessed into the room he had occupied during his school-days. This was at the rear of the house; as a further precaution, he had the windows leaded lest certain effects of flame and spark arouse the neighbors.

For a while he intrigued himself with the study of the nature of Life. For many months a procession of rabbits and guinea pigs came in through the kitchen in wire cages and left via the incinerator in ash-wagons. The problem proved elusive; neither the mechanists nor the vitalists held the answer. Nowhere in any of the little creatures could Edmond find any trace of a vital fluid or an essence of life, yet he saw more and more clearly that these beings he slaughtered were somewhat more than machines.

"Perhaps," he thought, "the vital fluid is more subtle than matter or energy for which my traps are set. Perhaps it partakes of both natures, or neither; yet I will not concede the existence of quantities called spiritual."

"The difference between living beings and machines," continued his companion self, "is in this: that life contains a sort of ghostly purpose, an imitation of a purpose that drives its subjects to prolong their own misery, to force others to live after them. This semblance of a purpose is the mysterious vital fluid which is of the nature neither of matter nor of energy."

During the progress of his experiments, he became interested for a time in the matter of intellect. He was curious to observe the relationship between intelligence and the brain, and to this end devised a means of stimulating the growth of a rabbit's cerebrum, by using certain pituitary extracts. He watched the miserable little monstrosity in its cage suspended on the wall, as its head grew out of all proportion, until it was forced to crawl pushing the unwieldy capital along before it. The thing grew slowly. After several months Edmond perceived or imagined that it watched him with a trace of interest; certainly it grew to recognize his feeding, and this was a recognition never granted by its companions. The abnormal creature kept its miserable black eyes incessantly on him. It cowered away in terror when he approached the cage with his syringe for the daily injections.

"Perhaps I can do as much for you," he told Homo, who chattered on his shoulder, "though I suspect the inflicting of intelligence is the greatest injury Fate can do to any being, for it is literally to thrust that being into Hell. You are doubtless fairly happy, Homo, and better off as you are."

As the experiment progressed, Edmond began to perceive the development of certain unpleasant-ries, and frowned often in his observation of the little monster. He was neither surprised nor very displeased, therefore, to enter the laboratory one day and discover that the rabbit had somehow contrived to spring the latch to its cage and fling itself to the floor. It lay with its delicate, misshapen skull shattered, and the abnormal brain crushed.

"Very likely it is better this way," thought Edmond. "The thing was miserably unhappy and I believe, more than a little mad."

Again he abandoned his line of investigation, turning now back to the realm of physics. He noted that metallic lead exposed to the weather for long periods became slightly radioactive. With this as a clue he produced lead with an activity nearly one fourth as high as radium, but was unable to proceed beyond that point. He wanted to solve now the mystery of atomic energy to see the effects of that colossal power to which all other sources were as rain drops to the ocean. He wanted to release this power and to control it, if control were possible. He set about to devise a method.

"A violinist can shatter a wine-glass if he plays the correct note," he thought, "or a few soldiers trample down the greatest bridge in the world if they time their steps rightly. I can doubtless shatter an atom if I use a properly sympathetic vibration. Where now am I to find a vibratory beam of the inconceivable frequency I require? Cosmic rays have it, but they dribble out of space in beams too uselessly tenuous. I must produce my own."

He turned his thoughts to a method of generating his beam. He considered the use of the bursting atoms of niton as his oscillators.

"Since the cosmic rays of space are generated by the birth-throes of atoms," he reflected, "I can certainly pervert them to be the agents of atomic death."

But niton, the deadly mysterious emanation of dying radium, was beyond his means. He needed perhaps ten grams of radium for its production, a quantity whose cost exceeded his financial powers. First, therefore, he found it necessary to procure enough money to purchase it.

This problem presented at first no outstanding difficulties to such a being as Edmond. He saw many methods. However, certain requirements had to be met. He wanted a continuous source of income that would require none of his time to produce; a royalty on a patent would provide that. But whatever device he patented must be proof against imitation or theft, and be readily marketable. It should moreover be foolproof to the extent of revealing no secrets which he considered dangerous to a society that rested on the rocks of the cave. He wished to introduce no destructive force.

"I am perhaps the greatest of all misanthropes," he reflected; "nevertheless I have no desire to destroy the society that enables me to live in comparative comfort, that prepares my food, maintains my dwelling, and supplies me with warmth and light. Let the beasts outside once learn the secret of the atom and the next little war will tumble civilization into the abyss."

He turned his twin minds to his activated lead. He produced a little rod of this material, perhaps the general size of a safety match. Removing a vacuum tube from his radio, he broke the glass bulb from the base and affixed his lead rod thereto, slipping it carefully through the tubular grid so that it replaced the delicate tungsten filament. With the more than human dexterity of his curious fingers, he replaced and evacuated the bulb, leaving the tips that carried the filament current disconnected.

"Here is a cold, unvarying and permanent source of electron

flow," he reflected. "Presumably I can interest a manufacturer in a vacuum tube which is completely quiet, practically eternal, and that consumes no A-current. Then there is the considerable advantage of simplified circuits."

He did not trouble himself to try the device, but placed a diagram and description in the hands of a patent attorney, and sent his model to the office of Stoddard & Co., one of the larger independent makers of vacuum tubes, with a letter describing it Thereafter he ceased to think of it, and turned his activities again to the problem of energy and matter. He prepared his apparatus, and waited for his fortunes to provide the funds he required.

2. Commerce

Perhaps a fortnight after the forwarding of Edmond's tube, he received a reply from the concern.

"We have received and tested a vacuum tube submitted by you..."

"The device fulfills your claims to some extent, and there is a possibility that we might be interested in its manufacture....Should you care to discuss the matter, we will be pleased to receive you at this office at..."

Edmond smiled his ironic smile, and dropped the letter in his pocket.

"One of the axioms of a buyer is to appear only casually interested," he thought. "Let their dignities be satisfied; I'll go to them."

Some three hours after the time designated, Edmond presented himself at the outer office of Stoddard & Co., and passed a card to the startled office girl. There ensued a delay of several minutes. Edmond guessed that the powers behind the door summoned an additional member. Then he was ushered in.

Four men rose as he entered, staring at him. He felt the instant dislike that was his common reception; it flooded the office with a tenseness, a chilly, unpleasant strain. He stared back unsmiling, and after a moment, the oldest of the group flushed and coughed apologetically.

"Mr. Hall?" he said. "I am Mr. Stoddard and this is Mr. Thwaites, our secretary. These two gentlemen," indicating a square-jawed, blue-eyed individual of forty, and a somewhat younger one with spectacles, "are Bohn and Hoffman, our engineers."

Edmond bowed slightly; the men nodded. Not one of the group had extended a hand. He seated himself.

The president interrupted another strained silence with a cough.

"We had expected you earlier," he said.

"It was inconvenient," said Edmond, and waited.

"Well, well, perhaps we had better get down to business. This vacuum tube of yours is—somewhat revolutionary. It seems to function satisfactorily, but you understand that in the event of our adopting it, it would mean the discarding and altering of considerable machinery."

Edmond nodded.

"You must realize that this entails great expense, and there is some doubt in my mind as to the value of the device."

"Well?" said Edmond.

"What terms would you consider, if we should decide to acquire the rights to your tube?"

"I will require," said Edmond, "a five percent royalty on the selling price of the tube, and will permit you to manufacture the device under an exclusive contract with me. I will retain ownership of the patent, and the right to terminate the contract should your production fall below a minimum of two thousand per day. I will further require an initial payment of a nominal amount— ten thousand dollars will be satisfactory, and you may if you wish check this against future royalties. Finally, I will myself draw the contract."

"Those terms are impossible!" exclaimed the president.

"Very well," said Edmond, and waited.

"Are you a lawyer?" asked Mr. Thwaites.

"No," said Edmond, "nevertheless the contract will be binding." He stared silently at the group before him, his incredible hands clasped over the handle of his cane. There was an aura of tension about the group. Each member felt an inexplicable aversion to this curious presence, and Edmond knew it. He smiled his saturnine and supremely irritating smile.

The president looked at him with a weary somberness.

"Will you listen to our offer?"

"I consider my terms equitable," said Edmond. "May I point out what you doubtless realize—that you have no choice? The concern to which I grant this tube will immediately possess a monopoly, since all other types are instantly obsolete. You are compelled to accept my proposal."

The four stared silently back at him. Bohn opened his square jaw and inserted a pipe. He lit it, and puffed a moment.

"May I ask some questions?" he snapped

"Yes."

"What's the source of your electron flow?"

"It is a disintegration product. The energy used is atomic."

"What's the material you use in your filament?"

"Radioactive lead."

"There's no lead that active."

"No," said Edmond, "I created it."

"How?"

"That," said Edmond, "I will not answer."

"Why not?" Bohn's voice crackled with enmity.

"Because the explanation is beyond your understanding."

The engineer gave a contemptuous snort at the insult, and fell silent, eyeing Edmond coldly. Edmond turned to Hoffman, who seemed on the point of speech, by the blinking of his eyes behind their lenses.

"May I ask what is the life of your filament?" he queried mildly.

"It has a half-period of about eight thousand years."

"What?"

"I say that it will dissipate half its activity in eight thousand years."

"D'you mean the thing's eternal?"

Edmond gave again his irritating smile with its intolerable undertone of superiority and contempt.

"You asked me the life of the filament. The useful life of the tube is very much shorter. Inasmuch as the emission is constant whether or not the device is in use, certain radiations other than the electronic, produce effects. There is a tendency for the plate and grid to become active under the influence of alpha and gamma rays; this sets up a secondary opposing electron stream from them which will gradually weaken the conductive effect of the primary flow from the filament. The loss of efficiency will become noticeable in about seven years."

"But man, even that's too long!" exclaimed the president. "It practically destroys the replacement market!"

"That need not worry a concern the size of yours. It will take many decades to saturate the market."

Mr. Thwaites spoke for the second time. "We are simply inviting legal trouble. The Corporation will never permit an independent to ruin its market without a fight."

"I will trust you to carry through the courts," said Edmond. "You will win, for the principle and the process of manufacture are both basic and new." He paused a moment, surveying the group. "Should it appear necessary, you may call upon me." His intonation implied contempt; the intolerable scathing smile returned to his lips. It amused him that none of the four had questioned his ability to oppose the rich and powerful Corporation, owner of most of the basic electrical patents. He noted Bohn's irritation and a certain tenseness in his jaw as he bit his pipe. "Your confidence is a high compliment, Gentlemen. Is there anything further?"

"Yes!" snapped Bohn. "I think this thing is a hoax!" He rose excitedly from his chair. "This man has bought or stolen some radium from a hospital or laboratory, and he's alloyed it with lead to make his filament! He's selling you about fifteen hundred dollars worth of radium for the cash payment of ten thousand dollars. Pay him and he'll never show up again!"

The four were on their feet facing Edmond, who still sat smiling.

"Bohn's right!" said Hoffman. "Radioactive lead—there isn't any such thing! It's a fraud!"

Thwaites opened his mouth, and then remained silent. The four angry men stood staring vindictively at the curious being who faced them still with his smile of cold contempt. There was a moment of pause bitter with hatred.

"I congratulate you, Mr. Bohn," said Edmond, his voice and expression unaltered. "Your deductions are admirable, but have the one flaw of being incorrect." He drew from his pocket a little disc as large as a silver dollar, wrapped in a dull, glinting lead-foil; he tossed this before the group, where it dropped on the table with a leaden thump.

"There is a two-ounce disc of A-lead. If it contains radium, its value will be considerably greater than your ten thousand dollar payment. I leave it as a token of good faith, gentlemen; it cost me perhaps three dollars."

He glanced at Bohn, who was unwrapping the foil about the piece with fury in his blue eyes.

"You may perform any tests you wish on this material, Mr. Bohn, but handle it gingerly. It burns—like radium!"

Edmond rose.

"I do not require your check at once, but will expect it within a week, at which time I will submit my contract for your signatures. During the interim, Mr. Bohn and Mr. Hoffman may call at my home," he indicated his card, which still lay on the table, "for instructions in the method and some of the principles underlying the preparation of activated lead. They will perceive that the cost of manufacture is surprisingly low."

"Why only some of the principles?" asked Bohn, glowering.

"Those that you can comprehend," said Edmond, turning to the door. "Good afternoon, gentlemen."

He departed, hearing with amusement the crescendo of excited and angry voices issuing from the closing door. The voice of the president—"What was that man? Did you see his hands?"

3. Market

Edmond stepped out of the building into the late afternoon sun that flashed at him from the windshields of ten thousand westbound vehicles. He shaded his eyes for a moment, then crossed Adams Street and continued south, merging for the moment into the stream of living beings that eddied around and between the canyon-forming buildings.

"This river flows its own way, bound by laws as definite and predictable as those that govern flowing water," he reflected. "Mankind in the mass is a simple and controllable thing, like a peaceful river; it is only in the individual that there is a little fire of independence."

He entered the lobby of a great white skyscraper. Disregarding the clicking of the elevator starters, he mounted the stairs to the second floor, turning into the customer's room of his brokers. The market was long since closed; he was alone in a room of vacant chairs save for several clerks casting up the final quotations, and an old man sweeping scraps and cigarette butts into a central pile. The translux was dark, but a ticker still clicked out its story of "bid-and-asked"; no one watched it as its yellow ribbon flowed endlessly into a waste-basket.

Edmond walked over to the far end of the room, where a smaller board carried the Curb quotations. A casual glance was sufficient; Stoddard & Co. had closed just below twenty, for a fractional loss from the preceding day. He stood for a few moments recapitulating his readily available resources—he found no need ever for written accounts—and walked over to the desk, to a clerk who had handled his occasional previous transactions. He nodded as the man greeted him by name.

"You may buy me five thousand Stoddard at twenty," he said.

"Five thousand, Mr. Hall? Do you think it advisable to speculate for that amount? Stoddard's only an independent, you know."

"I am not speculating," said Edmond.

"But the company has never paid a dividend."

"I require the stock for a particular reason."

The clerk scribbled on a blank order: "5000 Sdd. @ 20 O.B., N. Y. Curb," and passed it to him. He signed in his accustomed precise script.

"You realize, of course, that we cannot margin this stock, being on the Curb, and poor bank collateral."

"Of course," said Edmond. "I will provide sufficient security." So he departed.

4. Puzzlement

Bohn and Hoffman presented themselves at Edmond's home promptly in accordance with their appointment. Magda admitted them, and directed them to the upper rear room that served as his laboratory. They found him seated facing the door, idle, and toying with little Homo who chattered furiously at them. Edmond returned their cold greetings without rising, indicating two wooden chairs beside the long table.

Hoffman sat down quietly and faced Edmond, but his companion's eyes ranged sharply about the room. Bohn noted the blackened windows, and a peculiar shade in the illumination of the room struck him. He glanced at the lights—two bulbs of high capacity of the type called daylight, under whose blue-white glare the group assumed a corpse-like grayness. Their host was hideous, Bohn thought; curious thing, he continued mentally, since his features were not irregular. The repulsion was something behind appearances, some fundamental difference in nature. He continued his inspection, considering now the equipment of the laboratory. A small motor-generator in the far corner, probably as a direct-current source, beside it a transformer, and next to that the condenser and hollow cylinder of a rather large high frequency coil. A flat bowl of mercury rested on a little turntable at his elbow; he gave it a twist, and it spun silently, the liquid metal rising about the sides of the bowl in a perfect parabolic mirror. Struck by a sudden thought, he glanced at the ceiling; there was a shutter there that might open on a skylight. For the rest, jars of liquid, some apparently containing algae, a sickly plant or two on a shelf below the black window, and two white rabbits dolefully munching greens in a cage on the windowless wall. Simple enough equipment!

Edmond meanwhile had dismissed the monkey, who backed away from the group, regarded the strangers with bright intelligent eyes and scampered out into the hallway.

"You are not impressed, Mr. Bohn."

"Hardly," Bohn bitterly resented the implied sneer.

"The tools are less important than the hand that wields them."

"Let's get down to business," said Bohn.

"Very well," said their host. "Will you be so kind as to lift that reflector to the table?"

He indicated one of several wooden bowls perhaps eighteen inches across whose inner surfaces seemed blackened as if charred or rubbed with graphite. Bohn stooped to lift it; it was surprisingly heavy, necessitating the use of both his hands. He placed it on the table before Edmond.

"Thank you. Now if you will watch me...."

He opened a drawer in the table, removing from it a spool of heavy wire and a whitened cardboard square perhaps four inches to a side.

"This is lead wire. This cardboard is coated with calcium fluoride."

He passed the articles to Bohn, who received them with patient skepticism.

"I want you to see that the wire is inactive. I will extinguish the lights"—the room was suddenly and mysteriously dark—"and you will note that the board does not fluoresce."

Bohn rubbed the wire across the square, but there was no result whatsoever. The lights were suddenly glowing again; the wire and square were unchanged save for a scratch or two on the latter's white surface.

"Your demonstration is convincing," said Bohn sardonically. "We feel assured that the wire is innocent and harmless."

"Pass it here, then, and I will give it its fangs."

Edmond unwound some six inches from the spool, leaving it still attached, extended out like a little wand. He drew three cords from points on the edge of his reflector; at the apex of the tetrahedron thus formed he gathered the ends. To mark this elusive point in space he moved a ring stand beside the bowl setting a clamp to designate the intersection of his bits of string which he allowed to drop.

"A simple method of locating the focus," he explained. "As the black surface of my reflector does not reflect light, I have to use other means. The focal length, as you see, is about thirty centimeters. The reflector itself is not parabolic, but spherical. I do not desire too sharp a focus, as I wish to irradiate the entire volume of the lead wire—not merely a single point."

The two visitors watched without comment. Their host passed

the six-inch rod of lead back and forth through the point indicated by the clamp, back and forth perhaps a dozen times. Then he tossed the spool to Bohn.

"Hold it by the spool, Mr. Bohn. It will bite now."

Bohn examined the little rod, which seemed utterly unchanged.

"Well?" he said sharply.

"We will try the fluorescent screen. I will extinguish the lights"—and again the lights were dark. Bohn placed the rod of lead above the square; at once a pallid blue-white glow spread over the surface. The scratches Bohn had made were outlined in white fire, and the square shone like a little window opening on a cloudy night sky. The cold white flame rippled as he moved the rod above it.

The voice of their host sounded: "Try your diamond, Mr. Hoffman." Hoffman slipped a ring from his finger, and held it toward the glowing square. As it approached the wire, the gem began to glow in its setting; it glistened with an icy blue fire far brighter than the square. Hoffman withdrew it, but it continued to flame with undiminished brilliance. The lights flashed on, catching the two engineers blinking down at the glowing diamond.

"It will fluoresce for some time to come," said Edmond. "At least you may be assured that the gem is genuine; imitations will not react." He paused. "Is there anything further?"

"We are convinced," said Bohn shortly. "Will you explain your methods?"

"In part." Edmond drew a cigarette from a box beside him, and passed them to the engineers. Hoffman accepted one, but Bohn shook his head and drew out his pipe. Their host exhaled a long plume of smoke.

"Obviously," he continued, "the simplest way to break up an atom is through sympathetic vibration. The same principle as breaking a glass goblet by playing a violin above it at the proper pitch."

"That's an old idea," said Hoffman, "but it never worked."

"No; because no one has been able to produce a vibration of great enough frequency. The electrons of most substances have revolution periods measurable in millionths of a second.

"However, certain rays are known that have frequencies of this order; I refer to the so-called cosmic rays."

"Bah!" said Bohn. "I suppose you produce cosmic rays!"

"No," said Edmond, staring coldly at him.

"To continue: It has also been observed that lead exposed to the weather for a long period of years becomes mildly radioactive. All the fools now occupying chairs of research have attributed this to sunlight. Of course, they are wrong; it is due to the cosmic rays.

"Therefore, I have designed this reflector"—he tapped the bowl—"which brings the cosmic rays which enter this room to a focus, intensifying their effect a thousandfold. That is what starts the disintegration of the lead; once begun, the process is self-continuous." He paused again. "Do you wish to ask any questions?"

"Yes," said both men at once. Hoffman fell silent, and Bohn spoke, apparently somewhat subdued.

"I have always understood that cosmic rays have unparalleled penetrative power, passing far into the deepest mines, and that even gold is very transparent to them. It is generally believed that nothing will reflect them."

"Almost nothing, Mr. Bohn. My reflector will."

"But what material do you use?"

"Did you ever hear of neutronium, Mr. Bohn?"

"Neutronium!" both men spoke.

"That," said Hoffman, "is the stuff that's left after all the electrons are driven off. Neutronium is solid protons, and weighs about one ton to the cubic inch."

"But that stuff is simply hypothetical," objected Bohn.

"Not quite hypothetical, Mr. Bohn. It occurs in the dwarf stars, for instance, and in other places."

"Where, for example?"

"In this room, Mr. Bohn. I have caused an infinitesimal layer of it to be created on the reflecting side of this wooden bowl, a deposit inconceivably thin—perhaps only two or three protons deep. Nevertheless, it is sufficient. Doubtless you noticed the weight."

"Yes." He stared at the black concavity on the table. "By what means do you perform this?"

"By means I shall not reveal, because it is dangerous."

"Dangerous! You needn't be solicitous of our safety!"

"I am not, but of my own. The process is economically dangerous."

"Bah! That's what people thought about every practical advance, from steam engines on!"

"Yes," said Edmond, "and I know of none that has not been perverted to destruction." For the first time in the interview he smiled, and the men flushed angrily. "Would you place hand grenades in the paws of all the apes in the zoo, Mr. Bohn? Neither shall I." He crushed out his cigarette in an ash tray with an air of closing the subject, and turned to Hoffman.

"You wished to ask a question. Mr. Hoffman."

The other leaned forward, peering at Edmond through his eyeglasses.

"Will this process disintegrate other elements besides lead, Mr. Hall?"

"A few, but the process is infinitely slower."

"Why is that?"

"There are several reasons. Primarily, because lead is itself more or less unstable in structure. Then, neutronium in this very thin deposit reflects the particular ray that affects lead in greater degree; in other words, my reflector has a sort of cosmic color. Again, the lead radiations form the greater portion of the cosmic rays themselves, for a reason I have not bothered to ascertain; they too are leaden-hued. That is of course why leaden roofs and gutters are activated after long exposure to weather, while zinc or iron or copper ones are not."

"I see," said Hoffman slowly. "Say, how long have you been working on this, Mr. Hall?"

"About six weeks," said Edmond coldly, ignoring the look of amazement on the faces of his guests. He continued: "I think we have covered sufficient ground here. You may send for these four reflectors; they will treat enough lead for your present capacity. Should increased production necessitate any addition, I will supply them. You may install these in any part of your plant; the cosmic rays are but slightly diffused by passing through the building. The technique of the actual handling of the filament I will leave to you, but be sure to safeguard your workers with lead-foil lined gloves against radium burns."

He rose, and the others followed.

"I'll take this one with me, if you don't mind," said Bohn, lifting the wooden bowl from the table with some effort. The three passed into the hall. "Homo!" called Edmond sharply, and from somewhere in the darkness of the hall the monkey scampered, leaping to his shoulder, and crouching there. As they were descending the stairs, Hoffman noticed their host glance backward at the lighted rectangle of laboratory door; instantly the lights went out. The engineer made no comment, but drew a deep breath when the front door had closed upon them. He followed Bohn, who staggered ahead under the weight he bore, and helped him slide the bowl to the floor of their car.

"What d'you think of it, Carl?" said Hoffman, as the car moved.

"Don't know."

"D'you believe that stuff about cosmic rays and neutronium?"

"We'll damn soon find out when I get to the lab. I got some lead there that I know isn't doctored."

They were silent for several blocks.

"Say, Carl, did you see him put out the lights?"

"Trick. He did it with his feet."

"But he put 'em out from the hall when we were going."

"Switch in the hall."

But Hoffman, less solid in outlook, more mystical than Bohn, remained unconvinced. The curious Edmond had impressed him deeply, and he found his character far less repulsive at this second meeting. There was a sort of fascination about the man.

"Do you think he knows as much as he says he does?"

"If he does, he's the devil."

"Yes, I thought that too, Carl."

The car drew up before the Stoddard plant, and the two scrambled out.

"Lend me a hand, Mac, and I'll damn soon find out what this thing is."

But Bohn never did. He blunted innumerable knives on the black surface, and dented it very easily with a chisel, but never managed to collect enough of the stuff to analyze. The deposit was far too thin, a tenuous coating of something heavy that nothing could dislodge.

5. The Seeds of Power

Several weeks later Edmond sold his Stoddard at a fourteen point profit, and unemotionally watched it climb to more than forty. Then he set about securing his radium; part of it he was able to obtain from a domestic producer, and the remainder from Europe. He owned finally ten grams of a salty white crystalline powder—the sulphide of radium—and he had paid about fifty thousand dollars for this somewhat less than a spoonful. He had, however, a constant source of niton, in minute quantities it is true, but invariable and practically eternal. Nor was it an unwise purchase from any standpoint, for the radium was readily salable at any time.

He turned his energies again to the more complete solution of the mystery of matter. Niton, the gaseous emanation evolved by radium from its own decay, is in itself decaying, its own atoms bursting, consuming themselves in the long series of disintegrating elements whose end-product is lead. But niton is infinitely more active than its parent radium, and from its exploding atoms Edmond hoped to produce an intense beam of rays of the cosmic order by throwing these atoms into inconceivably rapid oscillation. To this end he enclosed the evanescent gas in a little globular bulb, on one hemisphere of which he caused to form an infinitely thin deposit of neutronium which was to serve both as a shield and a reflector for the beam. At opposite points on the globe's equator—the juncture of the black and clear hemispheres, he placed the slender platinum electrodes that were to admit to the gas an interrupted current of infinitesimal period; it remained now to produce an interrupter, a circuit-breaker, capable of breaking his current into bursts whose period compared to the almost instantaneous periods of revolving electrons.

Edmond resumed his consideration of the atom disrupter. He had now, in his niton tube, an oscillator capable of responding to the stimulus of such an electric stress as he contemplated; it remained for him to produce an alternator of sufficient frequency. He wanted now an alternating electric current of such short period that the already active niton atoms should be wrenched and strained so violently that the gamma radiations increase their hardness to the vastly higher scale of the cosmic rays. Out of their torture he wished to wrest those mysterious impulses that signal the birth-throes of atoms.

What agent could he use? Certainly no mechanical device could attain the nearly infinite frequency he required; even the discharge of a condenser fell far short. He discarded likewise the agency of chemistry; ions could not vibrate with violence sufficient to destroy themselves. His search limited itself of necessity to the more subtle field that lay within the atom; only electrons possessed the colossal, fluent velocity he needed. For many hours he sat toying with the problem, and the solution eluded him; finally he wearied of the glare of light in his laboratory and descended to the floor below. Evening was falling, unseen in the black-windowed room he quitted; its dusk was already in the hall and the library, though a low sun still gilded the living-room wall. Homo skipped frantically about his cage in the library; his chattering was a summons to Edmond, who released the exuberant creature, permitting it to scamper to his shoulder. He seated himself in his usual chair before the fireplace and gave himself to his thoughts. These were not sombre; the spur of obstacles, strange to his experience, gave a piquancy to the problem.

"It has long been suspected," he reflected, "that the laws of the conservation of energy and of mass are the same law; this means in effect that translation of matter to energy is possible, and conversely, one must be able to create matter out of pure energy. And of course, the relation becomes more obvious when it is realized that energy itself has mass; light, the purest form of energy known, obeys the laws of mechanics as docilely as a baseball tossed into the air."

Then he reverted to the immediate problem of his interrupter. By degrees, even this yielded to the inhuman ingenuity of his twin minds. By the time Magda announced dinner, he had a tentative solution, and before the end of his after-dinner cigarette, he had evolved a mechanism that might, he believed, serve his purpose. He returned to his laboratory in the evening and set about the business of constructing the device.

He took two tiny pillars of his A-lead, and caused the two electron beams to interfere; along the combined stream he passed his current. Thus he had an interrupter whose period was measurable in millionths of a second; by adjusting the relative positions of his

A-lead pillars, he could reduce it to billionths. His current traversed a stream of electrons that flowed in little instantaneous bursts, whose frequency he controlled. Thus Edmond constructed his atom disrupter, and only when it was complete did he pause to reflect, and question himself why.

"For what reason, to what purpose, do I create a device that, though it will release limitless energy for society's service, can also unleash power enough to tumble the earth out of its orbit? I neither love man enough to grant him the power of the gods, nor hate him so bitterly as to place in his hands his—and my own—destruction."

And he answered himself; "My only impulse in this creation has been the escape of boredom. I labor to no end at all; thus again I am faced by that which blocks all efforts everywhere—futility."

Nevertheless, he was avidly curious to watch the release of that power which was all but legendary, which had always glowed just beyond the horizon of physics like a never rising sun. The declaration of futility was a rational thing as yet; for this time he had no real sense nor feeling of it, but rather a resurgence of strong pride in his achievement. He felt indeed a species of elation very foreign to his somber nature; he alone held the key to the twin doors of salvation and destruction, his the decision. "I am the only being in this part of the universe who holds such a key; by virtue of it I rule or destroy as I will."

Then to watch the atom-blaster perform. He selected a tiny speck of potassium to disrupt—a piece smaller by far than the head of an average pin. This element he chose because of its comparative rarity; he did not wish to adjust his radiations to calcium or iron or aluminum and find stray beams disintegrating the walls of his house with perhaps enough accidental violence to blast into dust all that hundred mile city whose nucleus is Chicago. This tiny speck, still moist with oil, he placed on a square of tile at the estimated focus of his niton tube. He sat for a moment making his calculations, building in his mental view a potassium atom, selecting a key electron whose period he must determine. Then he adjusted the twin pillars of his interrupter with incredible delicacy, and thereafter stood with his hand on the switch of the motor generator surveying the various parts of the device. In a moment he dropped the switch and removed the speck of potassium from the tile; it had occurred to him that the tile itself might contain potassium salts, and certainly the allied sodium; a slight error in the setting of his interrupter wrould blast the sister element into a terrific volcano of destruction. It was the nearest to error he had ever come throughout his life.

He tipped the bit of metal to a leaden disc, stepped back to the far corner of the room, and threw the switch. The generator hummed; the tube of niton glowed with its characteristic violet; now through the clear half of the bulb he believed a stream of cosmic rays was pouring—not the diffuse and mild rays that flowed out of space, but an intense beam like that of a search-light. Yet the potassium remained unaltered.

He cut the switch, and again adjusted his interrupter, at a guess to a slightly lower frequency. Again he set the generator spinning.

Instantly it came. Where the speck of metal had rested hovered a two foot roaring sphere of brilliant violet light, whose heat singed his eyebrows, whose terrible flames were unfaceable. Reverberations pounded his ear-drums, and great lightning-like discharges leaped from his clothing. The room reeled in a crescendo of crashes; the terrific flaming ball that hovered above the table seemed to his half-blinded gaze to expand like a trap-door into Hell. A second—two seconds—it flared—then with a dying crackle of sparks it dissipated, darkened, dropped into nothingness. A strong odor of ozone swept the room and Edmond dropped his blistered hands from his eyes, to gaze dazzled at the aftermath of wreckage. A pool of molten lead lay on the table, about whose edge the wood flamed. He quickly smothered the conflagration with the contents of a flower pot, and examined the rest of the room's equipment. Surprisingly, the damage was less than he had anticipated. His niton tube was in splinters and his interrupter in fragments; no matter—they could be replaced should he ever desire.

He realized that he never would. The experiment was finished—completed—his interest in it had vanished. Let the earth-wrecker lie destroyed and unrecorded, let men suck the little driblets of energy they had always used. The spray from this ocean he had tapped; he wished neither to rule nor to destroy.

He called Magda to clean up the debris and went downstairs to the library. He summoned Homo to his knees and sat for a long time surveying the cold hearth.

6. Friendship & Humor

After the experiment of the atom-breaker and its culmination, that sense of futility which Edmond had reasoned but not felt appeared in reality. He grew weary of knowledge, since it led nowhere but only seemed to point a way, like a will-o'-the-wisp across a swamp. He perceived that all knowledge was useless, since all generalities were false. If no Absolutes existed, science itself must consist of merely relative truths. The pursuit of science was no more than the grubbing out of an infinity of little facts whose sum total was zero. All effort, he thought, was bounded by that one impenetrable spell that was called futility. His twin minds dissociated; he permitted them to trace out each its own ratiocinations.

"Every effort is foredoomed to be in vain," he reflected, "but living is only to struggle against this doom. Life is that which fights futility, and is to this extent free."

"Every effort is foredoomed," said his other self, taking this same point of departure, "and rational living is to recognize this doom and cease to struggle against it. This is to be really free."

Then his being merged into a unity, promulgating the conclusion he derived from these divergent courses of reason.

"Only one thing is certain; that truth is a subjective idea void of reality, and is wholly relative to the point of view."

For some time Edmond abandoned his laboratory, pursuing knowledge of a different sort. Thrust into a world peopled by human beings, he now devoted his time to a survey of their society, and an analysis of their functioning. He had of course, long since realized that he was somehow a being apart from these, one whose appearance, whose very mind, was alien to them. He wished, therefore, to acquire a viewpoint to enable him to understand those among whom he moved, or if they proved too utterly foreign, to at least appreciate wherein lay the differences. To Edmond who saw all things from two viewpoints, the world was a highly complex organization quite incomprehensible to beings of single minds.

"All creatures live in a world just greater than their ability to

49

conceive," he reflected. "The worm, blind and possessing only the single sense of touch, lives in a world of one dimension, but beings from outside stab at him and devour.

"I go now into that Elfhame of Cabell's, where things have only one side, but I anticipate the finding there of no Thin Queen."

So Edmond locked the door upon a room of wonders, abandoning there his quest for truth through the maze of natural things. For he foresaw that the facets of the jewel were infinite, and that a greater intelligence than his would yet fail to isolate truth in a laboratory. He opened another door upon the colossus of the city, and stepped into the streaming life that flowed about him.

Disregarding his roadster that stood at the curb, he walked east to Sheridan Road, to board a bus. The day was crisp late Autumn; leaves crunched underfoot as he walked. Trim women passed him with a single glance, a man or two with none at all. At the corner half a dozen people waited; Edmond scanned them with his instantaneous glance. He attempted to read their characters from their features; he failed and knew that he failed. Two of them, girls in sleek cloth coats with caressing fur about their throats were talking; the rest stood in that frigid silence characteristic of an unacquainted group. He listened casually.

"Paul's bringing two or three with him tonight—one's a critic on the State Herald."

That was the slender dark one speaking.

"Paul's the only one that's got anything. He's a thrill, Vanny."

"Think so? Come on over, if you like; it's just an informal bull-session."

"No bridge?"

"Not with this bunch of literary lights. The supreme egotists are your literati, and bridge requires a partner."

Edmond glanced at the speaker's face, unexpectedly meeting her eyes. He bowed in recognition, and the girl smiled a perfunctory smile. It was Evanne Marten of his school days, grown, he thought, rather lovely in a dark, lithe way. She had an air of being always taut as a watch spring, an elan, a vivacity, that had come of her childish sauciness. When the bus stopped, he watched the smooth flash of her legs as she mounted the step, watched without any emotion but with a distinct aesthetic appreciation.

The two girls turned into the interior; Edmond chose to ride above, where smoking was permitted. As he moved up the narrow stairway he heard the voice of her companion, "Who's the queer boy friend, Vanny?" And Vanny's answering laugh. He smiled a little to himself and thought no more of it for that time. He permitted his minds to roam at random, absorbing the unceasing roar of traffic, the buoyant life that flowed in a river of steel about him, in the middle distance the flash of the lake under a morning sun. The bus rumbled in heightened tempo as it spun at a suddenly increased speed into Lincoln Parkway. Over there the Elk's Memorial. An equestrian statue of someone, too distant to read the inscription. The overpass at the park's south limits; the Drake, the old watertower. He watched Vanny and her companion alight; they marched briskly along Michigan toward a row of shops, turned into one—"Veblis—Chapeaux". The bridge with its sentinel skyscrapers. After a few blocks he got off, turned west into the Loop. He drifted with the crowd and sought to identify himself with it.

After a time, he turned into a motion picture theatre—the first time since his latter childhood. He followed the play with interest, absorbed not by the puerile story nor the caricatures that passed as characterization but by the revelations of the minds that created and the minds that enjoyed these things. Through the play he saw both author and audience. He wondered mildly at what he perceived.

"If this level strikes the average of humanity's intelligence, then the world lies ready for my taking."

He reflected further.

"What I see here is again the crowd, and therefore no true standard by which to judge. The mob-man is the composite picture of his component men; all fine shadings are lost in the dominant and primal influences. A man may be intelligent enough, but the mob-man never; and it is this being I see reflected here, for audiences are in a true sense mobs."

He left the theatre and turned down State Street, passing gradually from the flooded noonday canyons of the Loop into streets of lower buildings and drab little shops. A panhandler sidled up to him with a low whine; Edmond tossed him a quarter without listening or looking. From a basement entrance a dog rushed out at him barking and snapping; with experienced skill, he dealt the cur a sharp blow with his cane.

"Man and his ally the dog both perceive in me the Enemy," he thought. "Why am I the Enemy? For what obscure reason am I placed here solitary, foredoomed to defeat, my only safety to assume the disguise of humanity? Something has gone wrong with the progression of the ages, and I am born long out of my time."

Thus he reflected, meanwhile watching the stream of beings about him, playing still the part of observer. For he moved through the stream but not a part of it; he was still alien, strange, unable to establish a rapport with the people of the stream. His viewpoint, he realized, was starkly different from theirs; it remained to find the common ground.

A window to his left caught his eye, a cheap little shop that did framing and sold the intolerable prints hung in the rooms of the neighborhood. There were a number of them in the window, but what Edmond saw was a little landscape in oils—a canvas no greater than six inches by ten. A curious little thing—nothing more than a tree, a rock, and a dusky sky, and these a trifle twisted, but somehow it seemed to convey a meaning. Something formless and inchoate, but a symbol nevertheless. It was an experience unique to him; he marveled that so simple a thing could arouse a tinge of feeling in his icy being. He entered, and stood before a dusty counter piled with framing. A nondescript man emerged from the rear.

"I want that oil you have in the window."

"Yes sir," said the man, and procured it, placing it before Edmond. "Very pretty little picture isn't it, sir?"

"No," said Edmond, examining it. Certainly it was not a pretty picture; there was an air of horror about the scene, as of some region foreign to reason, a glimpse of an insane world. He scanned the unusually lucid script—Sarah Maddox.

"Who painted this?"

"I don't really know, sir. They come in here to sell 'em when they're broke; sometimes I never see 'em twice. I remember it was a sort of thin woman, but most of 'em are that way." He frowned in concentration. "Wait a minute; I think I paid her by check, and sometimes I put the address on the stub, in case the work sells good."

He thumbed through some stubs, then shook his head.

"The check was made out to cash. I didn't think her work would take, you see."

"How much is it?"

The man looked at him appraisingly.

"Eight dollars, sir."

Edmond paid and left, carrying the picture wrapped in a square of brown paper. He wandered on. He was somewhat surprised at the unattainability of man the individual. How did one pick up acquaintances? He considered approaching one of the numerous idlers he passed, and rejected the plan knowing from experience how he would be received. He walked on, back toward the towered heart of the city. A bookstore. He entered, glanced over the shelves of volumes. A clerk spoke to him by name; he had made previous purchases there.

At the rear was a table piled indiscriminately with tattered volumes. He picked up the first to hand, a book thick as a table dictionary—the Apocalypse Revealed of Swedenborg. He glanced through it, reading with his accustomed rapidity, absorbing the meaning of entire sentences instantly, as one might read words. He was interested by the curious intricacy of the author's mind. "They call him a mystic," he thought, "epithet of all epithets the most inapplicable. This man is no mystic, but scientist wasting his talents on a dream; his mind to his work is as a sculptor's chisel trying to carve out of a cloud."

He tossed the volume back, stepped again to the counter. The clerk moved to serve him.

"What book," said Edmond, "do you find the most popular at this time?"

The clerk smiled, and tapped a pile of little booklets before him. Edmond recognized them from various references he had seen in the newspapers; they held the autobiography of one who specialized in a lowly type of architecture.

"I don't think you'd care for this, Mr. Hall," said the clerk recalling certain previous purchases of Edmond's. "It's supposed to be humorous."

"I want one, however."

He took the thin little volume to a chair beside a table; in half an hour he had perused it.

"I lack all humor save irony," he thought. "Until I can understand this element in men their minds will elude me. I think that humor in itself is the enjoyment of disaster to others; people constitutionally hate each other, and the reason they band together in tribes and nations is merely that they fear nature and foreigners more deeply."

He slipped the booklet into his pocket, picked up his package, and again departed. The early setting sun of Autumn was already behind the buildings; the streets were beginning to chill. He hooked his cane over his arm and walked toward the lake; he turned north on Michigan, walking idly, aimlessly. The sense of futility was on him again; he forebore even to think. It seemed to him that he could never bridge the hiatus that lay between him and humanity; alien he was, and was doomed to remain. To make friends was an impossible feat; among the millions about him he walked solitary. He watched the flood of impatient cars jostle each other in a vast medley of motion, and walked and walked; he was lonely.

He passed the Drake. Beyond, the graying lake broke close to the street; some benches caught his eye and he crossed over to rest, for the long walking of the day had tired him a little. He sat down and lit a cigarette, watching the play of shadows between the wave crests. He felt desolate, futile.

A figure passed before him, turned and repassed, seating itself on the next bench a few yards to his left. He smoked silently. The figure suddenly moved to his side; he sensed it now as a woman, but made no move.

"Got the blues, huh?"

He turned. She was one of the ageless creatures of the modern city, wearing a mask of powder, her cheeks bright even in the dimming light.

"Yes," he said.

"Maybe I could cheer you up?" It was a question.

"Sit here a while. I should like to talk to you."

"Gosh, no sermons, Mister! I heard 'em all!"

"No. No sermons. I merely wish to talk to you."

"Well, I'm here."

Edmond drew the booklet he had purchased from his pocket. "Have you read this?"

She leaned over, peering at the title, and smiled.

"Huh, and I thought for a minute you were some kind of a preacher. No, I ain't read it, but a regular—a friend of mine, he tells me about it. I got a laugh."

"It is very funny, isn't it?"

"Yeah, the part where he falls in." She laughed. "The girls nearly passed out, the way he told it."

Edmond passed her the book.

"You may have this copy."

"Thanks." There was a moment's pause.

"Say, ain't we going somewhere?"

"I want to talk to you a while."

"Well, I gotta live."

"Yes," said Edmond; "that is true, from one viewpoint."

"Talking don't buy no groceries. I gotta live."

"Why?"

"Why? What's the idea? Everybody's gotta live, don't they?"

"People seem to believe so."

"Say, what's the matter with you? Don't you like me?"

"As well as I like any person."

"Say, who do you think you are, anyway?"

"That," said Edmond, "is something I have often wondered."

He stood up; his companion rose with him. He drew a bill from his pocket—five dollars, he noticed, and passed it to her.

"Good evening," he said.

"Is that all you want?"

"Yes."

"Well, for God's sake! Turned down! I never been so—Say, I know what's wrong with you! You must be queer!"

Edmond stared at her coldly. Suddenly a flame filled his eyes. He raised his arm, holding his hand before her face. Above his palm, his fingers writhed and twisted like five little snakes. He wriggled them before her eyes; they coiled about each other. The woman stared in frozen fascination for a moment, then shrieked, backed away, and fled over the clipped grass toward the street.

"That," said Edmond, as he reseated himself, and reached for another cigarette, "is humor!"

7. The Study of Man

"An entomologist," thought Edmond from his chair before the fire, "studies one variety of insect after another, learning their different life cycles and diverse habits.

"I spend my time unprofitably observing this single ant-heap of Chicago; perhaps I can learn what I wish by comparison with others."

Thus, leaving Homo in Magda's care, Edmond set out to travel. He viewed New York with little interest, sailing immediately for Liverpool because at the moment that route was most convenient. Thereafter he visited France for some months, liking best of all regions the country of the Spanish border with its magnificent uplands.

French and German he had as a heritage of his school days; other tongues came to him with an incredible facility, so that as he wandered he absorbed the dialect of his locale with chameleon-like rapidity. Yet his quest was fruitless insofar as the study of men went, for he found no differences save superficial ones.

He visited the bookstores in Paris and Venice, and added greatly to his collection. Several times he found curious volumes that surprised him—a little undated manuscript detailing a queer jest of Gilles de Retz, a tiny volume of twelve pages describing Roger Bacon's experiment with a mechanical head. And there were others.

"Am I really the first of my kind?" he wondered. "Perhaps in other ages an individual or so of us may have existed, solitary as I am solitary, lonely as I." The thought imparted to him a feeling of great sadness. "Their works lie here neglected, understood dimly or not at all, while lesser genius is enthroned."

So he wandered, sometimes rewarded, sometimes prey to a vast boredom and a sense of futility that nothing ever quite eradicated. About a year after his departure, he suddenly abandoned his quest and sailed from Havre.

"*Homo Sapiens* is a single species," he concluded, "and the world over, there exist no important differences save those of custom. Herein lies the reason for the recession of romantic color; there is nowhere anything unique. All people are merely types, members of a class, and no one anywhere merits the article 'the'. The Kraken has vanished from men's consciousness, and instead we have whales. The Golden Fleece has sunk into a legend of tradesmen."

He arrived at the house on Kenmore some hours after Homo coughed a final weak cough and succumbed at last to the unnatural climate, and a window Magda forgot to close. Edmond was somewhat moved as he gazed at the little furry body.

"So passes my single friend, and the only being whose presence I could miss. To my one friendship, therefore, I now erect a memorial."

He took the small corpse to his long-locked laboratory, emerging some time later with a tiny articulated skull. Thereafter he sent for a mason, and had this strange memento inset into the stonework above the library fire-place, whence its hollow gaze was fixed forever on his favored chair. Here he seated himself at the completion of the work, turning contemplative eyes on the empty ones that had been Homo's. Thus he sat silent for a long time, following out a course of thought that lay mostly beyond the regions enterable by words. Finally he stirred himself, being weary of thinking, and lit a cigarette with dexterous hands.

"Homo," he said, "is released from the innumerable petty illusions that harrass life. He knows not even that he knows not, and is infinitely wiser than he was when he perhaps thought himself wise.... For the most barren of all is the illusion of knowledge, which is a negative illusion, so that the more a man learns the less he knows." His eyes turned to the little landscape by Sarah Maddox that hung to the right of the mantel; as he gazed at it obliquely, it seemed again that he looked through a window at a strange world.

After a moment, he stirred, picked up the mass of mail that had accumulated during his absence. A vast sheaf of advertisements, which he tossed to the fire, a few current bills—he had let Magda forward these monthly to his bank for payment—several envelopes bearing the letterheads of universities. Edmond smiled; he had expected inquiries concerning his A-lead from the various students of matter and energy. He put these aside unopened; Bohn could take care of the replies.

"What is to be done now?" he thought. "Let me take my cue

again from the naturalist—when he has studied the habits of his subject, he secures a specimen to examine at leisure, under the microscope if he will. It is for me now to secure myself a specimen."

But how? How should he, to whom even the making of a friend was an obstacle insurmountable, lure a human being to his side, to live with him, speak without reserve to him, that he might study at leisure the human mind? Magda? Too poor a specimen, he thought; too stolid and stupid to show the full phenomena of mentality, and furthermore, too unaesthetic.

"If I may not make a friend, I can at least hire one under pretext of needing a guide or instructor," he thought, and dismissed the matter for that time.

He heard the buzz of the doorbell, and Magda's cumbrous tread. In a moment she entered the library, bulking through the arch like a little planet.

"She moves in orbits," thought Edmond, continuing the simile, "and completes a revolution once a day. Her sun is the kitchen stove, her room and the front door her aphelion and perihelion."

"There's a man to see you, Mr. Hall. He's been here a dozen times. Oldish with glasses." She extended a card.

"Alfred Stein, Department of Electro-physics, Northwestern University."

A picture of the lecture hall returned to Edmond's mind, the amiable little professor bustling about with his chalk and pointer, his own rare interest. It was very recently that Stein had published his most revolutionary studies of electrons.

"I will see him, Magda."

Edmond noted that the professor had changed but little. The iron-gray hair, the thick-lensed spectacles, the droop of the shoulders, were all as they had been in the class room.

"Mr. Hall?" said the professor, with a smile. "I am Alfred Stein of Northwestern. I have done some work with radioactive elements, and that interest brings me here."

"I am familiar with your work, Professor Stein," said Edmond, "having attended several of your courses in 1920."

"Ach, I should perhaps have remembered."

"Not at all; they were simply lecture courses. I have followed your work since, however."

The other beamed.

"That pleases me, Mr. Hall. It is something I seldom hear. And you agree with me?"

"I do not question your figures," said Edmond, "but your inferences are erroneous."

The professor winced.

"Well, let us not argue that. When someone offers a better hypothesis, I will listen. Meanwhile I am satisfied with mine."

Edmond nodded, and was silent. The little man blinked at him through his thick lenses, and continued.

"I am very much interested in this stuff you call Activated Lead, that the Stoddard company is using for filaments in radio tubes. We bought some of them, and took out the lead, but frankly, none of us has been able to make much out of it. I went to Stoddard's plant and they gave me some, and also I got a fantastic explanation from a fellow named Hoffman, from whom I had your name. So,—" he spread his hands, "I came to you. For a considerable time I have been trying to see you."

"For what purpose?"

"Why, to learn from you the true explanation of this amazing phenomenon."

"I do not doubt that Mr. Hoffman's explanation was accurate to the extent of his knowledge."

"A fairy tale about cosmic rays and neutronium that one does not believe."

"I can offer you no other solution, Professor Stein."

"You say it's true?"

"Yes,"

"Bah! That is an impossibility!"

Edmond smiled in his exasperatingly superior manner, but it failed to irritate the other whose blinking near-sighted eyes did not perceive his face except as a blur.

"Listen, my friend! You have a duty to consider. You owe something to the advancement of knowledge, and it is unfair of you to try to conceal any important discovery. The tube is patented; you can lose nothing by explaining."

"You are thinking," Edmond said slowly, "that the material can be used to replace radium in medical work—the treatment of cancer and the like."

"Yes, I had thought of it."

"You would like to patent that application for your personal gain."

The little professor blinked at him in surprise.

"Why—I give you my word I had no such thought!"

Edmond was slightly puzzled. It was apparent to him that the other was speaking the truth.

"I meet for the first time a true scientist," he reflected. "Altruism becomes more than a gesture." He turned to Stein.

"Professor, you are as you say entitled to an explanation. If you will step upstairs with me, I shall endeavor to supply it."

They entered the dark little laboratory with the blackened windows. Stein peered eagerly about as the light flashed on. The fragments of Edmond's disrupter were still scattered about; the table still showed the blackened pit of the atomic blast. Stein was examining the remnants of the interrupter as Edmond found a small reflector and lifted it to the table.

He repeated in somewhat greater detail the demonstration he had given Bohn and Hoffman. Stein watched him silently, intently; at the conclusion he laughed.

"This much I saw at the Stoddard plant, but they never let me touch their reflectors. I think, if you'll pardon me, that there is a trick."

"One can hardly wonder at their solicitous care of the reflectors," said Edmond. "They are irreplaceable—except by me."

"I should like to know how you make this so-called neutronium."

Edmond shook his head. "I cannot reveal that."

Stein chuckled. "Either way I don't blame you. If this is a fraud, certainly not—and if it's true, the danger in the hands of industry is appalling."

"You have my reason."

"Which one?" said Stein, and chuckled again. "Well, we have reached an impasse."

"Not necessarily," said Edmond. "I offer you this reflector—in return for a service and under conditions."

"The conditions?"

"Primarily that you make no more A-lead than you must to study the device, as the element is dangerous, and as indestructible as any element."

"That is easy."

"Then of course the material must be kept out of the channels of trade. Should you accumulate a surplus, it must be delivered to Stoddard."

"That too is easy."

"That is all."

"But the service?"

"Yes," said Edmond, "the service. In return for the gift of the reflector, I wish your aid in some social research I am doing. I should like to know more about people and their lives, and you will spend a certain amount of time as my guide and instructor. We shall explore the human ramifications of the city."

Stein laughed. "Ach, at that I would be a failure! I know less than anyone about people and their lives." He paused a moment. "See here, I will do this. What you need is a young sophisticate, someone who knows the town and is in touch with the people you seek. Me, I am a hermit almost, but I know a young man who would serve well."

"I will pay for his services," said Edmond.

"You should know him. He was at N. U. about the same time you were. His father is in the English department—Professor Varney."

"Yes," said Edmond. "I remember Paul Varney. We were at high school together as well."

"I will send him to see you. He has been trying to make a living by writing and will welcome a little additional compensation."

"I shall be grateful," said Edmond. "This reflector is small and not very heavy. You may either take it or send for it."

Stein picked up the bowl, tucked it under his arm.

"Thank you," he said. "If this fails Paul won't be around to see you."

8. Guinea Pig

Several days later Edmond returned from a casual walk to the lake shore to find a slender blond young man awaiting him, who forced a smile to his sensitive mouth.

"Good afternoon, Paul."

Paul's grin became more strained as he extended his hand. A shudder shook him as Edmond's supple fingers closed on it.

"Strange," reflected Edmond, "that the few women I have encountered have not hated me so intensely." He formulated his own reply. "Men hate their masters; women love them."

He led the way into the library.

"Sit down, Paul."

Paul seated himself, gazing curiously at the titles of the volumes that lined the walls. The skull of Homo above the fireplace startled him for a moment.

"Professor Stein asked me to call here."

"Doubtless he explained what I desire."

"To some extent. I gathered that you wanted a sort of guide to Chicago's night life." Paul smiled nervously. "I supposed you were writing a book."

"Not exactly," said Edmond, watching his companion. "But that will develop later. I will undertake to pay whatever expenses we incur, and will give you, say ten dollars per evening." In his mind's background he was reflecting, "This one will serve; this is a good specimen. High strung and sensitive, his reactions show on the surface for my observation."

"That is more than fair," said Paul a little bitterly. "I cannot afford to reject it."

"Then it is settled. I shall require you for a month or longer, though perhaps not every evening." He reached for the inevitable cigarette; Paul shifted as if to rise. "I understand that you still write."

"I am trying, or rather failing, to make a living at it."

"What type of writing?"

"Mostly poetry. I try my hand at a short story now and then."

"Have you any with you?"

Paul shook his head.

"Perhaps a notebook? Or a few fragments?"

Reluctantly Paul drew a paper covered notebook from his pocket. "I had rather not show these. They are merely jottings for the most part, and nothing finished."

"I am neither writer nor critic. You need fear neither ridicule nor plagiarism; it is merely that I wish to understand you. It occurs to me that a glance at your work may supplant some hours of getting acquainted."

Paul silently passed the notebook to Edmond who spun the pages with his miraculous rapidity.

Twice he paused for a longer glance. Paul fidgeted in his chair, watching the facile hands. As always, they fascinated him. Finally he selected a cigarette from the box beside him, lit it, and smoked in silence; after a moment more his companion flipped the last pages, glanced casually at them, and returned the booklet.

"You didn't read a great deal of it," remarked Paul, as he dropped it into his pocket. "I read all of it."

The other looked his incredulity, but said nothing. "There is one fragment that merits completion," continued Edmond, "the ballad that begins:

Thotmes, loud tramping over Abyssinia,
Swearing an oath of vengeance on its king
Seized then the ebon monarch's first-born Musa,
Blasted his manhood as a shameful thing.
Thotmes of Egypt, mighty builder of images,
Graven at Karnak, Lord of the North and South,
Made of the tall black prince a slave, first tearing
The tongue that cursed him from the bleeding mouth."

His cold tones ceased for the moment, then continued.

"It will doubtless surprise you to know that something similar actually occurred, though not exactly as you have noted it in your synopsis." He turned his intense eyes again on Paul. "Would you like me to tell you the story as it should be written?"

"If you think you can." Paul's mouth tightened into the trace of a sneer.

For some minutes thereafter Paul listened with a growing horror and a curious fascination to the meters that flowed in icy tones from his companion.

"Thus it goes," said Edmond at the conclusion. "It is susceptible to much polish as I gave it, since I do not pretend to be a poet. The thing is yours to use if you wish, though"—he smiled—"I do not imagine that a very large portion of the public would approve of it. However, I am glad to note that your work escapes at least one fault; few creatures to my mind are so valueless as the poet who writes vapid optimisms about this somewhat horrible process of living."

Paul departed, feeling dazed, and not a little angry. He felt somehow as though he had been subjected to innumerable subtle insults, though exactly how he did not understand.

The following evening at the appointed hour he presented himself at Edmond's home, finding his strange employer twirling the leaves of a book and smoking.

"Tonight you shall take me to some place of amusement," he said as Paul waited, "where there is music and dancing."

"The crowd is going to Spangli's just now."

"Spangli's will do," said Edmond rising. "I have been there."

"Why on earth do you need me as guide, if you've been there?"

"You shall interpret for me."

They entered the low roadster; Paul marveled at the liquid ease with which the vehicle slid through traffic. The car seemed elastic and flexible as a living, sentient being.

At Spangli's they seated themselves at an obscure corner table, whence the panorama of the room was observable as from a vantage point. The orchestra was resting for the moment; a clatter of conversation and laughter assailed their ears. Paul was silent, a little puzzled as to just what was expected of him; Edmond smoked and watched the tables around him. A waiter came up; they ordered.

With a moan of chords, the orchestra swung into action. Several couples rose and moved to the dance floor, followed by most of the remainder. Everyone, it seemed, was young; skirts which last year had swept the floor were this year almost non-existent, and the girls moved with the slim charm of youth. They swung into their partner's arms with an eager buoyancy, merged into a rippling stream of dancers that drifted past. Paul watched them sympathetically; Edmond with a more critical observation.

"Do you like to dance, Paul?"

"Why—of course."

"What is the nature of your enjoyment?"

"Well," said Paul reflectively, "it is a pleasure allied to music and poetry, melody and meter. One naturally enjoys the harmonious mingling of sound, motion and rhythm. There is a pleasure in using one's muscles gracefully." He paused.

"Explain it to me as if I were utterly strange to any of these feelings you describe, like a being from another planet."

"You are," thought Paul, "or else crazy." But he continued: "Dancing is as truly a creative art as any other, since it produces the sense of beauty, if only for the participants. In the circle of the arts, it verges into dramatic art or acting on the one side, and into sculpture and painting on the other. It is an evanescent art, dying as soon as created, but so too is the playing of music. And of all arts it is the most widely practised; vast numbers of people have no other means of self-expression."

Edmond, who had followed this with apparent intentness, crushed out his cigarette and smiled. Paul wondered momentarily whether his every smile was a sneer because of some distorted facial muscles. "A sort of Gwynplaine," he phrased it to himself.

"I will tell you what I think," said Edmond. "I think that all dancing of whatever sort, is sexual, allied to the wooing dances of birds, and that ballroom dancing is most purely erotic. The pleasure therein is the sensual rubbing of body on body, the more alluring because it is conventionalized and performed in public. It represents a secret triumph over the conventions."

Paul smiled. "No woman will concede that."

"No, since a woman must seem to be passionate against her will. To be successful—that is, to create the strongest appeal to males—a woman must seem to yield despite her inclinations. This is in the nature of a compliment to a man's attractions." He exhaled a plume of smoke. "Some of our nicest conventions in the attitudes of men and women are based on this fact."

"Well, perhaps you're right. But I think there is a true beauty, a sort of poetry of motion, distinct from sex. The swaying of reeds in a storm, the rippling of a field of grain, these are very lovely things."

"Bah! Your mind translates them to the undulations of female hips."

Paul shrugged and glanced at the dancing couples on the floor. For the tiniest fraction of a moment he had a curious illusion. From the corner of his eye his companion seemed to duplicate himself; there was a momentary impression that two men sat facing him, four eyes regarded him steadily. Startled, he altered his oblique glance; his companion sat as before, with a speculative gleam in his bright amber eyes, and feathery smoke stream exhaling from his parted lips. The faintest trace of expression lingered on his usually stony face—amusement, contempt, triumph? Paul could not read it as the thin lips drew another deep draught of smoke. "Probably the lights," he thought, as he turned again toward the floor.

A mass of dark bobbed hair drew his eyes. The girl turned, glanced over her shoulder at him, smiled in recognition.

"Hello, Vanny," he called.

The slow drift of the dancing current brought her closer. She saw Edmond, nodded slightly.

"Come sit at our table," she said as she passed on into the crowd.

Paul's eyes followed her. The music stopped. Her companion took her arm and strolled to a table across the room. Edmond watched the two casually. He was a little charmed by the girl's grace; she bore herself with a pertness and spirit that he liked.

"That's little Vanny Marten. You must remember her from school. Shall we move to their table?"

"I remember her. No," said Edmond. "However, you may do so. This is sufficient for tonight, and I am leaving." He called their waiter and took the check.

"Now what do you suppose," thought Paul, as he watched his employer depart. "What do you suppose he got out of this evening's activities that is worth ten dollars?"

He made his way to Vanny's table still wondering.

"Hello, Paul. What were you doing with him?"

"Hello, Walter. My new job. Pushing him around to study night life."

Vanny laughed. "May keep you away evenings," she mocked. "Never mind—I'll manage without you." She smiled mischievously, and chanted:

There was a young fellow named Paul
Whom his friends told to hire a hall,
But the way things fell out,
They were twisted about,
For they found that a Hall hired Paul."

Walter laughed a trifle loudly, he was feeling the first exaltation of liquor. Paul grinned, somewhat embarrassed. Walter filled a glass below the table's edge, passed it to him, reaching for Vanny's almost empty one. She refused with a smile and a gesture.

"Practically on the wagon," said Walter.

"No, merely a desire to remain within my capacity."

"How does one learn that?"

"Trial and error. I prefer public trials and private errors."

"Smart girl. System no good for me, though. I always err on the same side."

Paul set down his glass nearly empty. He was still thoughtful, silent. Vanny turned to him.

"What's the matter, Paul? Are you stunned into silence by this brilliant conversation?"

Paul smiled at her.

"I can't get him out of my mind. He's so—well, so abnormal, physically and mentally."

"Ought to be an interesting job."

"Oh, I won't be bored!" He finished the remainder of his glass. "Say, Vanny, you've got a pat sort of mind for impromptu limericks; you should have heard what I heard yesterday afternoon. He reeled off a thousand lines just to show me how it was done."

"Was it good?"

"It was horrible! The man's mind is as agile and snaky as his hands!"

"I'd like to meet him again."

"You never will with my aid," said Paul, with a sudden dark sense of foreboding. He looked at Vanny, whose dark eyes gazed into his without their accustomed sauciness; there was a faint glimmer of anxiety in them.

"Why—Paul, I've never seen you so upset. How can any person affect you so?"

"Ugh!" said Paul, with a shudder. "He's inhuman!"

9. Futility

For several weeks, with occasional breaks in routine, Paul and Edmond appeared often together. Together they visited the various havens of the pleasure-bound—the hotels, cabarets, and night-clubs. They listened to numberless dance orchestras, watched an endless parade of dancing couples, consumed a multitude of cigarettes and a not inconsiderable quantity of poor liquor. And Paul was still puzzled; certainly his employer was not seeking this alone in his search for atmosphere. Nor, to the best of Paul's knowledge was he himself contributing much to this pursuit; occasionally, it is true, Edmond questioned him about certain phases of the panorama but for the most part their discussions ranged through theoretical and highly impersonal fields. As for example, one evening at Kelsey's Venice. They had been discussing creative man, man the genius.

"Great men are great," said Paul, "by virtue of an impulse that is overwhelming. No man is great simply because he desires to be. He must have in addition to a finely organized neural system and brain, an outlook and a sympathy that partakes of the universal. Genius is a oneness with life; expression follows inevitably. This is the greatest happiness possible to man."

Edmond smiled in amused contempt.

"You are wrong in every premise save the biological," he said. "Great men are great simply because they desire to be; that is your driving overwhelming impulse. Furthermore, genius is neither a oneness with life nor a universal outlook; far from this, it is a maladjustment to life and the most highly personal outlook imaginable. Nor is creation the greatest happiness possible to man; like its feminine counterpart, birth, it is the greatest misery. Genius is always unhappy, always out of place, always a misfit in its environment; and finally, genius is always psychopathic."

"You believe with the crowd, then, that all geniuses are crazy."

"I said psychopathic, which is to say abnormal by the standards of the crowd. To use your argot, genius is largely a gigantic inferiority complex. And it is always masculine."

"That's ridiculous. Schopenhauer was long ago discredited."

"By a generation of feminists. How many great women can history recall, and of these few, how many live other than through their influence on men, or a man?"

Paul thought a moment.

"There is some truth here. Of course the thing is largely due to woman's social and economic position in the past. She has been suppressed by lack of freedom, paucity of education, and being forced into youthful motherhood. These restraints are breaking down today."

"Your premise is wrong. Men have overcome difficulties as great and greater. Lack of freedom, social and economic position, you yourself can recall a hundred men who have battered down these barriers." Edmond paused, looked at Paul with his piercing eyes. "What restrains woman, the thing that prohibits the sex from greatness, is her physical organization."

"You mean her more delicate make-up?"

"I mean her ovaries. Whatever creative genius she has flows into them."

"Still," said Paul, "one can mention Sappho."

"Yes; Sappho, goddess of feminism, idol of feminists. Sappho, product of the dawn, dimly glimpsed through the dawn's mists."

"How do you explain her?"

"I do not."

"Then what of your theory?"

"My theory stands. Do you or I, does anyone now living know that Sappho actually produced the works we have? Do you know even that she was indeed a woman? Yet granting these things, granting that Sappho, with the abnormality that stamps genius, is the exception, it is still true that woman is on the average less creative than man. Less creative through media of art, I repeat, because more creative with the substance of life."

Thus for this period Edmond pursued his researches into the character of Paul, leading him into argument, promulgating generalities he knew to be abhorrent, rasping his sharp intelligence across Paul's nature like a file, to expose the metal of Paul's ego below the oxide. And finally his analysis approached completion. He drew his conclusions, put them to the test of experiment, and was satisfied. Paul, he decided, was no more than a complex mechanism motivated by desires and fears, and to a lesser extent by logical reasoning. He pushed metaphorical buttons, moved verbal levers, and observed the results; he was confident that out of his knowledge and powers, he could if he wished control Paul's actions as easily as those of Homo in the days past.

He was increasingly unhappy. He was like a man in a Chinese torture-chamber, unable either to stand up or lie down; nothing in the world offered him an opportunity to exert himself to the utmost. Things yielded too easily; he had no worthy competition.

Knowledge! He could keep on pursuing it forever like one chasing the horizon; however far he drove it, it hemmed him in forever with the unknown. Now his knowledge of humanity was as futile as any other; what could he do with it? Paul had nothing to give him worth the taking. Once more he was brought face to face with his own conclusion: "Knowledge is the most barren of all illusions. It is a negative illusion, in that the more a man learns the less he knows."

10. Lucifer

"What am I?" queried Edmond of himself, "I am certainly not a man such as Paul, and yet I am indubitably male. I am not human in the literal sense, for I possess qualities and capacities that pass the human. Yet I am very closely akin to humanity, since in appearance and in all physical attributes I am allied to them. Save for this, I should believe myself alien to this planet. Since I am unique among its occupants—I should think myself a changeling, a Martian smuggled here by some inconceivable art."

He sat before the skull of Homo, idling an afternoon away in his chair in the library. The empty stare of the little skull drew his attention.

"Your blood is in me, Homo," he continued. "In all respects we show our common origin. My skull is yours grown more capacious, my hands are yours grown extremely agile, my soul is yours grown out of all nature, and my sadness is your joy become intelligent. You are my incontrovertible proof of my own earthly roots, there is no gainsaying our blood relationship when the family resemblance is so strong."

Again he posed his question, "Then what am I?" He turned the problem this way and that in his minds, seeking a point of departure for his line of rational argument. "If I am of human origin but not myself human, there are but three possibilities. The first of these is this: that I am a survival, a throw-back, a reincarnation of some ancient, great race that merged itself with humanity in the dawn before history. The second is this: that I am no more than an accident, utterly unique and without meaning, a sport, a product of chance, with neither origin nor effect beyond the domain of chance. And the third is that I prognosticate, that I foreshadow the great race to come, that I am indeed the superman born ahead of his appointed time. The solution of my enigma thus resolves itself into the problem of the past, the present, or the future."

He continued, "I reject the first of these, the concept of the past, on grounds logical, since a mighty race in antiquity must certainly have left its impress on the planet that bore it, yet nowhere in the world do I see any ruins save those of human origins. Egypt, Babylonia, Greece, India, China, Yucatan—these remnants are those of human cultures.

"I reject the second possibility, the concept of the present, on grounds ethical, since I possess a strong pride of race and a bitter contempt for those around me. Were I a chance product in the world, should I not envy these other beings, placed here by nature under her own laws and protection? My differences then must be a source of shame rather than the inceptors of this strong pride, this derisive contempt.

"There remains the third possibility, the concept of the future. Since I reject the others, I must accept the last, and believe that I foreshadow the coming of my race, and that I am the harbinger of doom for humanity. I am the Enemy, that which will destroy; I am the replacer of mankind, and the future incarnate."

He stared back at Homo with sombre eyes, meeting the eyeless, vacant, insolent gaze of the little skull.

"I am to man what man was to you, Homo. I am that which devil-worshippers adore, as perhaps your kind adored man, in fear and distrust of a power implacable and beyond understanding. For what else to man is his destroyer, his Enemy? I am all evil embodied to the human viewpoint. I am the Devil!"

Book 2
Power

1. The Brief Pursuit of Power

One afternoon Edmond drove his car aimlessly north, through the interminable suburbs of the sprawling city. For a time the effortless speed and vigor of the supple machine diverted him; it was as invigorating to him as if his own muscles thrust him forward, until this too palled. He slowed the swift vehicle, permitted it to idle aimlessly along the white highway, which here paralleled the lake, visible at intervals as a sharp flashing far to his right. A narrow semi-private lane sprung out of the road toward it; at random he drove his car along through a crowding cluster of trees. Now the lane passed just above the lake; a long slope inclined to the top of a little bluff below. Edmond slid his car to the side of the road, and stepped to the ground, walking casually toward the bluff that overlooked the lake.

He stared for a long while at the unresting surge of waters; the sound of the breaking wavelets hummed accompaniment to his mood of melancholy. He sat down, stretched himself on the grassy hill, and watched a tree etch patterns against the sky above him. He gave himself over to his mood. Futility, he thought, hemmed in his every effort; he felt that he could take whatever he might desire, but nothing was worth the taking. Even knowledge and its pursuit had failed him. There remained what? Power? Any terrestrial power lay in his grasp for the using. For a few moments he toyed with the idea, visualizing the means, sketching the plan. Several courses lay open to him, within the limits of his ability—the financial or industrial, through the control of wealth. The martial coup, through the development of invincible weapons. The emotional control—such power as the great religious leaders wielded in more plastic ages. Or, he reflected, any combination of these three. The second plan held his interest somewhat more strongly than the others; it presented problems of technical difficulty—the design of a weapon and perfecting of an organization—to provide an outlet for his energies.

He entertained no doubt of his abilities. The thing he desired was foredone in his mind; there remained only the deciding to be accomplished. This presented no easy task, for behind the drive of his ennui, his frustration, he realized that he did not want power over human beings. He did not hate them enough to oppress, nor love them well enough to guide. He stared down at a little hill of busy red ants before his feet, watched the creatures scurry about the important business of living and perpetuating.

"As well call myself emperor of these," he thought. He kicked a little sand across the openings, observing the ensuing excitement.

"They fear me as much and know me as little as men. What satisfaction is there to me?"

He continued thoughtfully, "Yet certainly an intelligent ant would prize my power over his fellows; as a man would deride this, but prize that mastery of his own kind. Things devolve on the point of view; this is the only absolute in the universe, being the ultimate denial of absolutes."

He lay back in the grass, watching a pale afternoon moon pursue the sun toward the west.

"I rest solidly here on the grass," he thought. "The sun and moon revolve quietly about me; security and peace surround me. Let me alter my viewpoint."

He gazed again at the moon, seeing it now as a hurtling sphere, trying to visualize his own relation to the immediate cosmos. And suddenly his viewpoint changed; no longer did he rest in safety on a grassy slope, but clung to the surface of a colossal globe that spun at fearful velocity—off at unimaginable distances whirled others in a gigantic frenzy of chaos—giant spheres whirling endlessly through infinity—blazing and dying and being re-born in fire. He clung to the side of his particular atom—a mite, an insect,—while vaster shapes whirled and danced under the blind play of the cosmos.

A leaf drifted from the tree before him. Edmond fixed his attention on it, won back to his normal viewpoint. The sun and moon dropped their mad dancing, moved slowly and majestically once more, and were only a little way above him. He found himself shaken, with his fingers and heels digging into the soft earth in a frenzy of effort to hold on. He sat up, lit a cigarette.

"That is the abyss in which all things dance. What is a dream of power before that?"

He thought for some time of his two vain attempts at happiness.

"The path of Knowledge," he concluded, "while it starts apparently in the proper direction, loses itself and its traveler at last in an endless maze of meandering on an illimitable desert; and the path of Power ends in a blank wall, and is so short and straight that I see to its futile end from whatever point I stand, without the need of treading it."

Thus he abandoned untried his scheme of conquest. The atom-disrupter, that had risen in his mind as a world-shaking weapon, sank again to the oblivion of an experiment that was finished. Colossal things died in the conceiving, like an untold infinity of potential human genius.

"A sort of intellectual masturbation," thought Edmond, "in that I let the seeds of my thoughts die sterile."

There remained nothing. Was every avenue forever barred? Must he struggle to the end against the old futility that hemmed him, like one who battles a fog that closes about his blows?

"One road is still untried, though I am by nature ill-fitted to travel it—

"Happiness through pleasure. The satisfaction of the senses. This presupposes the incidence of sex on my experience, and the pursuit of beauty. I find myself not reluctant."

He rose and mounted the slope toward his car, a grotesque anachronism as he toiled upward, a being born out of his time.

"Paul must serve me here," he reflected moodily. "He shall procure me a woman."

Book 3

The Pursuit of Pleasure

1. The Seed Planted

"Listen to me a minute, Vanny!" Paul was expostulating. "I'm serious. You've got to answer me."

Vanny stopped humming, turned her pert features toward him.

"All right. The answer is maybe."

Paul stared at her a moment on the verge of anger, gave a gesture of exasperation, and strode to the window. Her laugh followed him. For a moment he stared down at the street, where a bat whirled and circled the solitary arc light trying, no doubt, to look like a dragon. Paul spun about, faced the smiling girl.

"You're certainly expert at the fine art of torture," he said. Vanny wrinkled her nose at him, toying with the great black Persian cat beside her.

"Listen to him, Eblis! He's accusing your mistress." She turned back to Paul. "I've been studying Torquemado."

"You could teach him a few tricks!"

"Don't growl at me, Honey. All I'm suggesting is the use of a little intelligence."

"Bah! What's the matter with me, Vanny? God knows I love you, and sometimes you seem to care for me. Why won't you marry me?"

"I thought we agreed last time to drop the discussion."

"But why won't you?"

She cast him another impish smile.

"Said then the little maid,
You have very little said
To induce a little maid for to wed, wed, wed.
So pray say a little more,
Or produce a little ore,
'Ere I'll make a little print in your bed, bed, bed!"

"Vanny, you're impossible!"

"But I mean it, Paul. Two of us can't live comfortably on what I've got, and your contribution would hardly suffice."

Paul dropped to the davenport beside her, startling Eblis into an ebony flash to the floor.

"I guess you're right," he said, dropping his face to his hands. A tinge of sympathy passed over the girl's face; she placed a hand on her companion's shoulder, touched his light hair.

"Snap out of it, Honey," she said. "All's not lost save honor."

Paul sat erect. "Very well, but I'm giving you fair warning, Vanny—this isn't going on much longer! I'll have you somehow."

She dropped her shining black head to his shoulder. "You have my permission to try—try as hard as ever you can, Paul."

For a time they were silent. Paul slipped his arm about her, drew her closer, but he still brooded, morose and unhappy. Best start a new train of thought, reflected Vanny.

"How's the night-work, Paul?"

"I'm through with it."

"Fired?"

"No; I quit. Couldn't stand it."

"Why not?"

"Something's wrong with that fellow, Vanny— something's very wrong. Either he's crazy, or—I don't know, but there's something unnatural about him. His snaky hands and all."

"I used to think his hands were lovely, at school."

Paul did not answer. He was still sullen; something weighed heavily on him. Vanny looked at him with a tinge of pity.

"What's really the matter with you, Paul?"

"Nothing I can tell."

"Don't be silly. I'm no prude, and I have the average gift of understanding."

"It sounds foolish, Vanny—but I'm afraid of that fellow Edmond Hall."

"For Pete's sake, why? You could crack him like a nut!"

"Well, the other night—that's when I quit—he wanted me to bring him here!"

Vanny stared at Paul's distressed face, broke into a peal of laughter.

"He wouldn't be the first freak you've dragged around, Honey!"

"All right," said Paul, again sullen. "You would have it, and there it is."

"But still, what's the trouble? Why not bring him over some evening? You're not jealous in advance, are you."

"Yes! I am!"

Vanny laughed again, with a taunt in her eyes.

"Not in the way you think," said Paul.

"Of course not." She was still teasing.

"Oh, I don't think you'd ever fall for him! He's too devoid of sex appeal."

"Then what?"

"I don't know," said Paul, "except that I feel he's an ill-omened bird. He's got a raven soul, and it croaks behind his every mood."

"Baa!" said Vanny. "You get tiresome. Your soul's an old woman soul, and doesn't take second honors anywhere in croaking."

She cast off his arm, rose, and pirouetted before him, ending in a curtsy.

"Come on, Paul. Switch on the radio, and let's dance."

"I don't feel like dancing."

Vanny crossed the room, spun the glowing dial. A dance orchestra swelled into melodious syncopation. She danced over to Paul, seized his hand and pulled him reluctantly erect, drawing herself into his arms as they swayed into the rhythm of the music.

"Paul"—she threw back her head to look up at him—"why don't you bring him over?"

"Never!"

"You don't have to be jealous, Honey. I'd just like to meet him again."

"You never will through me!"

"Well, you needn't snap at me so!"

"If you want to see him, call him up yourself!"

"It would be a bit presumptuous, hardly having seen him for ten years—not since high school days." They swayed easily to the music. "However—perhaps I will!"

2. The Seed Sprouts

Edmond felt no more anger at Paul's defection than he felt at the rain or wind or force of gravity, or any other natural circumstance. Indeed, he had anticipated it, perceiving in Paul's nature the emotional seeds from which the refusal sprang. Still, a quality in his own nature, either the goad of ennui or a certain grim persistence led him to maintain Vanny as his objective. His usual merciless scrutiny of his own motives led him to a realization that a certain preference lay behind his persistence; this girl offered a rather rare aesthetic appeal that drew him more, perhaps, than his original plan contemplated.

"I weave nets to entrap myself," he reflected, answering at the same moment in another part of his mind, "Surely I am strong enough to break any snare of my own creating."

Thus he set about the task of rebuilding an acquaintanceship of his past. He wished to arrange an apparently casual meeting, confiding thereafter in designs of his own, and he was content for the present to trust to chance to provide the encounter.

For several mornings he drove his car along Sheridan Road, past Vanny's accustomed bus-stop, but failed to meet her. Once he fancied he glimpsed her entering a lumbering bus several blocks ahead of him. He did not pursue; the chancy seeming of the meeting would have been destroyed—a subtlety he preferred to preserve.

In his complex mentalities he reflected, "Paul has beyond doubt informed this girl of my suggestion; let her vanity be a little flattered by my interest, and then a little piqued by my lack of it. This at least will give our ultimate encounter a spice of attention." Thus he reflected, and afterwards parked his car on a side street; spending the better part of the day watching a school of minnows that sported through the lagoon in Lincoln Park. He thought idly of many things, amusing himself for a time trying to imagine a feat impossible to perform in the world of the Material.

"All things are possible," he concluded, "given time and a price, and the greater the span of time, the smaller is the price required—

and this in effect is but saying that in eternity whatever can happen must happen. Flammarion glimpsed this truth, but his specious theory of past eternity and future is obviously fallacious."

The meeting was not entirely unexpected by Vanny. She sat at a table in Kelsey's Venice, with Walter Nussman. The orchestra, ensconced in its gondola, drifted silent in the fifteen-foot pool. Vanny was a little flushed, her black eyes a trifle brighter than usual; she had already taken four highballs from Walter's rather capacious flask. Walter was becoming a bit solicitous; indeed, Vanny seldom indulged very freely, yet here she was sipping her fifth, and the evening still young.

"Why don't you quit worrying about Paul, Vanny? He'll be around as usual!"

"Listen, Grandpa! My worries are my personal property! For your information, I'm not worrying anyway."

"What's the trouble between you? As your elder, I always thought you two made such an attractive couple."

"We had a spat—and besides, I won't be coupled with anybody! I'm a trust-buster!"

"Huh?"

"He was acting in restraint of trade, and I'm the Sherman Law. *Verstehen Sie?*"

"You're pickled," said Walter, with a judicial air. "You're soused, pie-eyed, blotto, besotted!"

Something in his remark seemed deliciously funny to the girl; she laughed unrestrainedly.

"Why I am not! I'm as sober as you are!"

"My God!" said Walter. "Then we'd better leave at once!"

Vanny raised her glass as the orchestra emitted a blare of introductory chords. Walter seized the opportunity.

"Put it down and let's dance."

"Sure," said Vanny. "You just whirl me around. That's as good as a drink."

They moved on toward the floor, joining the throng already swinging into the time of the music. Vanny was just a shade unsteady.

"Put some pep into it!" she complained; but the sedate Walter danced as he always danced, marking time as if the staccato blues were a Teutonic march. After a while Vanny succeeded in losing herself in the music; she hummed the piece to herself—the perennial St. Louis Blues—and achieved the sensation of drifting bodiless on a gently undulating sea. She closed her eyes. Walter's methodical steps required no effort to follow; all her consciousness flowed into the single sensation of rhythmic movement. She was dizzily content; there was a faint realization of the forgetting of something unpleasant. Paul! That was it. Well, let him do the remembering; she was well enough able to get along.

The undulations seemed to be lengthening, rising to a peak, and then a long downward slide. Not nearly so pleasant. Better open her eyes—so. The room was swaying a little; she forced her eyes to focus more sharply, and gazed without any surprise into the eyes of Edmond Hall. She flashed him a smile of recognition; he responded. Alone at a table; did he always come to these places just to sit and drink?

"There's Edmond Hall," she said.

Walter spun her around and gazed over her shoulder.

"The cat-eyed gent sitting alone? Is he the electrical inventor?"

"You don't have to spin me around so! I don't like it."

"I had to write a Sunday feature about his radio tube," said Walter. "Wrote it without an interview, too; he was in Europe. There's something deep about it. Half the authorities I called on said the thing didn't exist, and the rest said it was a fake. Finally got a little information out of this fellow Alfred Stein at Northwestern." He chuckled. "The paper's still getting peeved letters from professorial cranks!"

The music stopped. They joined the general exit from the floor. Seated again, Vanny toyed with the remains of her highball. It was nearly flat, she added a little ginger ale.

"I went to school with him," she said.

"With whom? Oh—Edmond Hall."

"He's funny, but not as bad as Paul makes out."

"Can't prove anything by me," said Walter. "Didn't we see him once before—at Spangli's?"

"Yes. Paul was working for him then."

She sipped the amber-fired glass before her.

"Listen, Walter. He likes me."

"How do you know?"

"I'm telling you. You're my father confessor. That's what started Paul and me quarreling. That's why Paul quit his job. Hall wanted to come over. And I said I'd ask him."

"I never saw you at the confidential stage before! You'll be crying on my shoulder next."

"I'm all right. I'm going to ask him over to our table."

"That's your privilege, my dear."

Vanny turned; Edmond was still regarding her with cold amber eyes. She smiled and beckoned, and the other answered, rising.

"Walter Nussman," said Edmond, at the introduction. "Do you write for the *Sun-Bulletin*?"

"Guilty as charged," Walter laughed. "You must have seen my feature on your A-tube."

"I did see it. If ever I want to conceal the mechanics of any device of mine, I will surely let you explain it."

"Perhaps the article was a bit inaccurate."

"A trifle so. I believe you did have my name correct."

"Now I wonder how that happened! I'll speak to the proofreader."

"Say, you two!" put in Vanny. "I'm being overwhelmed! Such mutual admiration!" She turned to Edmond. "Won't you sit down? I thought you looked lonesome."

"Thank you," said Edmond, meanwhile reflecting, "Paul has been playing my game, else I should have been compelled to make my own opening."

"I'm thirsty," announced Vanny. "Walter, mix me a drink."

Walter inverted his flask.

"Empty, my dear—and lucky for you that it is!"

"I have some," said Edmond, producing his flask. He was unobtrusively watching Vanny; she was still in control of herself, he perceived, though not with her usual cool self-assurance. "Her conscious self is relaxing," he observed. "Paul has forewarned her; let me use the means at hand to pierce this resistance." He permitted the girl to pour her own drink, while Walter grumbled.

"Don't say I didn't warn you! You'll suffer the consequences yourself."

"Listen to me, Old Man! Have I ever disgraced you? Have I?" she insisted.

"I guess not."

"Well! And I'm all right—a little dizzy, but perfectly all right!"

She raised her glass. A feeling of recklessness swept into her; she did not note that Edmond's eyes were fixed on her. "Whee!" she said, and drained the contents. "How do you like that, Ancient?" she taunted Walter.

"About as well as you will in another half-hour!"

"Quit croaking! This isn't an inquest, and you're not the coroner. I came here for a pleasant evening, and that's what I'm going to have!"

Edmond's flask still lay on the table. Suddenly Vanny snatched it, opened it, and raised it to her lips. Walter seized it, jerking it away with a trickle of tea-colored spots spreading down the crimson silk front of her dress. Someone laughed at an adjoining table. She wiped her lips with a napkin, dabbing at the spotted silk.

"Boor!" she snapped. But somehow the last swallow hadn't tasted right; the floor was gyrating too precariously. "I didn't want any more anyway," she finished.

Edmond stoppered his flask and removed it. "This is sufficient," he thought, and turned his mind to the furtherance of his designs. Vanny's control was at low ebb, and he fixed his eyes on her with a certain compulsion in his gaze; there was something he wished to impress on her mind, something he wanted her to say. She swayed in her chair, shifting her gaze as if to avoid some disturbing sight.

"I want to dance!" she said.

"Better not," said Walter. "We'd better be leaving."

Edmond was peering at the girl, apparently estimating her condition; Walter's near-sighted vision failed to note the intensity of the lambent eyes.

"She's all right for the present," he said. "I'll dance with you, Vanny, if I may."

They rose, and Edmond led her to the crowded floor. She moved erectly and steadily enough, but with an effort. They swung into the moving huddle of couples. Edmond danced for the first time in his life, but observation served him, or perhaps his partner was in too uncritical a condition to judge. They moved smoothly, however, and Edmond kept his curious eyes on Vanny's, gazing coldly persistently into hers with some unspoken command. The girl leaned more heavily on his arm.

"I want to sit down!" she said finally; he half-supported her across the floor to their table. She sank into her chair and dropped her face into her hands, while Walter watched with a look of consternation.

"My God, don't pass out here!" he exclaimed.

She looked up at him. "I want to say something," she said.

She felt, suddenly, a sense of foreboding. Decidedly, the world as expressed in her immediate surroundings did not seem nearly as pleasant as it had some minutes before. That last highball had been a mistake, as well as the fiery draught of straight whiskey. Walter was speaking to her; his words didn't register clearly in the blur of sensations. She was trying to formulate something, a thought that seemed trying to emerge by itself from a whirling turmoil of dizziness.

"Listen, both of you," she said, "while I'm still on deck. Tomorrow's Sunday, isn't it?"

"Certainly is," agreed Walter.

"Well, I want both of you to come over in the afternoon. About four. Paul's coming, I think. Both of you—especially you, Edmond Hall!"

She dropped her face to her hands again.

"It's hot in here. I want to get out."

There was a muddle of words about her. Walter— "No, we came in a taxi." And Edmond's voice: "I have my car." She did not see the triumphant gleam in his amber eyes as he took her arm to assist her. Walter stood at her left. Her last clear memory of the place was of a full-length mirror in the hall; she glimpsed herself very pallid, but the strangeness of the memory was of Edmond; he seemed to duplicate himself, so that he supported her from both sides. She stood between two twin Edmonds and Walter's reflection did not appear.

3. The Plant Flowers

Eblis stalked into the room, spat indignantly at Walter for daring to occupy his accustomed chair, and leaped to Vanny's lap. She caressed his black velvet fur with her hand, stretched out her pajamaed legs.

"Was I very awful?" she asked ruefully.

"Never saw anyone worse."

"I'm terribly ashamed. I only wanted to get a little happy."

"You succeeded. Remember the ride home?"

"Not very much. It was in Edmond's car." She thought a moment. "We stopped somewhere, didn't we?"

"Yeah. Several times. Once in Lincoln Park for your benefit, and once in front of his house. Say, speaking of that, how do you feel today?"

"Not bad at all. I've felt worse with less cause. Why?"

"Well, he gave you something. Don't you remember?"

"Omit the questions. I'm doing the listening."

"Well, he went into his house and got something, and I sort of supported you while he persuaded you to drink it. Said it'd ease off the after effects."

"It must have."

"Whatever the dope was, it laid you out like a black-jack. I was a little worried, but he said he'd studied medicine."

Vanny reflected. "I believe he did."

"Well, then he drove us here with you peacefully out on my shoulder, and between us we got you upstairs."

"And left, I hope, like good boys."

Walter grinned. "We held an inquest, and I was the coroner and you the *corpus delicti*."

Vanny flushed. "I remember the remark, but you don't have to rub it in. I was miserable enough this morning."

Walter relented. "We didn't do much after delivering you to the proper address. I was all for waiting around but he said the stuff would keep you quiet for five or six hours, and you'd come out of it fairly O. K. So—we parked you right there on the davenport and left."

Vanny gave another rueful smile. "That's where I woke up this morning—in a black and red dress that had seen its last party. I liked that dress"—she sighed—"and all I could think of was my invitation to you and Edmond to come over today. I remembered that perfectly. Think he'll come?"

"Why not? It's the gentlemanly thing to inquire as to your state of health." Walter paused. "Incidentally I came early, so that if you'd reconsidered— we could always leave, you know. Plead forgetfulness. I thought it might be a trifle unpleasant for you if Paul and he were present together."

"Thoughtful of you, at that," she said. "Of course I'm not sure Paul's coming since our spat—that's just a hunch. It's been a habit of his to drop in for a cold snack Sunday evening. Besides, I've a hankering to see Edmond when I'm sober; my impressions of last night are not of the clearest." She was remembering mainly the strange double image of the hall mirror. Do inebriates literally see double? And why twin images of Edmond at the expense of Walter's respectable reflection?

"The choice is yours, Dark Princess," Walter was replying.

"We'll stay, then," Vanny decided.

The bell rang. Walter rose to answer; glanced down the apartment hall. He shrugged, and stole a glance at Vanny. "Paul" his lips formed silently. She spread her hands in a quizzical gesture of resignation, and Paul entered. He was patently not over pleased to see Walter and greeted Vanny with, "I'd hoped to find you alone."

"I was just on the point of leaving," put in Walter, seating himself and ostentatiously packing his pipe. Paul glared at him as he lit up and puffed complacently, but Vanny flashed him a smile of gratitude; she would thoroughly appreciate his restraining presence should Edmond appear.

"Never mind, Honey," she soothed teasingly. "With your temper it's just as well to have the presence of a solid citizen like Walter."

"Sometimes my outbursts are justified!"

"All right, Everett True!" She turned to Walter. "Make some conversation, Ancient."

"I can tell you what a rotten business feature writing is. Or any kind of writing, for that matter!"

"It's not a business," said Paul gloomily. "It's not profitable enough to be called a means of livelihood."

"Then why'd you decide to try to become a writer?"

Paul ignored the implied slur. "As master Tristam Shandy says, 'I would not be a lawyer and live by men's quarrels, or a doctor and live by their misfortunes, so'"—he spread his hands— "'I became a writer'—"

"And live by their stupidity," said Edmond Hall in the doorway. In the startled silence the mantel clock chimed four, beating in dirge-like tempo to Walter's murmured, "My God, I left the door open!"

"You did," agreed Edmond, as the three stared at him. Paul's vindictive glare left him unmoved. He nodded coolly and inclusively to the two men, and turned to Vanny.

"I anticipated your recovery," he said. "I am glad to find myself justified."

Vanny sensed the question forming on Paul's lips, and felt a flush of embarrassment suffusing her face.

"Thank you," she said, and cast about for some means of forestalling Paul's question. Walter was nonplussed for the moment; Edmond's reference in Paul's presence to the debacle of the previous evening had surprised him. Edmond himself broke the momentary silence.

"I stopped by for just a minute or two," he said. "However, I should be honored to have you accompany me to dinner tonight."

Vanny felt Paul's gaze upon her. She formulated a polite refusal, and heard with genuine surprise the sound of her voice in answer, "I shall be delighted, Edmond."

"Thank you," he said. "I'll call for you at six-thirty."

He moved toward the door.

"Wait, Hall, I'm leaving too," said Walter suddenly. He felt his duty done with Edmond's departure, and had no stomach for the scene he saw foreshadowed in Paul's face.

As the door closed, Paul turned to Vanny. His stormy eyes surveyed her.

"Well!" he said.

"Let's have it," said the girl.

"What's that about your recovery? Recovery from what?"

"I'll tell you! I was soused last night."

"You—soused?"

"Well, pickled, then! I don't care what you call it."

"Vanny! You?"

"No one else! I didn't enjoy it. I passed out."

"But why?"

"You ought to know! I was just trying to forget our scrap. I was only trying to be happy for a little while!"

"Who was there?"

"Walter took me to the Venice. Edmond was there alone and he came and sat with us."

"Walter!" groaned Paul disconsolately, somewhat to Vanny's surprise. She had expected Edmond to furnish most of the fuel to his anger.

"What's wrong with Walter? He'll never say anything."

"That fat Philistine! I know he won't say anything! He'll be quiet simply as a favor! He just loves to do favors—the greaseball!"

"Well, no one'll know!"

"*He'll* know, and *I'll* know! He'll think I ought to be grateful because he's being a gentleman! He'll think he's in our confidence!"

"Oh my Lord!" said Vanny, a little relieved at the turn Paul's anger was taking. "I don't think that's such a vital point."

"All right! What about this dinner date with that fellow Hall? Why'd you accept that?"

"I don't know," said Vanny, wondering why she had. "I guess I was just mad at you. Our last fight was over him."

"You don't care much for my feelings!"

"You know I do, Paul!"

"Do you mean you won't go? You'll break the date?"

"No, I don't mean that," said Vanny, shaking her glistening black head. "I've got to keep the date."

"You're going with him?" Paul was almost incredulous. She nodded.

"Bah!" said Paul. He turned and slammed his way out of the door. Vanny watched him go with dark tearful eyes, and turned to bury her face in the deep fur of Eblis who still purred in the corner of the davenport. The great cat felt a touch of moisture; he drew back indignantly and leaped to the floor. Vanny flashed the animal a somber little smile: "Heaven knows you were well named, Eblis."

4. Jupiter & Leda

For some reason which she did not analyze, Vanny dressed with considerable care for her dinner with Edmond. With no idea of the type of restaurant he contemplated, she selected a severely tailored costume of wine velvet, with a collar as ebon as her hair, and after some consideration, violated the fashion by choosing sheer black hose and tiny black pumps. Edmond's prompt arrival found her ready.

The strange amber eyes surveyed her, and she fancied they held a gleam of admiration. Indeed, Edmond, deep lover of all beauty, found her not at all displeasing, but his cool mentality, pursuing its inevitable probing, searched out the reason Vanny had ignored.

"She previsions the conflict imminent between us, and arrays herself to sustain her own self-confidence. She uses her beauty not as weapon but as armor."

But aloud he merely greeted her.

"Will you have a cocktail before we leave?" asked Vanny.

The other acquiesced, permitting himself a saturnine smile as he noticed that she poured only one. She answered with a little grimace of distaste. "Not for a long time."

Edmond replaced his empty glass on the tray.

"Where are we going?" asked the girl.

"Have you any preference?"

"None at all."

"Then let me take you to a place which will perhaps be novel."

Vanny was quiet and a little ill at ease on the drive toward town. She felt constrained and embarrassed, the usual topics of conversation seemed thoroughly futile — the "What-have-you-been-doing's" and "How-have-you-been's" of former schoolmates. The phantom of Paul's anger, too, rode between them and conversation was restrained to simple generalities.

Edmond drove to a section strange to her, well westward from the Loop, and led her into a plain little second floor restaurant with no more than a dozen tables covered with red-checkered cloths. She glanced around curiously.

"Oh—Russian!"

She recognized a giant samovar, symbol to America of things Slavic. Two nondescript men held each a curious stringed instrument in the far corner— balalaikas, she concluded.

"Muscovite," answered Edmond.

They chose a table in a deserted corner—easily enough, for only two other tables were occupied. Vanny was charmed by the appearance of a bearded waiter, and amazed when Edmond addressed him in throaty Slavic. She was charmed again by the cuisine, delighted with the appearance as appetizer of apparently unbroken eggs that proved to contain a paste of caviar, a little startled by the borscht, and once more delighted by a curiously creamy, extremely rich pudding.

"Why, this is a gem of a place!"

She suddenly realized with what enjoyment she had eaten; she had not dared taste food during the day. With the cigarettes came a sensation of normalcy; she felt quite herself again. She resumed her usual self-assurance, and Paul's difficult temperament ceased to weigh upon her. She felt again her cool mastery of self and situation, and turned her attention to her strange companion. He sat regarding her with a half-smile.

"If I've made a pig of myself, the blame is yours for so perfect a choice of restaurants!"

"I hoped you would enjoy it."

Vanny pressed out her cigarette.

"Shall we leave?"

"At your pleasure. Have you the evening free?"

"Of course. My Sunday evenings have usually been reserved for Paul, but he knows of our date."

"Shall we try a theatre?"

"No," said Vanny. "I'm sick of purchased amusement. Let's steal ours. Let's ride. We haven't really talked yet, you know."

They drove northward through the cool autumnal air. The lake flashed, and a purple night-veil gave back the stars like an echo. Vanny turned to her companion.

"Why were you anxious to meet me?"

"Because you offer a certain beauty for which I have been seeking."

She laughed. The compliment placed her on familiar ground; she felt as easily able to manage this being at her side as Walter, or fierce, sweet, lovable Paul, who always came back apologetic and dejected. Would he tease as easily?

"Well, that's the first glimmer!"

"Of what?"

"Of deviltry. Frankly, Edmond, while you've been a pleasant companion so far this evening, you've not been quite the fiend I've heard."

"And while you're as lovely at close range as I believed, you've not proved the nymphomaniac women are supposed to be."

"That's a little better!" the girl teased, "but a bit too personal! Besides, I've been called cold before. I like the reputation."

Edmond turned his eyes from the road, looking for a moment into hers. "Perhaps the name is less warranted than you like to think."

For a short moment, when her eyes met the strange ones of her companion, Vanny felt a little thrill that was almost fear. Instantly it passed, but a stray chill breeze from the lake seemed to rise. She shivered.

"Now I'm really cold," she said.

"Shall we stop somewhere?"

She considered a moment. "I know! Let's stop at the apartment. We can talk there, and no one's likely to come on Sunday."

The agile car swung around, driving toward Sheridan and its banks of mountainous dwellings. They entered, and Edmond recalling the position of the furniture from the preceding night, switched on a single rosy lamp. For a moment they gazed from the window on the distant flow of traffic.

"I always thrill to this," said Vanny. "Life centers in cities."

"Civilization," said Edmond. "City-building. The word is its own definition."

Vanny seated herself on the davenport. The great Eblis bounded into the room; she stretched out her foot to toy with him, then noting the direction of Edmond's gaze, withdrew it, smoothing her skirt in some embarrassment.

"The lady has a prudish streak," thought Edmond. "I shall take pleasure in violating this inhibition." But aloud he continued the conversation. "This colossus called Chicago, and all of its species, is the outgrowth of power and its application. The cycle is self-perpetuating—great cities demand abundant power, cheap energy favors the expansion of cities."

"Paul was describing the city of the future to me not long ago," said Vanny. "Not like this, but a clean and beautiful place. He thinks large cities will die out."

"Being Paul, he is probably wrong," said Edmond. "The future is never explicable in terms of the past, no more than is the tree in terms of its seed. The elements, the germs, are there but the fruition is a thing apart." He was studying the girl as he had Paul, probing her mind and the subtle relations that are called character. Two evenings in her company gave him data; the conflict approached as he prepared to further his designs.

"Shall I describe the City of the Future, its glory and its horror?" he continued.

"If you think you're qualified," smiled his companion.

"Let us see," said Edmond with a curiously sardonic smile.

He began to speak in a low monody that droned in Vanny's ears like a murmur of distant waters. Gradually the sense of the words grew vague; the sounds of them merged into a continuity, but the pictures they evoked lived on, grew into a sort of reality. She wondered momentarily at this phenomenon, then lost herself in the magic imagery; it did not occur to her that she was being lulled into a quasi-hypnotic state.

"It is hot—sultry, on the ground level. Above us is no sky, but the span of the first tier, the swift stage of the delivery level, and the first level of Palace Avenue. This is the city Urbs, planet-capital, greatest of the world cities of that future era, and here buried in the depths of her steel entrails, lies the forgotten ground that bears her. We hear the muffled roar of traffic above us, the voice of that great Street and the hiss of liquid-air coolers sighs from the walls beside us.

"You turn to me. 'It has been a year since last I have had occasion to walk on the ground.'

"A great freight-bearer rumbles past, forcing us close to the walls. We walk on, since it is your fancy to walk, past masses of blank masonry, windowless but with many doors that gobble freight. Here in the dimness of the ground level the air of Urbs is foul with the breath of her thirty-five millions. Even the almost negligible costume of the day feels hot and moist about our bodies; you sweep back your black hair from your forehead with a gesture of petulance.

"'And yet I love it!' you murmur. 'This is the city Urbs!' And indeed there is a sort of splendor about the thing, even in its drumbeat voice echoing its vastness to the depths wherein we plod. There is a shouting behind us, and a crowd surges for a few seconds across the street. We watch for a moment, then move on; there is always rioting on the ground level, but a shade of trouble shows in your eyes.

"Ahead glows the red sign of the doorway of the Atlas Building, above a little stone-arched portal; for the great gates of the public ways are far above us. We seat ourselves in a lift for the ten-minute ride to Mile-high Gardens, half-a-thousand stories above the ground. The windows drop past, instant glimpses of the tiers that rise along the great Avenue, a moment's flash of a sky serrated by mist-capped towers, interlaced by the spider-web of the monorail. Then open sky and the cloud traffic of the city Urbs, and we step out into the sun and music and coolness of the Gardens. It is the hour of luncheon; the tables are well occupied. There comes a sudden burst of applause as we appear, for you are Evanne, called the Black Flame."

Vanny turned dark dreamy eyes on the narrator. "But part of the applause is for you, Edmond. Tell me why." Edmond smiled his saturnine smile; he perceived that his designs were succeeding, for it mattered little what story he told if only it seemed real to his listener, so that his twin minds could insinuate his appointed thoughts. So he continued.

"We seat ourselves, and a waiter brings the wines. A performer is singing—your song, Vanny, 'The Black Flame'—in queer, clipped Urban English. But we stare down the teeming length of that mighty Street to its far end, where the twin spires of the Palace rise even to our eyes. There is the dwelling of him called in Urbs the Master, and in the outer nations, the Overlord.

"'An hour—only an hour more,' you say. 'Must you leave again so very soon?' and I answer, 'There is revolution in Africa, and revolt in China. The structure of the Empire grows top-heavy like its City; some one must dance about on top to balance its teetering.'

We stare again at the Palace spires, symbol of the Master loved in Urbs, world-hated."

Edmond, who until this moment had no more than taken his companion's arm, now drew her closer, until the glistening black head lay unresisting on his shoulder and his arms encircled her. He droned on his story.

"The quarter hour strikes, and the great fans at our end of the Street spin into a sudden blur, sucking out the fetid accumulations of the past minutes. The city Urbs is breathing, four gasps to the hour. But this is of no import; what both of us watch with bitter smiles is the sinking of an airship between the twin spires of the Palace. It is my Sky-rat, and we know the hour of parting impends. I move my chair close beside yours, the better to embrace you, as is the custom among the rulers of the city Urbs. There is wistful sweetness in the lips you yield; parting grows less bearable."

Edmond now pressed his thin lips to Vanny's half parted ones; still dream-like she answered his caress, drawing herself closer. Suddenly she stirred, drew back. "Edmond," she whispered, "you are the Master!"

"Yes" said Edmond in tones quite different from those of his story, "I am the Master!"

The trance-like slumber dropped away from Vanny's mind, yet she still lay quiescent in his arms. A pleasant languor still held her; she was somehow intensely happy, and somehow contentedly helpless.

Her will had been given to Edmond; she felt her old mastery of self and situation slipping from her like outworn armor, and was content. And then both mastery and contentment slipped away indeed!

Edmond's facile fingers found the catch of her dress above her left shoulder, snapping it open. The wine-colored velvet dropped away from her as he drew her erect; a feeling of horror and violation pervaded her, yet the strange lassitude held. She could not resist, and only her stricken eyes pleaded with her tormentor to withhold from his purpose. For that which she had decried in others was overtaking her, and she was utterly helpless to forestall disaster.

But Edmond too was experiencing a revulsion of different sort. He had satisfied his self-given promise to violate Vanny's modesty; the thrill of her half-revealed body was highly pleasing to his senses, but another element appeared—the foreign emotion of pity. He felt the appeal of the girl's frightened eyes and quivering form, and found himself neither as cold nor as ruthless as he had hitherto believed.

"This is a needless cruelty," he thought. "Let me give her some means of self-justification."

He drew her close. "You love me, Vanny."

A straw to grasp at. "Oh, yes! Yes!"

"You are very beautiful, dear. Dance for me, Vanny!"

Strangely, without Vanny's being aware of it, the radio was providing a soft melody. Edmond drew back, seated himself, while Vanny half-huddled before him.

"I must justify her costume to herself," he thought.

"Dance for me, Black Flame!"

Vanny swayed, took a few faltering steps while Edmond watched the flash of light on her black-silk clad limbs. Suddenly she crouched sobbing, with her arms across her face. Edmond sprang to her, raised her in his arms, and bore her to the davenport. Still holding her, he thought, "Something lacks. I have not yet justified her complaisance to herself." He considered a plan. "After all, why not? The form means nothing at all to me, and she is really a very lovely creature."

He bent over Vanny's head. "When will you marry me, dear?"

She stirred, looked up at him with tear-bright and serious eyes.

"I have said I loved you, Edmond. Any time! Now, if you wish it!"

5. Fruition

The thrilling drabness of a Crown Point wedding was over; since morning Vanny had been a wife, and it was now mid-afternoon! She was alone now for the first few moments since the epochal events of the morning. Edmond had given her his car to drive to her apartment for such necessary packing as she had to do—things she would need in the house on Kenmore.

She ordered her trunk up from the cellar locker-room, and placed her key in the apartment lock with a queer sad little puckering of her lips. Things moved so swiftly! Who could have dreamed it two nights ago—or even last evening? How had Paul taken her scribbled note? Had he told the rest of the bunch? What had they said and thought—especially Walter, who used to call her Vanny the Invulnerable? Invulnerable! The joke was on Walter, and herself, too! How had it all happened, anyway?

"I don't care," she thought, as she entered the living room. "I just fell hard for him, and that's that!"

Eblis bounded in with a protesting squall; she had forgotten to feed him in the rush of the morning's events. She rectified the omission, and passed into her bedroom. There she paused at the sight of the wine-velvet dress draped over the foot of the bed, beside the black hose and the diminutive black silk dansette she had worn; an embarrassed recollection colored her throat.

"I don't care," she told herself again, picking up the lingerie. "I'm glad I wore it." She spread it against her, standing before the door-mirror, and turned a little pirouette. Black stockings must have looked somewhat less sensual, she thought, but there wasn't very much of the dansette. She tucked up her skirt, surveying her legs critically. Long, soft, rounded, nice!

"I'm glad!" she repeated. "I'm glad he liked the way I looked— glad he was man and I woman enough to thrill! And that I'm honest enough to be glad! In fact," she told her reflection, "I'm a complete Pollyanna, and what of it?"

She folded the garment, placed it on the bed, and proceeded

to bury it with others from various closets and drawers. The janitor struggled in with a flat steamer trunk, and she transferred the bed's burden to its hollow. She followed with an old hand-mirror of her grandmother's, a manicure set that was a graduation gift, a few other mementoes. For a moment or two she hesitated over a framed picture of Paul, finally laying it on the dresser. "If there's room," she thought.

The doorbell rang; she ran to answer.

"Oh—Walter!"

"H'lo, Vanny." He stood polishing his glasses. "Mind if I come in?" He entered. "Congratulations—or is it best wishes? I never remember which to offer the bride."

"I'll take a little of both," said Vanny. "You don't seem very enthused."

"Oh, I really am!" He paused again. "Only Paul, you know—"

"What about Paul?" she was a little anxious.

"Well, he asked me to see you. He got your note, and I guess it pretty well upset him."

"I should have been more tactful, I suppose," said Vanny, "but I didn't exactly know how."

"You certainly didn't! He came over this morning before I was up, and in such a state! 'You wormed yourself into this situation,' he said. 'You're Vanny's confidential agent! Now you see her for me!' Then he told me about your note, and he said, 'She even signed herself Evanne. To me!'"

"I didn't mean to do that," said Vanny. "I was rushed and excited."

"Well," said Walter, obviously ill at ease, and with a plunge-into-cold-water expression, "the upshot of his remarks is this: He thinks you married Edmond Hall because of your quarrel with him."

"Oh, that's utterly ridiculous!"

"Well, I'm just telling you. He said, 'You find out if it's true. I can't go around myself, and I can't write or call up, but you find out and if it's true, tell her we'll fix it somehow. Tell her not to worry, and we'll get her out of it!'"

"You tell Paul he's insulting!"

"Now listen, young lady," said Walter, "I can see Paul's side of it. You know the whole crowd sort of considered you two paired, otherwise there'd have been a few others on your trail. I might have had a try myself. And you did show a pretty sudden reversal of form."

"Paul and I were never engaged."

"He seemed to feel differently."

"Maybe I did encourage him some," admitted Vanny. "I liked him immensely and—I was wrong, I guess. I'm sorry."

"If I'm not presuming," said Walter, "just why did you marry Edmond Hall?"

The girl flashed. "Because I love him!"

"You kept it well concealed."

"I didn't know until last night! Besides, I'm not on cross examination, and I resent being questioned!"

Walter turned soothing. "No offense, my dear. I'll sing your requiem to the crowd." He turned toward the door.

Vanny relented. "Walter, you and Paul—both of you—must come to see me when we get back. Paul knows where."

"Oh, are you going somewhere?"

Vanny was a bit flustered. "Why, I suppose so— if Edmond wants to. We hadn't discussed it."

"'If Edmond wants to!' He certainly toned you down in a hurry! I wouldn't have believed it possible!"

"He's wonderful!"

"He must be. Goodbye, Vanny—The crowd'll be less of a riot without you!"

Men called for her trunk. She hurried a few last-minute articles into it, watched it closed, strapped, and borne away. She picked up the reluctant Eblis, and descended to her car, leaving Paul's forgotten picture still lying face downward on the commode.

6. Olympian Love

Edmond was sitting in his laboratory when Vanny returned, and she ran up the stairs radiant and flushed and a trifle heated from her exertions. She stopped in the doorway. Her newly acquired mate sat on a board bench peering into a spinning bowl filled with bright liquid. She tiptoed forward to peek over his shoulder, and glimpsed a distorted reflection of her own face.

Edmond turned, and she thrilled again to his glance of admiration. He drew her to the bench beside him. "You are very beautiful, dear."

"I am glad if you think so."

For some time they sat silent, Vanny content in her lover's arms, and Edmond turning various thoughts in the intricacies of his minds. "I strike closer to the secret of happiness," he reflected. "The pursuit of happiness through sensation, which is but the search for beauty, is the pleasantest and most promising of the ways I have followed. And this being whom tradition will term my mate is in all ways the most aesthetic, the most desirable means to my end."

Vanny twisted in his arms, to look up at him. "Walter Nussman came in while I was packing."

"Indeed. With a message from Paul, doubtless."

"Why, yes," the girl said. "The whole crowd was thoroughly surprised by the suddenness of the affair. In fact"—she smiled—"I was myself! Not that I'm sorry, dear—but I just don't understand yet."

"And that," said Edmond, "is hardly surprising."

"Were you as amazed as I was?"

"Not I." He had nothing to lose by frankness; the prey was trapped and caged. "I tricked you into it."

"You mean you fibbed a little," laughed Vanny. "Men always do to girls—especially men in love."

"I never lie," replied Edmond, "having never found the need. I planned your love beforehand. I took you at your weakest—at the Venice, when your resistance was negligible. I trapped you again last night—sated you sleepy with food, lulled you with words until you were prey to any suggestion of a stronger will, and then placed you in such a position that your own modesty, your own training, your own self-respect, forced you to admit you loved me. You could not have resisted; the experiment was too well designed."

He paused, noting the effect of his words. A trace of horror, a trace of hurt reproach, showed in his companion's face, but not the violent emotion he had half anticipated.

"Edmond! An experiment! You talk as if I were no more to you than these things around us!" She indicated the array of cages and instruments with a contemptuous gesture, watching for his answer.

"But you do mean more, dear! You are my symbol of beauty and my final bid for happiness. Hereafter these other interests shall be—diversions."

Edmond was satisfied. His bird was well trapped and tamed, and did not even comprehend the method of her taking. "And thus," he reflected, "ends the experiment's inception and begins its consummation. Now if I am indeed his prototype, let us explore the meaning of love to the superman."

Vanny rested content against him; she thought nothing of his confession, he realized, because the thing was done to win her; it justified itself because she was the desired object. He drew her close again, caressing her body with his long fingers. Again he stripped that unresisting body of its coverings. His twin minds reveled in an unaccustomed riot of sensation, and forgot for the time to be properly analytical. He raised the vibrant form in his arms and carried her to that room where stolid Anna had borne him.

The girl tensed in his embrace. "Edmond! There is someone else in the room!"

She had somehow sensed his duality. "There is no other, dear. You tremble at shadows." He soothed her, drowning her senses in a flood of passion; her breath blew against him in fluttering gasps. "Cheyne-Stokes breathing," he noted, and then forgot method and analysis as his twin minds fused in a riot of ecstasy; Vanny was murmuring, and for a moment a paean sang in his ears.

Then he lay panting, drawn and exhausted, in the silence of diminishing sobs; his fingers clenched into curious fists.

"The superman!" he jeered. "Nietzsche—Nietzsche and Gobineau! Was it your shades that gibbered around my nuptial couch?"

7. A Honeymoon of a Dream

Edmond awoke with an unaccustomed weariness and a heaviness in his limbs. A weakening lassitude sat upon him, and a somber sense of futility. "It is a truism," he reflected, "that pleasure is won at the expense of pain. The accounts of the cosmos balance, and for each thing that is granted, payment is exacted even to the last place of the decimal." And in his other mind: "To this extent at least I am human, in that my desires still exceed my abilities."

But Vanny arose radiant; she went humming about the house, presented herself to the stolid Magda in the kitchen, and felt only passing regret at the defection of Eblis. For the great cat had liked neither the house nor its master, and had quietly departed during the night without a leave-taking, vanishing mysteriously as is the custom of his kind.

Vanny explored her new demesne; she found much to admire in the old furnishings, and some items which she promised herself to change. The gloomy library with its skull-topped fire-place depressed her; some effluvium from the ancient volumes seemed to keep the place in deeper shadow than natural. She looked into several books; they did not interest her and she returned to the upper floor to proceed with her unpacking, to find Edmond risen and vanished, doubtless to his laboratory. She was happy; Paul, Walter, and her friends had disappeared from her memory almost from the moment of her encounter with Edmond, just three evenings before. It was as if she had been suddenly reborn in another character.

Descending to arrange a late breakfast, she found her new husband reading in the library. He had had a fire laid in the grate to relieve the brisk autumnal chill, and sat idly smoking, turning the pages of a gray volume, as if glancing aimlessly through it. Vanny watched him for a moment beyond the arch of the doorway; she saw something romantically mediaeval in the faint flicker of the firelight on his pallid intelligent features. "Like a student in ancient times," she thought, and skipped in to perch beside him on the massive chair. He placed his arm around her, and she peered over his head at the text he held. Hen-scratches! "What's that you're reading, dear?"

Edmond leaned back in the chair. "The only surviving volume of the work of Al Golach ibn Jinnee, my dear. Does the name mean anything to you?"

"Less than nothing!"

"He was an apostate monk, turned Moslem. His work is utterly forgotten; no one save me has read these pages for nearly five centuries."

"Ooh! What's it about?"

Edmond translated the page before him; Vanny listened almost incredulously. "Gibberish," was her first thought, but an eerie shudder made her tremble. Little of the mad blasphemy was clear to her, yet there was an aura of horror cast about her by the words.

"Edmond! Stop!"

He patted her hand, and she departed for Magda's kitchen, but she perceived a curious illusion; a gigantic shadow followed her just out of direct vision—a shape horribly winged and formless, yet never quite visible; it danced along almost behind her, and persisted for several minutes in the sunny kitchen. There finally she threw off her sense of depression in the matter-of-fact association of Magda, checking supplies of staples, planning menus for the following day.

After a late breakfast, they returned again to the library. Edmond sat in his usual place before Homo's skull, and Vanny on the foot-stool at his feet. She watched the play of shadow on the little oil landscape.

"Edmond, I don't like that picture."

"I'll have it moved to the laboratory, dear." He had long since ceased to speculate concerning the daub.

"And Edmond, dear —" He smiled at her.

"Shall we go somewhere for a while? Not, of course, unless you want, but I should like to have a little time to adjust myself—to get straightened out. Things happen so quickly."

"Surely, Vanny. I understand. Wherever you choose."

Vanny was never certain thereafter whether they actually traveled, and, far from adjusting herself to her altered living, reality seemed to be slipping away from her like melting ice in her fingers. The journey, if journey it was, seemed too incredible, though parts of it had color and solidity. There was a day and a night in New Orleans—she remembered the startling expanse of Canal Street—when she was deliriously happy in Edmond's love, and other periods when they were suddenly in the house on Kenmore, dream-like, without transition. But at other times she recalled visits to places and cities that she was sure had no counterpart in reality. They wandered apparently for many days through an unnatural bloody-hued desert, subsisting on the contents of a water-skin Edmond carried, and the meat of strange little fungoid things that bobbled about in the air like potatoes in water. And they wore heavy furs, and were bitterly cold by night; even the day brought only a wan half-sunlight, and the sun seemed small as a dinner plate. And once they stood very still while a great thing only slightly like the little airy mushrooms droned overhead; it was too high above them to see clearly, but it buzzed along with a purposeful tenacity toward some unguessable objective.

At another time they stood bathed in muggy clouds on a low hill, watching the misty lights of a curious city below them. Edmond whispered warnings to her; something evil was abroad in the city, and she gripped a six-inch dart in her hand. She never remembered the outcome of this adventure, but she retained the impression of terrific destructive power in the tiny dart, and a vague supposition that it was a little rocket of some sort.

And there were many nights in the house on Kenmore when Edmond reclined in his chair and she danced for him, danced with no thought of modesty now, but with a wild sense of grace and pleasure; the fire behind her limned her body in charcoal-like silhouette, and her strange mate watched her with an admiration that she would almost have died to create. On one of these evenings he stripped her white body of every covering and folded about it an iridescent robe of purple he had acquired for her; the room was in darkness save for a faint fire-glow, and that night she danced with her body gleaming like a metal sword. The eyeless gaze of Homo's small skull seemed to her to follow her movements, and the musty volumes on the wall-shelves breathed an incense. That was a night of ecstasy long remembered! There was never a night that Edmond seemed more human, more sincere, more vital in his loving of her.

But reality was dropping away. The very solid walls of the house were growing unstable; they wavered and shifted like stage-settings when her glance was not directly on them; the sturdy oak doorways went misty as she passed, and chairs were never quite where she expected when she sat down. Even the familiar street beyond the windows took on a smoky appearance, and she could not read for the shadows that stole out of corners. This dream honeymoon was befogging her tense little mind; reality and fancy were becoming confused and inseparable. The solid material of every-day life grew shadowy, while the shadows in the corner took on a terrifying solidity.

Edmond watched the progress of Vanny's unsettlement with an interest not altogether academic or unsympathetic; his experiment was striking emotional chords he had not known he possessed. And he himself was not wholly unscathed; his languor strengthened about him like a misty net; nor was he unaware of the reason. His keen analysis of situation had instantly developed the x-quantity in the experiment.

"We are alien beings, Vanny and I," he concluded. "She is not mentally capable of sustaining our intimacy, nor I physically. Ours is the mating of the eagle and the doe; each is in its own sphere a competent entity, but the eagle's beak is too sharp for the doe's lips, and the doe's hindquarters somewhat too sturdy for the avian physique." He twisted his saturnine features in a smile. "Yet there are certain compensations."

But a culmination impended, and arrived with an uncompromising finality. Vanny collapsed first under the strain of the unnatural union. Edmond entered the arch of the library one day to find her lying senseless before the fire-place in a limp heap of iridescence, with the flames almost licking at her robe, and a reddening bruise between her eyes. He bore her to his chair and used what means he had to restore her; for several minutes thereafter she seemed dazed, and clung fearfully to him.

"It came out of the wall," she murmured. "It came out on ragged wings."

"The fire has vitiated the air here," said Edmond. "You were overcome, and struck your head on the mantel."

"No! I saw it, Edmond! It flew out at me!"

"You fainted and struck your head," Edmond repeated. He drew the girl erect, led her up the stairs.

"I saw it! I saw it!" she was murmuring. "It came out on ragged wings, with eyes that bit —"

He supported her to her bed, easing her gently down. He placed long fingers on her forehead, and held her eyes with a gaze grown suddenly intense.

"There were no shadows, dear," he said. "There will be no shadows hereafter. You are to sleep now. You are very sleepy, dear."

Vanny obediently slept. Edmond watched her for a moment and then left her with slow thoughtful steps. He felt again the surge of unaccustomed pity; she was too beautiful to be thus tormented.

"I must not destroy her!" he thought in his complex minds, and repeated almost fiercely: "I must not destroy her!"

8. Old Eve

It was several days before Vanny felt quite herself again; she wandered about the house in her purple robe with a bemused air, but the shadows remained quiescent in their corners, and chairs and walls were properly inert. Edmond was pleasantly considerate, and spent much of his afternoons amusing her with dagger-like comment, description, or fancy, but there were no more visions. In the main, he held the conversation to commonplace topics and routine affairs. He had casually liquidated the bonds which had supplied her modest income, and purchased a variety of stocks for her. The two months of their union had witnessed a considerable appreciation of these, and he brought her a sheaf of certificates to endorse. He was going to sell them, he told her, as she reclined on her bed.

"Fools are patting fools on the back," he said. "The rise will not outlast the month."

He saw that the considerable profit cheered her; Vanny had never been close to poverty, but had likewise never hitherto known the carefree sensation of affluence. She was familiar with the argot of the Street; Walter and others brought the talk of the rampant market to the old gatherings.

"Why don't you sell short, dear? Wouldn't it be wise."

"Very wise. The balloon is inflated to the bursting point. However, your profit, and mine as well, is considerable even in this year and this city. More would be burdensome, and involve a routine of management I prefer not to shoulder."

Her confidence was complete; she did not question him further.

After a day or two she was up and about as usual; except for a dawning sense of distance in her black eyes, she was quite the Vanny of old, laughing again at the little incidents of living, happy again merely because it was easy to be happy. October was slipping quietly along with its unexpectedly early evenings; she had been alone with Edmond for eight weeks and had not yet missed her old companions.

Edmond, after her recovery, had fallen into his old routine. He spent his mornings in town casually taking care of the details of living, and his afternoons mostly in his laboratory or the library. She grew accustomed to his habitual comings and goings, and adjusted the machinery of housekeeping to them, though Magda, of course, bore most of this burden with the methodical efficiency of two decades of service.

But as the month closed, she was not always happy. Edmond had changed. He was kind enough, thoughtful enough, but the old wild nights of flame were no more. There was some barrier between them, something of his building that kept them apart as if in separate cells. Had he ceased to love her? Was her bright body already growing stale to his senses?

She worried a little as the days dropped one by one into the past; perhaps she herself was at fault somewhere—but in what respect? She was utterly at a loss, and thought wistfully of the nights that already seemed long ago.

She offered her body as a lure. She used it in ways of which she could not have dreamed in the days past; she danced for Edmond like a votary before her deity, improvising a costume of the half-transparent robe. And all her reward was an almost reluctant admiration, for she perceived that he was not entirely unmoved. The prey rose often to the bait, but would not strike.

And so October dragged into its final week. The days shortened, there were new songs on the radio, and the tottering market crashed with a world-wide rumble that she scarcely heard. She was puzzled and hurt by Edmond's indifference; the word "experiment" popped out of memory to harass her.

There entered another element, equally puzzling in their relationship—she began to perceive the strangeness of her husband's character. There was a difference between Edmond and other men, a subtle something that she could neither express nor identify. This was less to be worried about than his coldness, for it seemed to her proper that he should be a being above others; if this superiority involved certain physical differences in eyes and hands—well, that was as it was. At times, indeed, she was startled by stranger differences, curious inhuman distinctions in his very thoughts. She sensed these things occasionally even in casual conversation, and sometimes in rather terrifying manner. One night when she danced for him she became suddenly positive that two people stared at her; she sensed another presence that watched her with desirous eyes. She stopped momentarily to gaze startled at Edmond; it was for that instant as if four eyes stared at her from his lean face. Thereafter the thing recurred with unsettling frequency, and she began to imagine thoughts and presences of peculiarly disturbing nature behind Edmond's pale eyes. November was dawning on a puzzled, wistful, more-than-half-frightened bride, in whose nature an ancient Eve was struggling newly awakened and demanding sustenance.

9. Old Eve Rebels

Edmond was not unaware of Vanny's predicament. From his sympathy and knowledge he knew, almost to the wording of her thoughts. However, for perhaps the first time in his life he found himself helpless to solve a problem he might have attempted. Continue the deadly intimacy of their first few weeks? He foresaw disaster to both of them. Explain his position to her? Impossible, since he himself was not cognizant of it. Send her away? A cruelty as burning as that he was now perpetrating. He was surprised by the intensity of the love which he himself had evoked in this being who was his wife.

"I played Eros too well," he reflected. "My arrows wounded too deeply." And his other consciousness repeated its old admonition: "The fault is neither hers nor mine, but lies in this union unnatural to both of us. Too close an intimacy will end by killing me and driving Vanny mad. Our separate strengths attack each the other's weakness; we are acid and alkali which are mutually destructive even to complete neutralization. Neither of us can sustain the other."

So he followed his policy of procrastination, confident that in time elements would enter that might make possible a solution. The situation presented a deadlock; only a disturbing force could upset the balance to permit his intellect to play. He had no presentiment as he left on his customary morning's visit to town that this force was about to emerge. He diverted himself by reasoning out certain trends he pre-visioned in the world of finance.

"The system has passed a climax," he thought. "Of the several rational methods to rebuild the structure of prosperity I see none likely of adoption save that of a population-devouring war. The little minds are too well in control of things, though doubtless they will muddle through as in the past. This is a rather hospitable planet, and provides a large margin of safety for the errors of its inhabitants. Likely enough in the next several years some new industry will rescue the phantom called prosperity, which was aided by the automobile and abetted by mass credit."

Vanny felt a surge of real pleasure as she greeted Paul, who entered looking rather woebegone, with his yellow hair in greater disarray than usual.

"Oh, Paul! I'm glad you came."

Paul was somewhat ill at ease, and too buried in his own unhappiness to look directly at Vanny. She led him into the living room, sat facing him on the davenport.

"Tell me about yourself, Honey."

Paul shrugged. "I starve on."

"I'm sorry." Vanny felt his aversion to pity; she turned to another subject. "What's happened to Walter?"

"Walter's nearly nutty! He was in the market—cleaned out last Thursday."

Vanny felt a thrill of pride. "Edmond sold out both of us ten days ago. He told me what was coming. He says it's not over yet."

"Then he's Babson, or the Devil!" He looked sharply at Vanny, his attention drawn by her sudden start. For the first time he noted the distant look behind her dark eyes. "What's the matter, Vanny?"

"Why, nothing, silly! What should be?"

"You look different. Not so sparkling—more serious."

"I was sick a few days, Honey. Nothing important."

"He treats you all right?"

"You're being ridiculous!"

"Are you happy, Vanny?" he insisted. "You've changed so!"

The girl looked at him, a trace of speculation in her eyes. She was surprised to discover that her trouble was plain in her face—or was it simply that Paul loved her, shared her feelings? She felt a rush of compassion; surely she had treated him shabbily enough! This was Paul, her Paul, who loved her, and whom she had casually and cruelly kicked aside. She reached out her hand, ran her fingers through his yellow hair. With the gesture, Vanny felt a strange stirring within her; her body was aching for the love her mate withheld. She drew back her hand, closing her eyes with the intensity of her aroused desire. Paul was leaning toward her, watching her.

"What is the matter, Vanny?"

The question recalled her.

"Nothing. I guess I'm still a little under the weather."

"Listen to me a minute, Vanny. I'm not welshing on the deal. I've lost you, and that's that. But you do see I was right in refusing to bring him around, don't you? I wanted you, and I had to fight. You see that."

"Yes, Paul. You were right."

"I was angry and bitterly hurt, Vanny. I thought it was a scurvy trick of yours to toss me aside so—well, so carelessly. I thought that at least I was entitled to a warning, a chance to plead my case." He paused. "Now—I don't know. You've changed. I hardly recognize you as the same Vanny. Perhaps you acted in the only way you could."

"I did, Honey. Believe me, I did not try to hurt you."

"It's all right; what's the difference now? But it was an awful wrench at first, with the feel of your lips still poignant. Your kisses haunted me for days."

"You may kiss me now, Paul."

He smiled wryly. "No thanks, dear. I know these married kisses with the fire carefully smothered. About as much kick as an extinct cigarette."

Vanny pursued the discussion no further in that direction; she smothered an unexpected impulse to insist, to repeat her offer, and returned to casual topics. For an hour the two sat talking; their old intimacy, the easy frankness of their long friendship, blanketed them, and Vanny was aware of a decided enjoyment. Paul was so solid, so real! He who thought himself a poet, an aesthetic spirit, and lover of beauty—how simple he was after all, how simple and human and understandable! No wizard here to evoke dreams and practise demiurgy and summon terrible and not-to-be-understood shadows out of corners! Just Paul, plain and lovable.

"But he's not Edmond!" she thought. "He's not Edmond. I master Paul too easily—he's a sweet, normal, intelligent youth and he loves me, but he's not the flaming, dominating sorcerer I happen to love!" And again, while Paul talked of something—she scarcely knew what: "But oh God! I wish Edmond loved in the same way as Paul!"

And an hour passed. As noon approached, the press of household duties made themselves felt; she could hear old Magda clattering in the kitchen. Paul, she recalled with a smile, never had any conception of the exigencies of time; she'd have to remind him.

"It's near lunch-time, Honey. I'd ask you to stay, only I wasn't expecting you, and there's hardly enough for you and me and Edmond." She hesitated to voice her actual doubts as to the advisability of his encountering Edmond—not that she mistrusted Edmond's finesse, but she was skeptical of Paul's delicacy in such a situation. However, Paul himself realized the conditions.

"Thanks," he said wryly. "I'd be uncomfortable anyhow, under the circumstances."

He rose to depart; Vanny followed him to the door with a curious reluctance, for he seemed to take with him a sense, a memory, of the old carefree days. Not that she regretted their passing, for she knew that she was Edmond's, flesh and spirit, utterly, for so long as he demanded; but the past too had its charms.

"Paul, Honey!"

He paused at the door.

"You'll come back soon, won't you?"

"Of course, Vanny. As often as you'll permit—tomorrow if I may."

"Not tomorrow." It would be pleasant, she thought. "Come Wednesday morning, then."

He was gone. Vanny watched him for a moment through the glass of the front door, watched with a reflective smile that was somehow a little wistful. But Edmond was due to arrive; she turned toward the kitchen and Magda, and the ancient spirit of Eve slept very quietly within her.

10. The Apple in Eden

Edmond was not entirely unhappy in his marriage, nor on the other hand, did he find his complete fulfillment in it. While he still delighted in the flashing loveliness of his mate, he still lacked the companionship he desired, and was almost as lonely as in the solitary days. Nowhere could he find understanding, and conversation was of necessity limited to topics and viewpoints that seemed to him elementary. As always, his recourse was his own self, and his conversation was constrained to the give-and-take possible between his two minds. He still read, but with lessening interest and growing boredom—philosophy, literature, science, all had a familiarity and a sameness that disgusted him, and the rare jewel of novelty was becoming almost undiscoverable. He began to perceive that he had exhausted human resource; the nature of man and his works were too familiar to intrigue him longer. So, for the most part, he sat and thought his own thoughts. These mostly devolved upon highly theoretical and extrapolated deductions, since he had abandoned for the time his routine of experiment. His esoteric labors were largely in the field of philosophy, as for instance, when he reflected in this fashion:

"Flammarion, a nice thinker, glimpsed one interesting fact, though it is a truth based rather on man's limitations than on actuality. In eternity, says Flammarion, whatever can happen must happen, which is to say that all possible combinations of events will occur if only enough time be granted. Then, he reasons, since there is an eternity behind us as well as before, in the past as well as in the future, it follows that everything possible has already happened. Specious and logical; let us consider it."

And his other self at the same time promulgated its answer: "The error is obvious. What Flammarion has done is merely to consider Time as one-dimensional. In effect, he takes an infinite line, places a dot on it to represent the present, and argues thus: Since there is an infinite number of points on this line to the left of my dot, it follows that every possible point is located there. A fallacy, obviously, since there is an infinity of points, to one side or the other, not on the line at all! There exists, in fact, not one Time but innumerable parallel times, as Einstein infers in his pleasant little fantasy. Each system, each individual, possesses his own little time, and these may be curved as Flammarion argues, but certainly not in the sense he believed."

So Edmond amused himself with his own cogitations, finding a dim and unsatisfactory companionship within his own mind. For here Vanny failed him as utterly as all the rest of the human world; however much she wished, she was simply unable to enter into an understanding conversation with her strange husband.

Not that she didn't try; she strained her bright little mind to its capacity in an endeavor to interest him, retailing scraps of knowledge she had culled from her reading, questioning him, and listening with tense attentiveness to his sometimes incomprehensible answers. Edmond was always ready to listen to her, and always kindly explicit in his explanations, yet she realized the perfunctory nature of his interest; she sensed always an attempt at simplification, as one might explain to a child. The thing worried her, puzzled her. "I'm no moron," she told herself. "I've always held my own with the old crowd, and some of them were considered brilliant. It's just that Edmond's so much more wonderful than anyone else in the world!"

However, an element that troubled her in far greater degree than his intellectual casualness was his physical indifference. He seemed satisfied by the optical sensation of beauty; when Vanny presented herself in a guise she thought becoming, he was ready enough with admiration, but his caresses were dishearteningly rare. There were few of the nights of ecstasy; little indeed of the glorious abandon of those early weeks! Edmond refused to revive that disastrous intimacy, knowing that neither could sustain it, and Vanny danced in vain before the grinning skull of Homo.

"I am no more than an ornament, a pet, or a dancing doll," she thought unhappily. "I have nothing of companionship to give, and now already my body palls." She was puzzled, weary, and wistful. Her body, having once known the caress, ached endlessly for it.

Paul's rather frequent morning visits were in some ways a solace, for at least he provided a sort of friendship she missed. His devotion bolstered her waning self-confidence, and kept alive the spark of pride that Edmond had nearly smothered with his indifference. Somehow, too, Paul sensed her perturbation, and his ready sympathy failed this time to anger her. A pent-up emotional volcano was threatening to burst its crust of convention and training; a crisis approached.

Occasionally as in the past Paul brought bits of poetry for her criticism; he used to enjoy her ready approval and encouragement. Somehow of late she found this hard to give; was her taste changing under Edmond's dark influence, or was Paul's work, lacking perhaps some lost inspiration, deteriorating? As for example, this particular morning. They sat on the living room davenport, Paul in his usual careless disarray, and Vanny, interrupted in her morning routine, in a simple housedress. He was reciting a short poem that he called merely "Autumn".

"Her eyes with their unanswered dreams
Are bitter, and her face is old,
But from her withered body gleams
A brazen mockery of gold
Shining like ancient wealth untold;
There is a coolness in her breath.
The handmaiden is she of Cold—
The harbinger is she of Death."

Paul paused for her comment as he concluded the octet, and his silence roused Vanny, who had been listening half in reverie.

"Do you like it?" he asked.

"Why—it's very pretty, Paul, but isn't it a trifle—well—obvious?"

"Obvious!" He looked hurt. "Why, Vanny! It's not supposed to be subtle; it's just an impression."

"I'm sorry, Honey. I wasn't paying very close attention, I guess. Perhaps I read a meaning into it that you didn't intend."

Paul looked at her. He noticed the distraction in her features, the curious haunted look in her dark eyes, the unsettlement in her aspect.

"Something's troubling you, Vanny! Won't you tell me, or let me try to help?"

She returned his gaze, seeing as if in memory the fine blue eyes, the sensitive features, the yellow hair she had loved. Old Eve, somewhere deep in her being, complained bitterly at that moment; Vanny's body ached for that which Edmond denied it.

"Perhaps," she replied. "Paul, do you still love me?"

"You know I do!"

"Do you still find me—attractive? Could I still thrill you?"

"Vanny! Is it clever or kind to torment me with suggestive questions?"

Something alive behind the turmoil that was Vanny's mind was urging her on. That part of her which was Eve prodded the part which was civilized, the being born of training and heredity opposed the being born of the first primal cell. She reached a sort of decision. From her position properly at the far end of the davenport from Paul, she dropped one small foot to the floor, leaning toward him. The light wash-silk housedress strained against her body; Paul was not oblivious to the lure she dangled before him.

"Kiss me, Paul. I want you to."

He leaned forward. Suddenly her arms were about him. He felt her lips against his with a burning softness, and she pressed her body close to his. There was an abandon, a fierceness about her embrace; this was certainly not the Vanny of old! His arms tightened, pressed her more closely.

Suddenly she threw back her head; her eyes with their strange light burned close to his. "Have I smothered the fire, Paul?"

"Vanny!" he was a little breathless. "I don't understand! Don't you love him?"

She disengaged herself, drew away, and faced him with her eyes still burning and her cheeks flushed.

"Yes, Paul. I love him. I love him as greatly as it is possible for me to love."

"Then why—?"

"Listen a minute, dear. I tell you I love him. I am not cheating, not stealing anything from him. What I am giving you is nothing to him, it is a part of me he doesn't want, a part he has rejected. Do you understand?"

"No," said Paul, "I do not, but neither do I question."

"I am stealing nothing from him," repeated Vanny, as if to herself. "I am living in the only way I can live. I am doing the only thing it is given me to do. I do not think there is any higher wisdom than that; if any exists, it is Edmond's province, not mine."

She seemed suddenly to realize Paul's presence.

"Honey, I want you to go now. Come back tomorrow morning. Promise me."

"Of course," said Paul, still amazed as she hurried him out of the door.

She turned back through the living room, wandered into the library. The skull of Homo grinned at her with a replica of Edmond's sardonic smile.

"All right, if you know so much!" she snapped at it. "What else can I do?"

The little skull grinned silently at her.

11. Conversations on Olympus

Edmond watched the writhing market as it slid closer to the edge of the second precipice. There was a crowd at the customer's desk; those fortunate enough to be in position to buy were grabbing for bargains that seemed unbelievable in contrast with recent prices. A wave of buying was cushioning the drop.

A customer's man stood beside him.

"You were certainly lucky, Mr. Hall. You got out just in time."

"I allowed myself plenty of time," said Edmond. "The break came almost a week later."

"Hmph! Maybe! Are you buying today?"

"Not yet."

"Not yet! Why she's already rebounding. You'll buy your line back fifty points higher!"

"Did you ever review the history of past panics?"

"Yes, but this is different! Earnings are good—business is good. Money's plentiful. This break is the result of internal technical conditions!"

"So," said Edmond, "is an earthquake."

For some time longer he remained, observing rather the crowds than the quotations. The frenzy of the first break was over; some watched the gyrating prices with a dull lack of interest, others with a buzz of comment on each upward flurry. The Morgan group was buying, Rockefeller was buying, rumor told of a colossal banker's pool formed to support the market. He listened idly for a while, and then wandered out into the street.

He stood at the corner of Adams and Michigan, and watched the jostling autos crowd each other, or scuttle into side streets with audible grunts of relief.

"There is the germ of a true civilization in this," he reflected. "A truly civilized man would be in effect a free mind in a body of machinery."

And at the same moment his other self was objecting, "But the existence of a free mind in a mechanical body would in itself eliminate or prohibit the existence of all art. Art is simply a reflection of man's instincts and training. Poetry and music and dancing are the wooing of birds and fish, and are inextricably tangled with sex. Literature in general is the migratory impulse, the urge to explore, as are painting and sculpture. Philosophy and religion are self-preservation.

"This free brain of ours lacking the instincts that are a part of body could see nothing of beauty, and to that extent is not a truly civilized being."

And his first self, answering, "After all, art is not beauty, since beauty *per se* is not existent. Doubtless, sunrise is the acme of horror to an intelligent bat, and the inhabitants of planets of the red star Aldebaran would consider our green earthly verdure a monstrous and obscene thing. Beauty and truth are not one, save in that each is relative to the observer, and neither exists but in his perception. Thus our argument is its own refutation, and civilization is truly of the mind and not of the instincts."

So Edmond picked his way reflectively through the separate entities flowing around him, when of a sudden, like an awakening crash to a sleeper, his twin minds fused, and he found himself staring with a curious absorption at a figure half a block before him. He quickened his steps; a sensation unique to his experience flooded his being.

The woman turned. Their gazes met and mingled like the mingling of molten metals. Two eyes, light like Edmond's, intense as his—a figure slim, and shorter than his own—an awkward and unnatural masculinity somehow inherent in it. Her hands were gloved in black, but the revealing suppleness was there—Edmond was staring at a woman who was in every physical respect his counterpart!

And even while his consciousness reeled to adjust itself to this astonishing presence, some impish brain cells in the background were grinning. "Dog scent dog!" he thought sardonically, and raised theoretical hackles.

Then he spoke. "I did not dream you existed already."

The woman smiled, still holding his gaze with an intensity equal to his own.

"I have felt your nearness," she said.

Silently the two curious figures moved northward with the

crowd, but no more a part of it than two molecules of hydrogen in a current of air. Unspoken, they knew their destination—the woman's dwelling place. North of the river, they turned west through the streets of little shops and decaying buildings, and into one of these.

Upstairs, Edmond found a room, a cell like countless others save in the profusion of sketches, pastels, and small oils that covered the walls and lay piled in corners. And these pictures he recognized.

"You are Sarah Maddox, then," he said. "I might have guessed."

The woman smiled.

"I have two minds," said Edmond, "or a dual mind, but not such as the beasts call a dual personality."

"Yes," said Sarah.

"I have known a City, not past nor present, but a place where I am at one with life."

"I know," said Sarah. The two remained staring at each other; there was a comfort in their proximity, as of two friends meeting suddenly in a far place. Then Edmond spoke again.

"I do not think these are cities of reality in their sense. They are symbols, rather, of what may be. They are that world toward which we tend, for now I perceive our meaning, what we two imply."

"You need not explain," said the woman. "I know."

"Colors and objects are your media. I must phrase my thoughts, having but inadequate words."

Sarah smiled.

"Our implication is this," said Edmond. "That we are a mutation. We are not prototypes of things yet unwombed of Time, but part of a change that is. Weissman glimpsed the truth, and Evolution is not the slow grinding of environment on the clay of life, but a sudden unspringing of higher forms from that clay. The age of the giant reptiles—then suddenly the age of mammals. A fern, and then a flower. Things stable and stationary for a geologic age—then the crash of a new and stronger species, and catastrophically, that age is ended.

"*They* out there in the street will bear more like us, and we shall replace them. The age of the dominance of Homo Sapiens shall be the shortest of all geologic eras. Five hundred centuries since he sprang from the Cro-Magnons and destroyed them, as our kind will destroy him. There will be disorders and turbulences, and the grindings of a deep readjustment as world power passes upward to us. Shall we employ it better than the beasts?"

"How to judge? By their standard or ours?"

For a time these two smiled silently at each other; understanding blanketed them, and was sufficient. Then again Edmond spoke:

"There is that possible to me now which before was undreamable. That is intelligent conversation. Let us converse of realities, such things as the world of humans discusses not at all, save mystically or sentimentally, or in the gropings they believe philosophy. Let us speak of all things that are, their beginnings and endings."

The woman smiled.

"I speak," said the superman, "in poetry—not because, as some have believed, it is the natural mode of expression, nor because it is beautiful, but for this only: that in poetry alone can I imply the ideas which are otherwise inexpressible in language. Meter and symbol can suggest what words in themselves cannot convey; to these beasts this becomes emotion, but we perceive the implicit thought."

"Yes," said Sarah.

Edmond, who until then had stood as he had upon entering, now seated himself, and cupped his chin upon his incredible hands.

"Before there was anything, there was Something, for there was the possibility of being—an *existability*, without which all things were impossible. Nowhere conceivable does that state now exist, but on the remoter worlds, as Neptune, it is approximate. Neptune is thus the symbol of my thought."

Then Edmond gazed intently at the floor as one reflecting, and spoke again slowly.

"I am the Planet eremite, the gaunt repulsor of the light
That falls like icy rain at night, from frigid stars and moons a-cold.
Ye have not seen a world like this—the blank and oceanless abyss,
The nameless pit and precipice, the mountain very bleak and old.
Yet ah—my silence murmureth! Oh, Inner Orbs, ye have not heard
That stillness where there is no death, because no life hath ever stirred!
'But here God's very name is dead!' wept Heaven's mighty Myriarch,
Then trembling turned away and fled, for Something gibbered in the dark!"

Edmond raised his head from his cupped hands, and gazed with the old fiery intentness at Sarah. Comprehension surged between them, and he smiled, satisfied.

"There was a beginning," said Sarah.

"Creation is simpler to the understanding than Pre-creation," responded Edmond. "Even mankind is to some extent creative, though the fools unknowing worship in their Creator a goddess instead of a God, since creation is a feminine act. Yet there is more to be said:

"Dawn amid darkness, while afar
The little lights in scimitar
Lit up an age-old barren sea,
Of nothingness infinity.
Incipient air and pregnant storm
Embodied then a giant form
Still trembling with the power that gave it
Intellect *to damn or save it.*
Sentience, *from its twi-formed birth*
*Of **male** and **female**, air and Earth."*

Sarah—

"Mine the torch, and yours to light it."

Edmond—

"Yours to save, but mine to blight it."

Sarah—

"Yours the seed, but mine the flower."

Edmond—

*"Yours the years, but mine—**the hour!**"*

Another pause, as Edmond fused his twin minds into a questing purpose. He spoke again: "You are right in saying that masculinity is of inceptions, and femininity of growth. The sperm is mine, but the child yours. You are right, too, in saying that there is a compulsion laid upon us, not in the sense of a duty, but as a tenet of nature. We two have received a trust, that our kind survive. We must reproduce."

Now Sarah's eyes, still gazing with unwinking intensity into Edmond's own, flamed with a deeper light, a universal light that glows in the female of all species. That, too, Edmond perceived, and to his consciousness there seemed a discordant note, but he said nothing.

"There will be an ending," said Sarah.

"Endings are simpler than Existence," said Edmond, "and Destruction, like Creation, is feminine; I deal with things already created and not yet destroyed. Beginnings and endings are your province; mine, things as they are. Yours are birth and death, but living is mine. As you and all women are closer to the emotional primitive, so are you more in accord with Creation and Destruction, for nature, which is the most creative, is of necessity the most destructive of forces. Therefore, do you tell me of the ultimate end and the return of chaos."

Again Sarah smiled that fleeting and intense smile. Then, folding her hands, she spoke softly.

"There came a night when all things lay
As if some wind had swept away
All vestiges of pulsing life,
And left cold bodies to be prey
To primal elements, while they
Renewed their immemorial strife."

"That," said Edmond, "is approximate truth. The music of the spheres is a gigantic crashing as they pass into existence and out of it."

But his other self was reflecting, "Intellectually she is all that I desire. Physically she possesses no tiny trace of appeal. Why?"

He stood upright. "There are things to be done. I must go."

Sarah smiled without reply. Both understood that other meetings were inevitable, desired by both. Edmond passed again into the streets of jostling vehicles.

12. Satan

Meanwhile Paul and Vanny again reclined before the fireplace of the monkey's skull, and Paul spoke of such things as poets speak of. Vanny listened, though a little wearily, yet withal indulgently. She had not colored her cheeks, and her eyes had still more of the inexplicable distance that had been growing therein.

"So that if poetry is but meter—a tom-tom beat,—then beauty itself can be reduced to mathematics," said Paul, and paused for a reply.

None followed. Vanny turned her luminous eyes upon him.

"You haven't listened to a word," sulked Paul.

"I have, Paul. All you say is true—very true—childishly true. But—Paul, you are only a child—all of us are children—to him!"

"Can't you forget him for a minute?"

Vanny did not answer.

"That devil!" said Paul.

"Yes—his name is Lucifer."

"No,—Caliban—Vanny, he's mad, and he's making you mad,!"

"Often," said Vanny, "I have wondered if that were the explanation. Perhaps! Only there is something else—something inexplicable—either divine or infernal. Something—"

Her voice dropped. Suddenly she looked at the man with a deeper luminescence in her eyes, so that Paul started back aghast.

"Paul, Paul—he is different—inhuman, somehow! At times," her voice grew tense, her eyes desperate, "at times, Paul, he is two people!"

"What, Vanny?"

"No, I mean it, Paul! I can feel it, sense it! Not physically, but I can feel the presence, and both are he! I am afraid of him, Paul, but I love him like—like a dog his master—like—." She fell silent, leaving her simile mysteriously incomplete.

"He is unbelievably powerful," she said, after a long pause. "Nothing ever bars him from the attainment of his purposes. Think, Paul, how he has defeated you at every encounter from earliest school days, and sometimes in rather terrible fashion!"

"Do you think so?" returned Paul. "I thought—" He paused, reconsidering the idea he had been about to phrase. It had occurred to him that in this present encounter he was worsting his redoubtable opponent, winning from him the greatest of his treasures. But was he? Was he not rather contenting himself with the leavings, with a part of Vanny that Edmond, for his own insane reasons, had rejected? "He ravishes her soul like the orthodox Devil," Paul thought, "leaving her body easy prey with the spirit drained out of it."

"I know this," said Vanny; "that if the whole world were set on one course, all the ministers, scientists, rich men, generals, and statesmen wanted one thing, and Edmond opposed it, he could sit in his black-windowed room upstairs and contrive a means to defeat them. You see, Paul, this sense makes his companionship very poignant, but also blasting and withering like a desert sun; and his love is languid and insufferable!" Some rising emotion shook her; tears were beginning to glisten in her eyes. "But I love him, Paul! I want his love and I am miserably cheated!" She was panting in an effort to suppress her tears; an old phrase of Edmond's, the word "experiment," had returned in memory to harass her.

"Whatever he wants is inevitably his," she continued sadly, and then, with a sudden flash of insight: "His one weakness, and like a curse on him, is never to know his desire, to want nothing at all badly enough to make its attainment a satisfaction—not me nor anything in the world!" She was weeping bitterly now, and her emotion burned rampant on its own fuel.

Paul seized her shoulders, shook her, held her close, so that her eyes were hidden. Her hysteria subsided.

"Vanny, you must come. This is madness."

"No, Paul."

She lay in his arms as many times before, and Paul felt as always the seductiveness of her.

"Paul—"

"Yes, dearest."

"Give me love again—human love—like men and women and natural things!"

Minutes passed—Edmond entered quietly and stood above them with his old ironic smile.

Paul rose pallid and dishevelled, and faced Edmond, who said nothing, but only waited with a smile of bitterness, his blazing eyes on Paul. Vanny crouched in terror, her eyes on Edmond, her hands fluttering frantically.

Silence.

"Well," said Paul at length, "after the manner of such gentlemen as I, I had better ask what you are going to do about it."

Edmond did not reply nor vary his gaze.

"Don't blame Vanny," said Paul. "Blame me, and mostly yourself. You're not fit for her, you know."

Edmond did not reply.

"It's your fault," said Paul. "She wanted your love and you withheld it. She's told me. She needs it, and you made her desperate." He felt a surge of panic, and his voice rose. "You've got to let her go! You're making her as crazy as yourself—Don't you see it? She can't stand it! Let her go, I tell you!"

Edmond did not reply.

"You devil!" Paul felt as if he were screaming. "Will you let her go? You don't want her! Let her find what happiness she can!"

He choked. Edmond did not reply.

An outburst of deep terror was flooding Paul's brain, as he understood that he faced something unnatural. He uttered a cry that was curiously shrill, and drove a clenched hand to Edmond's face. Edmond fell back against the wall and the ironic smile seemed to grow more bitter in a driblet of scarlet from the crushed lips, but there was no change in his intense gaze as Paul fled sobbing.

Edmond turned his eyes on Vanny, who through usage found them bearable. She smoothed her hair and garment, and stood before him like an ivory statue, a pallor on her cheek and a question in her haunted eyes.

"For that he should have died," said Edmond, speaking at last, "but that he spoke the truth. You must be released. I will go."

"Do you think, Edmond," answered Vanny slowly, "that anywhere I can now find companionship or love other than that I know with you? Because through you I have almost understood the inscrutable things, other men are as children or the beasts of nature."

Edmond shook his head sadly.

"Do not part us, Edmond," said Vanny. "I love you, Edmond."

"They think we are both mad," she said, "and I too think so,—

sometimes; but often I know otherwise when I perceive that you are an angel or a devil, or something more than a man. Nevertheless, I love you, Edmond."

And at his silence, she continued, "Do not punish me, Edmond, because I have these several times yielded to the stubborn bestial clay within me; I have more of the beast than you, but now I swear it is dead, Edmond. I will ask no more of you, no more than you will give."

And again, "Will you understand me, Edmond?"

At last he spoke, gently.

"I am not angry, Vanny, nor do I fail to understand. There is something else between us, something ineradicable and fatal to any further union of ours.

"Vanny, I am not human!"

"You are telling me that you are the Devil," she said, "but I love you Edmond."

"No, Vanny, it is less comprehensible than that. You and I are alien, not in race, but in species. This is why you are unable to bear a child by me, nor ever will be able. We are fortunate in that, for a child of ours would be far worse than any mixed breed; it would be a hybrid!"

Through his other mind flashed a comparison of Vanny's pale body and his own deformity.

"When the horse and ass breed," he said, "the offspring is a mule. Vanny, our child would be—a mule!"

And as her desolate eyes still gazed into his: "Perhaps I am the Devil, inasmuch as I am mankind's arch-enemy, and that which will destroy him. What else is the Devil?"

A sort of comprehension was born in Vanny's mind. She glimpsed the meaning of her husband, and a feeling of the inevitable disaster dawned in her. Henceforth, they were enemies, alien species, like the lion and the lamb, but with no ultimate lying-down together!

"Then goodbye, Edmond."

For once Edmond vocalized the obvious.

"Goodbye, Vanny!"

As he moved again out into the street, he was more utterly miserable than ever before.

13. Lilith & Adam

Edmond and Sarah, two strange elements in the fantastic quadrangle, seemed for the brief ensuing period to be more perfectly aligned, to possess a greater degree of harmony than the stormy combination that was the origin of their union. Sarah, cold, languid, impersonal, seemed to her companion a fit and desirable consort, and a haven of peace and quiet intellect. Not yet had the demands of his body made themselves evident, and the pleasant poison he had imbibed was yet to run its course in his nature.

Still, a remnant of the sorrow Edmond felt at the loss of Vanny survived to sadden him. Sympathy and pity were emotions that had grown less foreign to his character, and he was coming to know a sort of familiarity for their twin dolorous faces. Yet the first bitterness of his renunciation passed with the inception of Sarah's completer understanding. He managed to suppress for the time being that sense of beauty which was the one trait that had so far yielded him a modicum of satisfaction. Sometimes, however, the urge returned to plague him, and he wondered anew at the self-borne inconsistency that caused him to find beauty in an alien creature.

"There is a sort of Satanic majesty about Sarah," he thought, "and her self-sufficiency is admirable, and proper to her kind. There is also a very precious element in understanding and companionship, and Sarah only, of all created beings, has that to offer me. It is irrational for me to seek in her a beauty her heredity denies her, the more irrational since her body, and not human woman's, is my appointed lure. And yet, rational or not, I miss the white wistful loveliness that is Vanny's! I have twisted my own nature into hopelessly unnatural channels!"

So he entered into this new union, part of him satisfied, and part of him prey to a longing that survived out of his old life. He moved Sarah away from her drab little room into an apartment overlooking the Park on Lake View Avenue. He doubted whether the change to more commodious quarters affected her at all, for so self-contained an entity was she that her surroundings were of all influences the most negligible. Not that she was a stranger to beauty, her artistry denied that supposition; but she drew her inspiration from a source far removed from reality, somewhere in the depths of her own complex character. She found, in her quiet and complacent duality, compensations that Edmond for all his restless seeking was forever denied.

Their wooing was a languid, and to Edmond, a disappointing affair lacking both the stimulus of obstacles and the spur of uncertainty. Sarah was acquiescent but unresponsive, yielding lackadaisical caresses in return for Edmond's own unenthusiastic offerings. There was none of the fiery ecstasy that made Vanny's love like to a flaming meteor burning the very air in its passage. That compulsion to reproduce, which had seemed originally noble and worthy of fulfillment, hung now about Edmond's neck like an iron collar, deadening half his pleasure in Sarah's companionship and reminding him insistently of the delights he had forsworn.

"If this is the measure of my race's capacity for enjoyment," he reflected, "then whatever their attainments of the intellect, they have much indeed to learn from their simple human progenitors!"

As summer progressed, the feeling of discontent deepened, and even the high and Platonic intimacy with Sarah was embittered by it.

"Sarah has failed me now," he thought. "There is no release anywhere for me who am doomed forever to tread a solitary path."

He continued his gloomy reflections. "It is a curious fact that all speculators concerning the Superman have made the egregious mistake of picturing him as happier than man. Nietzsche, Gobineau, Wells—each of them falls into this same error when all logic clearly denies it. Is the man of today happier than Homo Neanderthalis in his filth-strewn cave? Was this latter happier than Pithecanthropus, or he happier than an ape swinging through Pleistocene trees? Rather, I think, the converse is true; with the growth of intellect, happiness becomes an elusive quantity, so that doubtless the Superman, when he arrives, will be of all creatures the most unhappy. I, his prototype, am the immediate example."

It was with a feeling of relief that he realized Sarah was pregnant; part of the compulsion was satisfied, part of his responsibility was behind him. Sarah too seemed to feel the lessening of the tension;

their mutual interest in this purely rational undertaking of producing offspring bound them a little closer together. But Sarah withdrew more closely into herself after the event; she seemed to have less need than ever for a presence other than her own.

Often, during the months of summer, Edmond brought out his grey car and drove for many hours and many miles in an effort merely to escape the dullness of thinking. For his very thoughts palled upon him at times, seeming to him a rather wan and sickly substitute for certain realities he had known. He was seldom successful in his attempt, for the curse of intellect pursued him with speed easily sufficient to outdistance the mechanism in which he fled.

Still, the curious union was surviving. His nature and Sarah's never met in open conflict, since Sarah's desires were never deep-rooted enough to resist his own impulses; she gave way to him equably, quietly, and without rancor, yielding everything and finding recompense in her unborn child, her art, and herself. So the strange menage ground itself into a sort of stability as summer closed.

14. Eve & Lilith

Vanny sat miserably silent after Edmond's departure; the house seemed as still as the depths of a pyramid, and as old and lifeless. She was dumb, dazed, by the impact of events. The whole impulse that drove the wheels of her life was rendered powerless by her loss, as if she were a motor whose current had been suddenly cut off. She sat unmoving while the clatter of Magda setting the table for lunch scarcely penetrated her consciousness; a long time later she heard the stolid servant removing the untouched dishes. Edmond gone! It was incredible catastrophe. The words were as meaningless as if one should say, "The sun has gone out; the world is condemned to darkness."

The afternoon waned, and still she sat hopelessly, without thought, knowing only the depths of her misery. Finally she was aware that the doorbell was ringing, had been ringing for some time. She would have risen when Magda's heavy tread forestalled her. A moment later she looked uncomprehendingly at the figure that entered the room; realization came slowly that it was Paul, very excited.

"My dear!" he said. "I came at once, as soon as I found your note."

"Note?" Vanny said vaguely, tonelessly.

"Of course! Here!"

She glanced indifferently at the missive he presented; truly enough the script was her own, confuting in its accurate familiarity the very testimony of her memory. A single line, "Come back, Paul," and her own signature, perfect to the shading of its letters. Why had Edmond inflicted this irony on her? Was he, she wondered, attempting a mistaken kindness, or, out of the depths of his wisdom, did he indicate to her the course he considered best? No matter, she concluded dully; it devolved on her to follow his implied command.

"He's gone," she said, turning vision-haunted eyes on Paul, who still panted in excitement.

"And a good thing, dear! We'll have you free, start proceedings immediately!"

"No," said Vanny. "I don't want that."

"Why, dear! That's the only course!"

"No," the girl repeated in the same monotone. "If Edmond wishes to be free of me, he'll contrive it himself."

"Of course he will! And at your expense, Vanny—at the cost of your character!"

"He won't do that, Paul. He'll find his own means, if he desires it."

Now, with the presence of a friend whose sympathy she trusted, the apathy was transforming itself to an active misery, a poignant, unbearable pain.

"I'm terribly unhappy!" she muttered, and began to weep. For a long time Paul, sensitive to her needs, made neither sound nor movement, but when she began to quiet from sheer exhaustion, he moved close to her, held her in his arms, and tried to comfort. After a time she was pale and dry-eyed and calm.

"You will stay here tonight, Paul," she told him.

"Not here! You'll come away with me!"

"Here," reiterated Vanny.

The afternoon dragged slowly into evening; night fell on the city, and still they remained in a room grown somber with shadows. Vanny would not yield to appeal or argument to leave the house, and Paul had not the heart to abandon her. In the end he stayed, feeling somehow as if the girl had won a victory over him. Nevertheless, the next night found him still present, and the following night as well.

So there began a queer period in the lives of these two. Paul was nearly happy in the possession of the being he desired. He worked with unaccustomed energy at his writing, using Vanny's desk in the living room, and it seemed to the girl that his work was of more merit than heretofore. He was elated too with the acceptance of a short story by a magazine of small circulation but of decided literary repute; shortly afterward the same publisher accepted a poem.

As for Vanny, she was far from happy, but her misery drove her to Paul for comfort. She clung to his companionship with a sort of despairing avidity, feeling her loneliness insupportable without him. He was simple, affectionate, understandable; sometimes she experienced a feeling almost of relief at the realization that his thoughts were of her own degree, human and comprehensible. More than that, she could hold conceptions beyond his powers, and could if she wished master his nature as Edmond had mastered hers. There was a grain of comfort in this, for she perceived that she retained something within herself of Edmond's more than human abilities.

Magda, third member of the unusual household, worked on as stolidly as if she had not noticed the change in personnel. She prepared the meals as usual, served and removed them, and collected her wages each Saturday. It was as if she served not the tenants, but the house, as she had done for nearly a quarter of a century.

During this quiet and unhappy interlude, Vanny was relieved at least of the necessity of financial worry. She had her own account at the bank, and her own deposit box. An inspection of this revealed a surprisingly thick sheaf of securities, considerably more than she had believed she owned; it did not occur to her that Edmond possessed a duplicate key.

So life dragged along; the new year passed into being and the planet swung through the spring and summer arcs. Little by little the distant look was fading from Vanny's dark eyes, as the incredible sensations and events of her dreamy life with Edmond slipped out of the grasp of her memory. She realized their passing as her recollection of certain elements grew misty, but she had no power to fix them since they included conceptions alien to her mind. She was drifting back, away from both the horrors and the beauties she had known; she watched these latter vanish regretfully, but the turning of time seemed only to measure their disintegration. She was helpless either to aid or hinder the process.

Sometimes she helped Paul at his work with an incisive criticism or a suggestion full of possibilities. More often she read while he labored, for her husband's great library was at hand for her use, but the things she dug out of the volumes seemed usually meaningless gibberish, lacking the interpretation of a greater insight than her own. At other times she simply sat and dreamed; Paul was sometimes amazed by the stretch of time she could while away in this fashion—she who had been of old so active, so impatient of idleness. She found the library a solitary retreat, since Paul seldom entered it; the skull on the fireplace grinned at him with too ironical a smile.

Of late she had grown careless of her appearance; she employed no cosmetics, and her clear skin seemed always ivory-pallid. Mostly she wandered about the house wearing that iridescent purple robe that Edmond had draped about her; her hair drifted like black velvet around her face, and Paul thought her more lovely than ever. And then, as autumn sent a preliminary chill into the air, she perceived a restraint in Paul's manner; with something of Edmond's unbelievable perspicacity, she understood that he was concealing some unpleasantness from her.

"Paul," she asked him suddenly as he sat at the desk, "have you seen him?"

"Seen whom, dear?" He looked up perturbed.

"Edmond, of course! Where is he?"

"What makes you ask that, Vanny? How can I know?"

"Where is he, Paul?" she repeated.

He surrendered gloomily. "I saw him, dear. He's living in an apartment on Lake View; I think he's living with a woman."

Vanny's pallor increased so violently that Paul was startled; he sprang toward her from the desk, but her eyes met his steadily enough.

"Tell me where, Paul," she said, "or take me there I want to see her."

"I won't! You can't ask that!"

"I want to see her."

"She's ugly," said Paul. "Thin and shapelessly angular, and she looks like him."

"I want to talk to her."

"But he'll be there!"

"Not in the morning." She rose, moving toward the hall; Paul gave in with a sigh and followed.

"I'll go with you then," he said with a wan smile of surrender.

Edmond had taken his grey roadster; they found a taxi, and sped silently along Sheridan. Vanny spoke not a word until they angled off the teeming Drive to Lake View, and halted before a brown brick apartment building.

"Wait for me," she said then and walked unhesitatingly toward the boxes in the hall; his name was there; he had not deigned to alter it. She pressed the button beside it; a long minute passed without result. Again she pressed it, steadily, insistently, and waited; finally the door buzzed in mechanical invitation. She pushed it open; there was an automatic elevator, and she stood tense during the interminable ascent, half hypnotized by the long bee-like drone of the mechanism. The apartment door opened as she approached. Sarah looked out at her with intent, expressionless eyes, and instantly Vanny perceived the nature of this being for whom Edmond had abandoned her. This was a woman of his own sort, able at once to be companion and mother, capable of permitting the fulfillment of his life. Her mood turned suddenly to extreme melancholy. Now indeed, with such an opponent, it was a hopeless task to win Edmond back!

The woman Sarah still stared without speech, and Vanny felt constrained to break the silence.

"I am Mrs. Hall," she said. The other nodded silently, swinging the door wider and moving aside. Vanny entered, and the door closed. She stood surveying a room obviously of the better furnished-apartment class. Here and there about the walls were oil paintings, pastels, and crayons, and she recognized the handiwork; this was the same twisted artistry that had produced that disturbing landscape, once in Edmond's library, that yet hung in his laboratory. Sarah motioned her to a chair and sat herself facing her. The tense silence settled over them again. "I wanted to see you," Vanny said finally. The woman nodded.

"I wanted to understand," said Vanny, "since I have lost him utterly—lost him," she added in bitterness, "because I was a fool!"

"Do not imagine," said the woman in a voice of curiously flat intonation, "that your little peccadillos could drive him away. They are without meaning to him."

"Do you love him too?" Vanny said.

The woman spoke. "I have that which I wish," she said, and was again silent.

"You do love him," said Vanny. The other made no reply.

"I am sorry," said Vanny finally, "that I came here on such a hopeless errand. You understand that I must do what I can to draw him back; at the least, I must try."

The woman turned her strange eyes on Vanny, and spoke.

"No need to try," she said, "since you have never lost him. He seeks an illusion called beauty which he finds in you but misses in me."

A tinge of joy showed in Vanny's face. "Did he say that?" she asked.

"He says nothing. There is no need. Now do leave here and try no more to draw him from me, since you will inevitably succeed, and the course is disastrous."

"Disastrous! To whom?"

"To each of the four," said Sarah, "but mostly to Edmond." Again she was silent, while Vanny wondered dimly how she knew of Paul.

She rose to depart. "I've got to try," she said, moving toward the door. The woman Sarah watched her silently, though Vanny fancied she saw a glint of regret in the curious eyes.

15. The Loss of Beauty

Sarah was to bear Edmond's child in March, and late September found their curious establishment as settled as any normal household.

But as the period of her pregnancy progressed, Sarah drew more and more into her own being. Her minds, always introverted, turned their twin backs on reality, to dwell in a world within themselves and bounded by their own configurations. Never oppressed by that craving for an understanding companionship that drove Edmond, Sarah now found still less need for any outside entity. Yet she did occasionally seek his caresses, and these he gave, although hopelessly and indifferently. And the old loneliness returned to Edmond with a strange new intensity born of disappointment.

"Beauty has vanished out of my world," he thought, "and nothing is left me save a being who is to be a mother, and therefore is no companion."

But his other self meanwhile was regarding a visual memory of Vanny, with her body that curved, and was reminiscent of glades and sunlight and things earthly.

"The curse of the Cave still persists," reflected Edmond, "though differently in me than in men who daily go out to the hunt leaving their females to tend fires. Life moves in cycles and each individual finds his little circle encompassed by the greater circle that is society."

Instantly his other mind visualized his concept, thus:

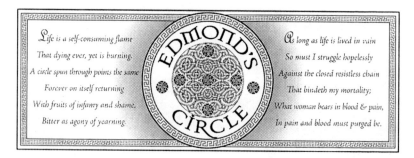

Life is a self-consuming flame
That dying ever, yet is burning.
A circle spun through points the same
Forever on itself returning
With fruits of infamy and shame,
Bitter as agony of yearning.

EDMOND'S CIRCLE

As long as life is lived in vain
So must I struggle hopelessly
Against the closed resistless chain
That bindeth my mortality;
What woman bears in blood & pain,
In pain and blood must purged be.

One night he saw Vanny on Michigan Avenue, walking with Paul, and moved by that pity which he had come to know, he slipped back into the dark entrance of the North American Building, that they might not meet. An ancient longing surged through his duality, and the sight of Vanny's pallor twisted in his breast like an oriental kris. Nor did he fail to notice the questing glance of her luminous eyes, peering here and there in a hopeless search, while Paul talked earnestly of something negligible.

"She feels my presence like Sarah," he thought. "The suppleness of her mind amazes me; who can limit the potentiality of the simplest brain? She has learned more of me than I had believed possible."

But the anguish of his loneliness persisted below the icy speculation. He wanted again the virile love of humans, and Sarah's languid caresses seemed ever less desirable.

"I have tasted an opiate," he thought. "Human love is not for my kind. Vanny and I are as poisons to each other, and as I kill her mind with forbidden visions, so does she destroy my body with fatal pleasure.

"Alien are we, natural and appointed enemies; no good thing may ever come out of this brief union of ours."

He followed with his burning eye Vanny's diminishing figure.

"Silver flame of Attic woodlands," he thought. "Why does she, of an alien species, draw me as Sarah should? I who should call kind to kind, as mare and stallion, woman and man?"

And his other self supplied the answer.

"Because all my associations have gathered around the normal woman-body. Beauty is to me what experience has trained it to be, and Vanny, not Sarah, is its embodiment."

Often a vague idea of suicide beckoned, and as often a stubborn pride of race rejected it.

"Surely no race whose first member is suicidal has any survival value. On me lies the primary burden of proving my species' fitness."

And his other self replied, "This is the primitive idea of Duty that misleads me. This is patriotism, and pride of blood. Peace is a thing infinitely more to be desired; and peace is easy of access, and I know the way."

But his first mind, considering: "Still, the idea is in itself repugnant, as it confesses the weakness of my kind. Better for me to live and suffer, that the coming of my race be easier."

And his other self again, "Why aid these successors into unhappiness like mine? If come they must, then let them, but do not usher them into Hell. Cerberus had three heads, not two."

And finally, "Neither the pursuit of knowledge nor that of power is happiness. Happiness hides in its own pursuit. Happiness is the quest; content, the achievement. But for me, who come before my appointed time, there is neither the one nor the other, since the goal is in a not yet extant future."

But always in part of his mind the image of Vanny persisted. He perceived that love had two components, companionship, which is the intellectual, and passion, which is the physical element.

"My love is thus sundered, so that I love one with my brain and another with my body."

And he smiled his ironic smile, whispering to his idle self, "Of these two, the bodily love is sweeter!"

"There is a delight I can never know," he reflected;—"the unity of these two elements of love. Sarah's mind in Vanny's body—"

His idle mind envisaged for a moment a dark thought, to be toyed with an instant, weighed, and rejected. He perceived that in certain things fate is inexorable, and monsters are always to be abhorred.

Then his twin minds reverted to Sarah—placidly intelligent Sarah, who alone could accompany him through the mazes of his thoughts, but could not follow the broad and easy way of the body—Sarah, whose pleasure in the bearing of a child was greater than that in its conception—Sarah, who knew nothing of strong human love, and desired nothing of it, her mind unpoisoned by forbidden pleasures.

"She is normal of her kind," he thought. "In the placidity of pure intelligence, she is unaware both of the pits of despair and the peaks of pleasure; her existence is an equable flowing out of ideas, unruffled by any emotional breeze. But I am a creature of the depths, toiling forever toward shining heights that recede horizon-like before me. I have in a sense perverted myself with alien joys; my nature should have been as Sarah's, but that I tasted the poison."

16. Edmond Refuses to Follow His Fancy

Again one afternoon Edmond returned to his lake-cresting hill, whence he had watched the planet spin under him, and seated himself once more on the remembered slope. He watched the posturing of a golden finch, a laggard in the migration, in the tree above him, taking a sort of pleasure in its instantaneous grace. He answered its twittering, and reply brought forth reply, for all beings save Man and the man-ridden Dog were drawn to Edmond.

"I am less of the Enemy and somewhat more of the Master," thought Edmond. "I am of nature the user, where man is the destroyer."

But his other self sat within like a statue cast in lead, and struggled to think of things remote from that vision which was unforgetable. Like the migratory bird, his thoughts were drawn inevitably to the tropics of his mind; returning from the zones of cool speculation to that torrid equator where the two hemispheres met. So at last Edmond gave himself to his misery, and wrung therefrom finally a sort of dusky pleasure.

"Suppose now," he thought, "I should evoke for myself an illusion, as I know how to do—a mental materialization of her whom I desire, and suppose I endow this image with the qualities of my senses, why should that vision not satisfy me? For I know that it would not. Is it that her thoughts and her personality would be my own? No; for the thoughts and character of the fleshly Vanny are mine."

His other mind replied, "What is lacking in the image of my own mind is Vanny's admiration, her worship and love. These are things I can never endow, for God knows I have none of them for myself!"

Nevertheless, Edmond did evoke for himself a vision of Vanny, and by means of faculties for intense concentration made her seem real and external to his minds. For he found a pleasure in the contemplation of her white loveliness that logic could not argue out of him; therefore the image that sprang into being was that Vanny who had danced for him by night, with her body gleaming sword-like in the dusk. Edmond made the quiet autumn afternoon into an evening about the two of them, and watched his evocation dance as Vanny had been wont to dance. Thereafter he summoned her, so that she lay warm against him with a well-remembered pressure, and he kissed her and spoke with his vision.

"Are you less unhappy with me than with Paul, Vanny?"

The image replied, "I am the Vanny who was yours, and I have forgotten Paul."

"But do you like to return? To recall things as they were?"

"How can I return? I have never been away."

"That is bitter reproach, Vanny! I am empty enough, lacking your presence."

"I am yours whenever you will it, Edmond."

"No," said Edmond, after a long moment, "my course is wiser in that it contains less of evil. It was the rational thing to do."

"But since when, Edmond, has that been a criterion of yours?"

Edmond looked into the dark eyes of his evocation with an expression that held unmistakably a trace of doubtfulness; it seemed to his perceptions that in that moment the vision spoke not with his words, but with its own. As if, he thought, he had performed some of the functions of creation, and played on a diminutive scale the part of deity—so real, so living, did this being made out of his longings and imaginings seem to him! He felt a strong temptation to do a thing his reason forbade, to adopt in fact the suggestion of this lovely fancy, and abandon reason as his criterion.

"Suppose, now," he argued while his vision nestled in his arms, "suppose I forswear reality, and take as my own this dream I hold, and dwell hereafter in a world of dream, as I can if I so desire. Perhaps happiness is to be found only in such a world, a conclusion not void of logic, since it is but saying that happiness is a dream. If this is true, is it not the part of wisdom to enter the world of visions, where all the law is my own desire, and only that same desire measures either my companion's acquiescence or my own capacity?"

Out of the depths of his intricate mentality, a part of his mind sneered an answer in grim irony: "Nietzsche, here is your Super-man who wastes his caresses on a phantom and indulges himself with a dream, like a morbid child! To forswear reality, to dwell in a self-created, phantasmic world, is simply to welcome a voluntary madness!"

He turned again to his vision, and the eidolon smiled into his eyes, as if grateful for his attention.

"It is neither wise nor sane that I dally here with you," he told it, "to cloy my senses with a nonexistent loveliness, as is the way of a madman."

"But why not?" replied the image. "Indeed, it is your own statement that beauty, like truth, is a relative thing, and exists only in the mind of the observer. If you must have reason as your guide, will you spurn the implications of your own logic?"

For a while Edmond regarded his creation with that intensity which had been Vanny's terror, and then spoke in the tones which had been her delight.

"Vanny! Vanny!—Say the answer to the question I am thinking!"

The vision trembled, the deep eyes glowed back into Edmond's unfaceable gaze.

"I love you, Edmond. You are not as men, but greater. Demon, or not, I love you. Do not be unkind—"

"Pah!" said Edmond. "I am deluding myself with my own fancy! These are my own words it gives me back!"

He dismissed the image, rose and returned to his car above the hill, but to his backward glance the vista seemed not wholly depopulated. For beneath the tree of the finch there still lingered a misty glory, as if the intensity of his concentration had bound some wandering atoms for a while into a semblance of a form, and for a little distance this golden mist pursued him beckoning. Edmond knew better than to heed, but watched with a certain speculation in his eyes as it danced with a diminishing glory in the sun.

17. Conversation on Earth

Edmond drove south along Sheridan Road with that miraculous dexterity which characterized all his relations with machines. These were to him simply extensions of his body; impulses flowed as easily through his limbs to the thrusting wheels on the road as to his finger tips. He and his vehicle moved as a single being, and thought of other things.

The car paused a moment at a light-controlled intersection, and Edmond noted the spectacles and cane called Alfred Stein waiting patiently for a bus. Edmond motioned for the professor to enter, and the cane and spectacles relaxed against the seat with a tired blinking and a grunt.

"These little electrons that I weigh," he said, "they can be very heavy to an old man."

"Your reward will come later, when others will seize on your results and draw inferences and formulate theories which will endure six months or more."

Stein grinned amiably. Sometimes he felt a reluctant liking for the curious Edmond.

"Experimental science—you do not think very much of it?"

"Your science," said Edmond, "is approaching the state of Chinese science—a vast body of perfectly good rules for which the reasons have been lost. The snowball of knowledge is growing too big for you to push, with all your specialists."

"Well, what is to be done? At least we must keep on pushing."

"What is needed," said Edmond, "is a new Aristotle—a new Roger Bacon, whose province is all knowledge—someone to coordinate all the facts you have amassed into a rational structure of things that are."

"And of course that is impossible because no one person can possibly be cognizant of all the infinite little facts we have dug out of nature. It is a lifetime work to acquaint one's self with a single minor specialty."

"Do not be too sure."

148

"Well then, who is the man?"

"Myself," said Edmond, and was a little startled by Stein's chuckle. "I have no humor," he thought in his other mind. "The things that amuse these beings are at times surprising."

"Listen," said Stein. "If you know everything, perhaps you will explain for me some of our traditional mysteries."

"Perhaps," said Edmond. "Specifically what?"

"Any of several. For instance, how to liberate the energy of matter—atomic energy?"

For a moment Edmond hesitated, balancing the idea between his twin minds. It would be so simple—a key couched in a few words might unlock the portal for the man beside him, had Stein but the perspicacity to understand the hint. Out of his mind rose a picture of a certain experiment—a flaming power that might be uncontrollable. In his other mind formed the very words of the suggestion—"Use atoms of niton as your oscillator." His first self toyed with thoughts of the results of revelation. "Jove's thunderbolts in the paws of apes; they will certainly consume themselves." And his second self, "However amusing, this eventuality is undesirable, since it dams the spring from which my own race is to flow. A people's gods cannot survive their race."

So Edmond temporized. "I have made a vacuum tube which in effect satisfies your problem."

"I know," Stein answered. "Frankly, I do not understand your filament, but it is active like radium on a lesser scale. It releases energy, but only in a single degree, and that a low one. What I mean is energy to do—well, this."

He waved his hand to embrace the scene about them—the humming lines of traffic, torch-bearing in the dusk, the persistent lights that were everywhere, the block-distant rumble of an elevated train. Power on every hand, energy run rampant, flowing like blood through the copper veins of the Colossus of the Lake Shore.

"How many little activated filaments," asked Stein, "would you need to create this?"

"Indeed," replied Edmond, "I am not denying the benefits to be derived from an illimitable source of power; but for every advantage there is a loss and a danger. The same energy that vitalizes a city can be inverted to destroy it. You have seen or perhaps experienced the effects of present military explosives, which are instantaneous; what of an atomic bomb that keeps on exploding for several weeks?"

"With unlimited power, there vanishes the economic need for war, my friend," said Stein.

"The need vanishes, but not the desire."

Stein chuckled again.

"Sometimes," he said, "I am tempted to take you at your own valuation, Mr. Hall, and yet I do not always like you." He paused, and then continued: "Suppose now I grant your claim to know everything. Have you evolved any philosophy out of your knowledge? Can you, for instance, give me one statement that is unalterably true? Can you give this—" his hand moved in another all-embracing wave—"this thing Life a meaning or a purpose?"

"Well," said Edmond slowly (while his other mind taunted: 'Observe: I have degenerated to the use of expletives'). "Well, naturally I have evolved a certain interpretation of things as I perceive them. I do not believe my viewpoint to be unalterably true, as absolutes are non-existent. Do you believe that any statement is possible which is wholly true?"

"No," answered Stein. "I believe with your Oscar Wilde that nothing is quite true."

"That statement is a paradox," said Edmond, "since to be true it must be false. However, there is one statement that is utterly true—a sort of pragmatic Einsteinism, but applicable not merely to pure science but to all things that are." He exhaled an eddying stream of blue cigarette smoke, and continued.

"Cabell also bothered himself with this problem, and produced a fair solution: 'Time gnaws at all things; nothing is permanent save change.' However, a moment's analysis will show that this statement too is only relatively true."

"Ah," said Stein. "Yes."

"The one finality which is absolute—the one truth which is quite true—is this: All things are relative to the point of view; nothing is either true or false save in the mind of the observer."

"Ach," said Stein, "I do not believe that!"

"Thereby proving its truth," replied Edmond.

Stein was silent, staring at the thin-lipped ironic countenance beside him.

"As to your last question," continued Edmond, "of course the answer is obvious: There is no meaning at all to life."

"I think all young men have discovered that," said Stein, "only to doubt it when they have grown older."

"I do not mean precisely what you imagine," Edmond replied. "Let me ask you a question. What becomes of a straight line projected along one of the three dimensions of space?"

"It follows the curvature of space, according to Einstein."

"And if you continue it indefinitely?"

"It completes a circle."

"Then if time is a dimension of space?"

"I see," said Stein. "You infer that time itself is curved and repeats itself."

"That is the answer to your question," said Edmond gloomily. "This little arc of time that you call life is a minute part of a colossal, hopeless circle, with neither beginning nor end, cause nor objective, but returning endlessly upon itself. Progress is an illusion and fate is inexorable. The past and the future are one, merging one into the other across the diameter of the present. There is no escape even by suicide, since it is all to be done over again, even to that final gesture of revolt."

Silence. Stein, infected at last by the pessimism of his companion, gazed somberly at the river of steel flowing around them. He glanced again at the satyric features of that figure beside him, on whose thin lips flickered for a moment an ironic smile.

"My God!" he said, after a few moments. "Is that your philosophy?"

"Only that part of it which is susceptible to words."

"Susceptible to words? What do you mean?"

"There are two kinds of thoughts," replied Edmond, "which evade expression in language. Words, you must realize, are a rather crude device, a sort of building-block affair, piled together in the general outline of a thought, in phrases or sentences. They are neither flexible nor continuous nor perfectly fitted together, and there are thoughts which lie in the crevices between words—the shades, the finer colorings, the *nuances*. Words may blunder around the borders of these thoughts, but their expression is a question of feeling or mood."

"Yes," said Stein, "I can comprehend that."

"There is another class of thoughts," said Edmond, so somberly that Stein glanced again at him, "which lies entirely beyond the borders enter-able by language, and these are terrible thoughts, which are madness to dwellers in Elfhame."

Stein, following out the course of his own reflections, forebore to answer or question further. A block or two slipped behind them. After a while he spoke.

"Can you think these thoughts?"

"Yes," answered Edmond.

"Then you are claiming to be something else than human?"

"Yes," answered Edmond again.

"Well, I think you are crazy, my friend, but I am not denying the possibility that it is I—." His eyes turned to the incredibly delicate hands, one casually guiding the wheel, the other poising a cigarette. "Certainly there are differences—. Let me off at Diversey, please."

The car rolled quietly to the curb, and Stein opened the door. He stepped out, standing for a moment with his foot on the running board.

"Thank you for the lift and the lecture," he said.

"Always from our rare conversations I take away one gem. To-day it is this: That there is no hope anywhere, and the sum total of all knowledge is zero."

Edmond smiled again his thin-lipped sardonic smile.

"When you have really learned that," he said, as the car started slowly forward, "you will be one of us."

For some minutes, Stein stood blinking after the gray car.

18. Edmond Again Follows His Fancy

With the discontinuance of Alfred Stein's distraction, the old longing against which Edmond had struggled flowed back again. The low purr of the motor became intelligible: "Vanny....Vanny.... Vanny," it muttered in endless repetition. The strident horns about him shrieked a cacaphony whose endlessly recurrent theme was "Vanny"! So he came unhappily to Lake View, and to the apartment building that housed his strange domicile.

He slipped his key into the lock of his letter-box; Sarah never bothered to have the mail brought to her, for it was inconceivable that it should contain anything of interest to her. On Edmond, however, fell the responsibility of keeping oiled the machinery of living—there were bills to be paid, and occasionally a technical communication or royalty check from Stoddard. Momentarily Edmond paused startled. Out of the customary series of typed addresses slipped one whose directions appeared in delicate mauve script—an unassuming gray little envelope—thin to the point of transparency. Vanny!

A rare thrill of pleasure rose and subsided in Edmond's being. Whatever Vanny might write could not alter circumstances, could not make those two alien creatures into a common kind, nor break the unbreakable circumference of the circle Time.

He slipped the letter among the several others, and stepped into the automatic lift. In a moment he was entering the apartment which at present sheltered Sarah and himself. As always, Sarah was not in evidence; she would be in the rear, in the second solarium, engaged with her curious little landscapes, or turning obscure thoughts this way and that between her twin minds. It was seldom that they two saw each other now; Sarah was satisfied to be relieved of the burden of procuring food for herself, satisfied in her pregnancy, self-satisfied in her art. Her not very coercive sex tissues were content with Edmond's infrequent praise, his occasional commendations, and his negligible caresses.

Nevertheless, Sarah was a great artist, Edmond admitted to him-

self—a worthy Eve for her generic Adam, the superwoman intrin-
sic. She was unharassed by her environment, adjusted, happy, where
Edmond was of all these the antithesis.

Thus Edmond reflected in one of his minds, while the other still
surged sea-like about the fact of the letter. He opened it and drew
forth a single thin sheet of gray paper, at which he glanced, absorbing the few lines with his accustomed instantaneous perception:

"The love that is too faint for tears,
And scarcely breathes of pain,
Shall linger on a hundred years
And then creep forth again.
But I, who love you now too well
To smile at your disdain,
Must try tonight that love to quell,
And try in vain."

For the third time a surge of pity overwhelmed Edmond, as he
stood gazing now over the deep streets of the torch-bearers, over
a dark and passive park, to where Lake Michigan split the cold fire
of a rising moon into a coruscating path. Vanny! Poor Vanny, with
her ice-and-ivory body only half-tenanted! Sweet Vanny, whose
life-cycle had so tangled with his that she had lost the thread of it!
Dear, human Vanny, who wanted only to live out that cycle in love
and peace, like birds and beasts and things natural!

Edmond crumpled the paper into a ball and tossed it from the
open window, watching it spin downward a dozen stories like a little planet—a world peopled by the hypotheticals and conditionals
of his life with Vanny—the ought-to-be's and might-have-been's.
Then his eyes turned again to the Satellite, on which he seemed to
gaze downward as it lifted gigantic from the far end of the moonpath. He watched it pour down its rain of silver that the wave crests
cracked and flung back in fragments like white petals.

"The dead world strews flowers on the grave of the dying one,"
he thought, and suddenly perceived this moon as a world ideal.
Lifelessness—the happy state toward which all stars and planets tend,
when this miasmatic Life-disease had vanished cured. The smaller
world yonder, burned clean by solar fire, scoured clean by the icy
void—a world of airless rock—there hung the ultimate, the desired
end. Heaven and Hell swinging forever about the common center;

Heaven the world of annihilation, Hell the world condemned to life. He crystallized his thought:

"Long miles above cloud-bank and blast,
And many miles above the sea,
I watch you rise majestically,
Feeling your chilly light at last.
There's beauty in the way you cast
Split silver fragments on the waves,
As if a planet's life were past
And men were peaceful in their graves."

A simple conception, reflected his other self—nothing to imply, naught of the terrible inexpressible, a thought bound neatly into language. And yet, in some way, a lofty thought. Edmond was in a measure satisfied, as one who has at last conceived the solution of a difficult problem. And suddenly he was aware of Sarah's presence.

She stood behind him as he turned, her gaunt little body merging with the gloom, her eyes blazing in the lamp light with their accustomed intensity. Strange and alien and rather hideous she seemed, with her fleshless limbs and ashen skin. "I have known a body that was vital, with the curve of ivory and the flash of fire," he thought, "but Sarah's glows only with the pale gleaming of the intellect, which is but a feeble little glimmering that shines through the eyes."

In the moment that their eyes met, Edmond perceived that Sarah was aware of his longings and his misery, and that she held this knowledge without rancor, without anger, because she possessed all of him that she desired. This Sarah understood, having perceived the poison in Edmond's soul, but she perceived without sympathy, comprehended without appreciating, since emotions were things outside of her being. She saw, even as Edmond had seen, the harm and the danger to himself from thus playing with forces unnatural to him, but she had resources and outlets which were denied him; she was within herself sufficient, where Edmond was driven by his unhappiness. Seeing him thus troubled, she spoke:

"This is a cruel and foolish thing you do, Edmond; you stand at the window overlooking life and are at odds with yourself."

Edmond answered, "But half of me stands overlooking since half of me struggles in the stream of life wherein I cast myself."

"Being as you are, it is your privilege to soar above that stream."

"But it is my pleasure to bathe therein."

"It is a poisonous stream, Edmond. Whomever it sucks into it-self, it draws out that one's strength, soiling his body and rolling his soul and his soul's dreams into the mud of its bottom that these things may add themselves to its flood. It is a poisonous stream and its proper name is Phlegethon."

"This that you say is true," answered Edmond in a low voice, "but it is also true that for all that it exacts, Phlegethon renders a certain price, paying its accounts with the scrupulous exactness of a natural law. In the filth of its bed are hidden jewels that are very brilliant, and in all ways desirable, and those that are rolled deepest in the mud are granted the most lovely of these."

"They are ill-starred gems, and are the very essence of the poison."

"Nevertheless," said Edmond, "they are extremely pretty, and sometimes retain their luster for many years."

Sarah moved close to Edmond, gazing into his eyes with the terrible intensity that was her heritage. For a long moment there was silence between them, as they sought to establish that aura of sympathy and of understanding that once had blanketed them. They failed, for the inevitable slow spinning of the Time-circle had twisted them a little apart, so that their twin minds no longer faced squarely each to each. Sarah dropped her eyes; lacking the requisite rapport for that meeting, the communication of the inexpressible was denied her. In her low and equable voice she spoke again: "Ed-mond—Edmond—it is a very terrible and obscene thing that you are thinking; I foresee but one outcome."

Edmond stood silent, staring outward at the moon which had now ascended perhaps twice its diameter above the coruscating lake. Then Sarah continued: "It is far better for you to fulfill your destiny, remaining in your appointed sphere; and it is the poison in your body and minds that calls you elsewhere."

Then Edmond replied, turning bitter at last, "You who speak from pure theory, who lack all experience of these things, what can you know of the fierce pleasures and pains of humanity? What can you know of that pleasure which burns so madly that it is pain, that pain so exquisite that it is delight unbearable? How can you know that these are not worth all that I surrender—even to that outcome you threaten?"

"I want none of this," said Sarah, "having watched the poison run its course in you."

"No," said Edmond, again passive, "you want none of this, being of your kind perfect, and having no emotion save one. In you emotion is rarefied to languid little tastes and preferences, likes and dislikes that incline you this way and that, but have not the fine irresistible thrust of emotion that is known to each of those down below on the street."

"What have they that we should envy them?"

"Only their capacity to bear suffering," replied Edmond, "and this is a great and ennobling quality, the one quality that may defeat our kind. For this capacity makes of their lives a very poignant thing, so that they live more intensely than we, and cling fiercely to their pauperous lives only that they may suffer longer."

The two were silent again, sending their minds through strange and not-to-be-understood regions. There was no longer a blanket of sympathy about them; something lacked, some common ground on which to meet. Edmond stood in the plane of silver moonlight which could not lend his face a greater pallor. Beside him in the shadow, Sarah waited silently—passive inscrutable Sarah, whose passions were languid and ineffectual things! Edmond broke the silence: "I have sometimes wondered whether intellect is indeed worth its price, and whether after all it is not merely the old curse of Adam, divorcing us from the simpler and far nobler things that were long ago. I have a half-memory of such things as are incomprehensible to you, Sarah, who have only a perfect intelligence with which to understand—I confess I do not know."

He turned abruptly and moved toward the hall, while across the moonpath on the lake there seemed to flicker for a moment a curious misty glory that danced and beckoned.

"By your standards, and doubtless by all rational ones, this that I go to do now is very foolish, and void of wisdom; nevertheless, I go not entirely without assurance. For this stream of life you hover above is a deeper flood than you know, and there are reasons buried therein that are outside the grasp of our minds,—even, Sarah, of yours—even deeper than the inexpressible. Therefore I go to face that inevitable outcome not wholly without hope, and go indeed with a pleasure greater than I have ever known."

He moved out into the dark hall. Sarah, on whose face the silver dagger of moonbeams now fell, stood silently gazing after him, with no rancor, no ire in her face, but only a languid little regret glinting about her eyes, and a faint puzzlement therein.

19. Return to Olympus

Edmond stepped from his car before the house on Kenmore Street, and gazed up at it. There flickered the light of a hearth fire from the library—the blue glow of cannel—symbol of warmth and cheer and welcome flung out into the chilly autumn evening. No other lights—did the room hold Paul and Vanny together? Edmond wondered idly with half his mind; it mattered little. He moved toward the entrance, producing his key. Down the street he glimpsed a lurking figure with something of desolation about it; he turned a suddenly intense gaze upon it and it retreated, vanished.

Edmond unlocked the door, entering; he dropped his coat and hat and ever-present cane upon a chair remembered in the dusk, and turned toward the library whence issued low music from the radio. Vanny stood before the fireplace of the monkey's skull, her figure outlined against the glow, in an attitude poised, expectant. She wore that purple silken robe which Edmond had himself draped about her, through which her limbs were half-outlined by the flames in long lithe shadows. Her hair was a jet helmet, circling the haunted wistfulness of her eyes. She stood waiting, while Edmond paused a long moment on the threshold, for to his vision the scene held a breath-taking beauty.

He moved into the room, closer to Vanny, studying her. She had grown a trifle thinner, a shade paler, but surely her eyes were less haunted. His second self supplied the answer: "Lacking my presence, the unbearable things she learned are dissipating like heavy gases; having no words to fix them, she cannot recall them clearly, and they grow dream-like." Vanny dropped to the low fire-bench, looking up at Edmond timidly to read his expression, then with a flaming gladness. Edmond smiled, and for once there was little of irony in his smile. He bent to kiss her, slipping beside her on the bench. There was the scent of wine in her breath and her cheeks were beginning to flush.

"She has bulwarked her brain against my coming," thought Edmond sadly; "my very presence is an assault on her sanity."

159

Vanny spoke. "Oh, Edmond, I hoped you would come. I have been wanting you."

Edmond's delicate long fingers caressed her; something of beauty had entered his life again, and he was content.

"First I only hoped you would come, Edmond; then when I realized your approach, I sent Paul away, and that was hard to do, and he was very bitter; but by ways I learned of you, I made him go."

Then, "Do you come to stay, Edmond?"

"For as long as is permitted me, dear."

"And is that long?"

"It may be forever—for me."

"Then I am happy, Edmond."

For a space of minutes they were silent, Vanny happy without thought, content in the presence of her loved one. Edmond sat not without thought, but as happy as might be, and whatever of sadness entered him he lost in the mellow flow of music.

"Dance for me, Vanny."

She rose, dropping the purple silken robe, so that it lay glistening like an iridescent pool of oil about her feet, then moved from it like an emanation in the breeze. Edmond watched her dance, reveling in the delights of beauty he had thought to deny himself forever. Thereafter he summoned her, so that she lay warm against him with a well remembered pressure, and he kissed her, and spoke with her.

"Are you less unhappy with me than with Paul, Vanny?"

"I am the Vanny who was yours, and I have forgotten Paul."

Startled, Edmond's other self recalled that very afternoon when he sat on the lake-cresting hill and spoke with his vision. He noted too that a misty glory had entered the room, dancing and beckoning in the fire-light.

"But do you like to return? To recall things as they were?"

"How can I return? I have never been away."

"That is bitter reproach, Vanny. . . ." He paused, suddenly pallid. "Stop, Vanny! The Time-circle is slipping, and it will be all to do over again! Pour me a glass of wine."

Vanny reached the silver decanter that was fashioned like a fantastic Bacchus, filling two glasses. They touched glasses and drank.

"Another, Vanny."

Again they touched glasses, smiling over them at each other, draining the tart Riesling to the bottom.

"And another, dear." Again they drank.

"No, that is enough now."

A pleasant ruddy mist settled over Edmond's minds, blanketing the terrors that had been rising therein, smothering them, so that the inexpressible was no longer conceivable to him, and the Time-circle slipped smoothly back to its appointed place and the dancing mist was no more. Vanny came to him again in the robe that flashed red and violet in the fire-glow, and he reached out his thin wiry arms, his incredible serpentine fingers, to draw her to him. Her eyes were bright with wine, and the deep terrors behind them were hidden; her cheeks were flushed, and through her half parted lips her breath flowed over Edmond bearing the perfume of wine. So for a little while they were a unity, flesh and spirit merging like separate notes in a chord, into a pagan paean, a rhapsody.

Vanny lay finally passive against him, the flush of her cheeks paling, her eyelids drooping, her lungs gasping in the too warm, over-sweet air of the room. Above the arch of the fireplace, the skull of Homo leered sickeningly at her.

"Your coming, Edmond—the wine—they are going to be too—much!" Her head drooped.

Edmond rose, and with an effort raised her, bore her unsteadily up the broad stairs. He felt a peculiar pleasure in the weight of her body, always so vibrant and tense, now listless and unresponsive against him. He lowered her to her bed, and by a means known to him, cheated that body of the pay it would have demanded for an evening of ecstasy. But he himself lay tossing most of the night despite a deadly languor.

20. Living

There began now for Edmond a new sort of life, a dreamy indolent existence through which Vanny moved like the shadow of his fancy. Day after day slid quietly below the threshold, so peacefully that nothing marked their passing save Edmond's increasing weakness, and a lassitude that grew with deadly steadiness. For this, of course, there were compensations.

He had dusted off his tubes and wires in the laboratory upstairs, and sometimes spent a whole day pursuing his old will-o-the-wisp of knowledge that danced before him now very far over the swamp of the unknown. At times he surprised himself by curious discoveries that lay far beyond the borders of science; and in these hours labored with a vigor and enthusiasm that he had almost forgotten. But at other times he sat most of a day idle with his head upon his hands.

Occasionally Vanny came in, seating herself soundlessly and timidly in the corner, never daring to speak in this mysterious sanctum unless Edmond first addressed her. She witnessed many great things, but saw them only as rainbow shafts of light and flaming bits of metal; of their import she comprehended precisely nothing. Once she saw him fling a leaden ball against the ceiling by an invisible force, and press it there until its outline marred the plaster, though nothing apparent held it. Another time for her amusement, he twice caused her to slumber so deeply that she seemed to awaken as from a distant world; when she revived the second time, flushed and happy from not-quite-remembered dreams, he told her that she had been dead. For this miracle he used a small shiny gold needle that trailed itself into a copper wire.

Still other times, by means of a little spinning bowl of mercury, he showed her knife-sharp crags and a disastrous landscape on the moon; and once, when he bade her peer therein, she looked down upon a wild roseate glade through which two winged beings moved, not human-like but of transcendent beauty, swift and iridescent. She felt a strange kinship existing between these and herself and Edmond, but he would not tell her on what world she gazed, nor on what sort of creatures.

The terrible things of their former days together were forgotten by Vanny, and Edmond guarded carefully against the vision of the inexpressible, marshaling his thoughts into selected channels lest she sense implications dangerous to her tense little mind. He was not always successful. One afternoon he returned to the library to find her trembling and tearful over a very ancient French translation of the *Necronomicon* of the Arab. She had gathered enough of the meaning of that blasphemy colossal to revive the almost vanished terrors of her old thoughts. Edmond soothed her by ancient and not at all superhuman means, but later she noticed that half a dozen volumes had been removed from the library, probably to his laboratory. One of these, she recalled, was the *Krypticon* of the Greek Silander in which Edmond had once during the old days pointed out to her certain horrors, and another was a nameless little volume in scholastic Latin by one who signed himself Ferus Magnus. With the removal of these books, an oppressive atmosphere vanished from the library and the room seemed lighter. Vanny spent more of her time there, reading, listening to music, keeping her household accounts, or simply day-dreaming. Even the skull of Homo above the fireplace had lost its sarcastic leer, and grinned as foolishly as any dead monkey. One day she came in quietly and surprised a sparrow on the window ledge; this was a portentous and significant event to her, as if a curse had been lifted from the chamber.

Alfred Stein, too, had unearthed Edmond's latest whereabouts, and sometimes dropped in for an evening. Edmond was somewhat amused by the puzzlement of the brilliant little man, and found a mild pleasure in confounding him. At intervals he demonstrated some marvel from his laboratory or propounded some thesis that left the amiable professor sputtering and choleric but nonplussed. He grinned sardonically at Stein's rather desperate attempts to fathom mysteries that were simply beyond his potentialities, knowing that to beings of a single viewpoint even the nature of matter must remain forever incomprehensible. After a while Stein reconciled himself to the deadlock, though Edmond perceived that he still considered himself the victim of chicanery; he never abandoned the attempt to pry out some bit of knowledge or information. He had come to accept Edmond as Vanny had, a being to be enjoyed as one enjoys music, without analysis, without questioning the technique of the creator. His initial dislike had vanished with familiarity; he had acquired a taste for the superman.

Vanny loved these visits. Little desire for human association remained to her, but she reveled in the sense of relaxation that Stein induced; it was breath of sea-air to a dweller on the mountain peaks. She had learned to serve wine or an aperitif, since alcohol seemed to temper Edmond's knife-like presence; under its rosy touch he seemed milder, more understandable, less inhuman in his icy cerebration. Often they sat a whole evening while discussion ranged over the gamut of mortal experience, all sciences and arts, social theories, politics, and the eternally recurrent sex. Vanny and Stein bore the burden of the conversation; Edmond mostly smoked silently, following their trend idly with half his mind, sometimes replying to a direct question with an incisive finality that seemed to bury that question forever, or again pointing out an absurdity with his scathing smile.

One night Vanny picked up a volume of Swinburne and read aloud from it. Stein listened fascinated—"The Hymn to Proserpine." The piece was new to him, and flowed into him like music. Vanny, intense vitalist, lover of all things sensuous and beautiful, breathed an exaltation into the long, musical, mystical lines that she half murmured. Even Edmond felt the sonorous liquid syllables agreeably, though assaying them in the scales of intellect he found them wanting.

"Ach," said Stein, as she finished, "that is great poetry. 'The last of the Giants' they call him, and that is right. They do not produce such things today—nobody!"

"Times fall away," answered Vanny. "Poetry flourishes when men are stirred to the depths; we fritter away our emotions in the too vast complexity of the machine city."

"Yes," said Stein with his slight accent. "Even a great upheaval of a war is dissipated into a billion little units, and we get a lot of hysterical mush and some mediocre literature. But there is no outstanding figure to dominate his time."

"I think the spirit of a time must be embodied in one man or a group, and that is why in this too swift, too powerful period there are no great artists." Vanny spoke thus, while Edmond sat smoking, staring into the shadows beyond the lamp. "Am I right, Edmond?"

Edmond crushed out his cigarette. "My dear, you and Stein take your poets like cheese: They have to moulder a bit before they're palatable."

Vanny smiled; she was always proud of Edmond even when his mockery turned on her.

"Then you think some current literature is permanent?" queried Stein.

"I do not doubt it, but like all else, the term is relative. A change in fashions of thought or schools of criticism can elevate mediocre work to greatness or doom great work to mediocrity." He lit another cigarette. "I always have found difficulty in discriminating between what you term great and mediocre literature. The differences are rather negligible."

"Ach, the man-from-Mars pose is working again," grinned Stein. "Our poor little human efforts are all about on a par to him."

Edmond smiled and fell silent again. Through his other mind ran a series of disquieting thoughts, and the growing languor oppressed him with its inertia.

21. Sarah

During the latter months, Edmond had husbanded his little store of vitality, loosing it drop by drop like a man dying of thirst. Vanny's hungry human body drained it like dry sand, but something of desire had gone out of her, to be replaced by a more intense love of all beauty. Denied the common lot of women, seeking other pleasures, finding different sorrows, she adapted herself thereto and considered herself happy. She demanded less of Edmond's waning strength, and found her compensation within herself.

Edmond too found himself content with his renunciation. He lived surrounded by that sensuous beauty for which he had surrendered his hereditary self, and found it sufficient. His audit balanced; when the moratorium was over he could render full payment for value received to a certain River creditor.

Twice Edmond had glanced from a window at night to glimpse a desolate figure lurking about the house—a figure that invariably fled before his gaze. This bothered Edmond not at all; he held the opposition of humans inconsiderable.

But Sarah had not forgotten him. Four months after their parting, in middle Spring, she came to him in a manner possible to her, and told him his son was born. She came long after midnight, while Vanny slept and Edmond lay tossing and weak, in such fashion that he was suddenly aware of Sarah standing beside him, regarding him with that intensity he knew of old. His eyes ranged languidly over her spare masculine form, her awkward carriage.

"He is born," said Sarah wordlessly.

"Show him to me."

She obeyed; Edmond gazed without interest at the curious little tearless whelp, lean as Sarah and himself, the little wrinkled brow and eyes already somber with the oppressive weight of mind yet to come. It clutched Sarah's thin hair with tentacular fingers, and stared back at its sire with a premonitory hint of his own fiery gaze.

"Enough," said Edmond, and the imp vanished.

"Edmond," said Sarah, "the outcome is imminent. I perceive

your weakness, and I see that you are foredoomed. Nevertheless, there is still time—if you return."

Edmond smiled wearily, and wordlessly denied her.

"Then you are lost, Edmond."

"I have that which compensates me."

Sarah gazed with the fusing of her twin minds, probing Edmond's brain, seeking for some clue to his incomprehensible refusal. That one should with open eyes approach the foreseen end—welcome it!

"I do not understand you, Edmond," she said, and departed with a trace of puzzlement in her eyes.

Again he smiled a weary and somewhat wistful smile, with no trace of irony.

"Beauty is a relative thing, and certainly only a dream and an illusion of the observer," he reflected, "but to that observer it is a reality unquestionable. I should be more unhappy than I am could I believe that this beauty that costs me so dearly is less real than life and knowledge and power, and certain other illusions."

At irregular intervals Sarah came again, and one night brought news that she had found two other men of the new race, and that they bided their time until the change had brought forth more. This night Edmond sat facing the skull of Homo in the library, rather too weak to rise and retire. Vanny was sleeping some hours since. Sarah came by that way which was open to her, and gazed long at Edmond without disclosing her thoughts; then she told him the news which had brought her. Edmond answered nothing, fixing his eyes silently on eyes that returned neither malice nor longing, but only a faint puzzled questioning and a languid little regret.

"The outcome is very near," said Sarah.

Edmond silently assented.

She swept closer, murmuring in that wordless speech she used. "There is yet time, Edmond. You are needed; out of your knowledge you are needed. Return to me where I am even now waiting."

Again and again Edmond denied her.

"I have chosen my course, and it yet seems to me that I chose wisely," he replied. "The things I gain outvalue those I lose."

"This is an incalculable madness and a delusion," said Sarah. "Ruin faces you."

Edmond smiled in a weary fashion. "I do not argue," he said. His eyes sought Sarah's thin awkward form as she stood erect and facing him; there was something of suppliance in her appearance, but her eyes were cold and proud. He scanned her, his twin minds probing and seeking; he perceived with a tinge of astonishment that Sarah too was unhappy. And again after many months, the aura of sympathy descended upon them, the inexpressible lay open before their minds. They had found a common ground.

Sarah felt it, and her cold eyes lit up with their ancient fire; she leaned tensely forward and sought to convey to Edmond what thoughts were in her minds.

Sarah:

"This is a concourse of dead gods—
They gather wraith-like in the night
Summoning futile powers."

Edmond:

"Synods
Of half-forgotten names of might,
Of names still potent to affright—
Sarah, defy them not!"

Sarah:

"Their rods
Are broken and their priests are fled
Save only you!"

Edmond:

"I serve my gods.
I will not see them starved and dead—
I make my ancient sacrifice
And drink my ancient anodyne."

Sarah:

"But only you must make it twice
Since only you know other wine!
Edmond; your deities have failed.
Rise from the River! Cast off the slime
Of Life; look down with eyes unveiled!"

Edmond:

"I think my thoughts and bide my time."

Thus Edmond again denied Sarah, and having ceased, deliberately broke the cords of sympathy that bound them so that their conveyance of thought was constrained to language. Sarah was pale and cold before him, regarding him with deep unwinking eyes.

"I shall not ask again," she said.

"I have fulfilled my destiny with you, Sarah," replied Edmond wearily. "Why do you not go back to those others, to weave your nets with them?"

"Once," said Sarah, "you told me that there were truths beyond my grasp, and thoughts outside the reach of my minds. Now I say to you that while your intellect may reach out and circle a star, yet there are simple and unassuming little facts that slip through your mental grasp like quicksilver, and you are as incapable of grasping these as if they lay buried at the uttermost bounds of the world."

She vanished. Edmond sat staring at the skull of Homo, with a faint wonder in half his mind. "Certainly," he thought, "it is surprising to hear Sarah so bitter. I had not dreamed she was capable of even such mild emotional disturbance as this; there is something wrong with my analysis of her."

And his other self brought forth the answer, a solution so banal, so hackneyed, that he smiled again his slow, weary smile. "Like all women, Sarah is reluctant to admit defeat. She is still feminine to the extent of wanting her own way!"

Nevertheless he felt that some element in Sarah had eluded him. He was aware of a certain doubt as he dragged himself erect and betook himself to Vanny.

22. Diminuendo

So things spun out their course in a peaceful diminuendo for Edmond; his vitality dropped from him as easily as from an aged man, with as little bodily discomfort. His intellect remained unclouded, even, he thought, clearer than before; certain veils that hung there of old had vanished, opening vistas hitherto obscured. The old hunger for knowledge grew less as he perceived its ultimate futility, but the love of beauty remained.

"My last reality is a sensation," he thought, "and so I complete the cycle that lies between the superman and, let us say, the oyster. For now the only difference remaining is that I possess a slightly more varied repertory of sensory organs. But doubtless a truly aesthetic oyster finds its compensations for this; it drinks more deeply of the wine at hand."

And his other self replied, "Beyond doubt the oyster is the happier, since it makes full use of the body it possesses, and fulfills its destiny completely, as I do not."

He sat now in his chair before the fireplace. Behind him the early autumnal dusk was darkening the window; the usual fire of cannel glowed its reflection on his face. His languor was not unpleasant, as he sat in a dreamy half-reality, a reverie; his twin minds ranged at random through devious courses. He wandered from memories of the past to hypothetical visions of might-have-been. Images of old experiments in fields he had wished to explore came to him, carrying breath-taking intimations of things incredible; of that diffuse cosmic intelligence which is everywhere, called Natural Law, or God, or the Law of Chance, according to one's nature. And this universal Entity, Edmond reflected, breathed a fiery purpose and vital fertility in every part, but in the infinite aggregate was sterile, purposeless and static.

Pictures of Vanny—flaming, incoherent visions that burned in an aura of emotion! Vanny dancing before the fire—Vanny's eyes with the haunting terror in them, and then those eyes lit up with an ecstasy. Vanny sleeping—Vanny laughing—Vanny's body tense and sweet and vital, or that body warm and languorous, with the perfume of wine upon her breath.

"I have made a good trade," he reflected. "Now I pay without regret that which I value little, for this that I prize highly."

Instantly a memory of Sarah moved quietly into his minds, her dry little voice sounding almost audibly her dolorous admonitions. "Edmond, the way of glory was my way; now at the end look back upon the ruin you have made of that which might have been a noble thing."

Edmond replied: "I look back upon a ruin indeed, but I see a charm about it. For the austere pale marble is softened, its outlines merge into the background which is living, and about the broken columns trail the vines of the grape. There is an air about ruins that the structure never owns; Sarah, do wild doves nest in a temple that is new?"

"Words!" said Sarah. "You blanket your life with verbiage, and tuck it in soft and warm while about you the lightnings flash. You argue with your own reason and temporize with your body, and are in all ways unworthy of your heritage—a beater of bushes and a trapper of flies!"

"Doubtless you are right," said Edmond, and dismissed her presence from his minds.

Now he sat for some time weighing Sarah's remarks, and his rational self saw their justice, but he found no real meaning therein. Sarah spoke from a viewpoint he could not assume; understanding was possible between them, but sympathy never. Edmond smiled again as he reflected that between himself and Vanny, exactly opposite conditions obtained; there was sympathy without understanding.

Vanny and Sarah—his physical complement and his intellectual. "It is true, then, that bodily things are far more than intellectual; the important elements are not the highest. The mental is not the fundamental."

He reflected in this vein, lapsing again into a reverie, until Vanny returned from some errand. She dropped a package or two, and slid to the footstool between Edmond and the fire.

"Of what do you dream, Edmond?"

He told her, since the thought was harmless.

"I think you under-value those things, Edmond, because they are what you possess in abundance. To me, everything else is a foundation for the intellect you despise."

He smiled at her, gently as his thin lips and satyric features could manage. "I may not explain further."

Vanny flushed. "Oh, I know!—I'm not a thorough fool! But you see that's why I prize this quality of understanding." A trace of the old haunted light showed in her eyes, and her mien grew a little wistful. "See, Edmond, I traded my soul for the chance to understand you, only the price I had to offer was not great enough."

23. Evening on Olympus

Winter found Edmond's vitality, which he had poured out so freely at first, now at very low ebb. He lived out his days in a pallid half-dream, and it was only with effort that he could call his twin minds to clarity. That vigor which remained he hoarded carefully, spending it like a miser's pennies, seeking full value in pleasure for each coin expended. No longer the spendthrift nights of ecstasy, but an avid grasping at sensation that grew ever more dream-like and elusive. He was perforce content to watch the will-o'-the-wisp of knowledge dance and beckon without pursuit; he remained mostly in his chair before the fireplace of the monkey's skull, engrossed in dreams and memories like a very old man. He who had dwelt so thoroughly in the future found himself squeezed into the past, as that future foreshortened and the past lengthened.

He could no longer disguise his illness from Vanny, but her anxiety was tempered by a sublime faith in him. To her he was as he wished to be, and his wishes remained beyond her understanding. That he chose to weaken himself was merely a mystery, not a danger.

Sarah came at intervals, standing before him unspeaking, regarding him silently with cold eyes.

The time for words had long passed, and she watched Edmond's doom roll upon him now in silence. Sometimes she carried with her their child, and then the already half-intelligent imp backed up its mother's silent stare with an intense little silence of its own. Edmond was too weary to raise his head, but he noted a dawning bitterness in its eyes. A sense of pity and regret smote him, as he caught a fore-glimpse of this little being's life.

"Far better for you to kill it," he told Sarah once, while the imp stared fixedly at him. She made no answer, but continued her gaze for a minute or more and departed.

One day thereafter he called Vanny to him, strengthening himself by means of an alkaloid of his own synthesis. For some hours the drug offered him a modicum of vitality, though he knew that payment would be exacted.

"My permitted time draws to an end, Vanny."

Into her eyes swept a look of terror and a glistening of tears. She dropped to the stool before him, gazing up at him, but saying nothing.

"Remember that when I depart, dear, I go the way of my own devising, and do not grieve."

"No, Edmond!—No," she murmured. "Do not abandon me again! Had I more to offer, you know I would give what you demand, and more, but I have traded all I am for your presence; do not deny me it!"

"I would not," said Edmond, "but that I must. Nevertheless, this parting is but temporary; there will be another union and another—forever."

"Then the parting is hard but not unbearable."

Through Edmond's other self flashed a memory of a chance remark of Stein's dropped long ago when discussing Edmond's picture of a circular Time; "How do you know the curvature is constant? Nothing else in nature is absolute; why must Time return exactly on itself in a perfect circle?"

His slim fingers caressed Vanny while his twin minds seized the thought; here at last might come the way of escape, the little crevice in the hopeless circle that bound all things! Perhaps Time moved not in a circle through a fourth dimension but in a spiral through still another, and things did not repeat themselves forever without point or outcome, but varied a little through each repetition. Perhaps this spiral spun in still another spiral, and that in another, and so through greater and still greater spirals mounting in unthinkable dimensions toward infinity.

Progress and hope—two illusions that Edmond had denied throughout his life—were born for him. He perceived at last the ultimate implication of his own philosophy: that the price demanded to make anything—absolutely anything—possible is truly a very small price, involving merely the shifting of the observer's point of view from one angle to another, from this valley to that peak.

A surge of exaltation revived him; the untasted poignancy of hope was like a strong drug in his body, and in those moments he was close to happiness. He reflected that after all he had made of his life no ruin, but an edifice of beauty, since he alone of all the millions had uncovered Truth. His other self murmured the one true statement—once terrible, but now inspiring (thus again proving itself!): "All things are relative to the point of view; nothing is either true or false save in the mind of the observer." He turned back to Vanny.

"This shall be only a little parting, and not for very long as we judge time. A few score years for you, Vanny, and it may be only a few hours for me. And then all this shall be again, and perhaps on a happier plane. This I promise, Vanny, and you will believe me."

She smiled a quiet and tearful smile. "Yes, Edmond."

"Think, dear—has not all this been in the past, not very long since? Your memory runs back some twenty-five years; was it not just before that time that this was again? Do you recall?"

"Yes, Edmond; I recall."

"What matter then the unthinkable ages intervening, since we are oblivious of their passing? When again in eternity the circle or the spiral spins back to this arc, we shall be together again, and perhaps happier. This is my promise."

"Yes, Edmond." Smiled again, wistfully, "If only I were sure."

"I am sure."

"Then it is enough. I shall go with you. What is there for me to fear in Death who have met Him twice already?"

Edmond considered this thought carefully, since it had about it a specious logic. He turned it about in his twin minds, reformulated it in the inexpressible, and then somberly rejected it.

"No, Vanny. For you is reserved the difficult part; you must live out your appointed time to the very end of the arc."

"But why, Edmond? To what avail?"

"Because, dear, I do not fully comprehend the terrible and obscure laws that govern Fate and Chance in their relations to Time. Because there is a danger that the foreshortening of both our arcs—the obliviating of both our futures—may condemn us through what you call eternity to an endless repetition of our act. The future grows out of the past; let us not dry up the spring from which it flows. More than this I cannot tell you."

"As you wish, Edmond, but this will be a cruel thing."

Edmond took her hands in his incredible grasp. The strange fingers twisted about hers like tentacles, but she thrilled to them, to the inhuman delicacy vested in them. She gazed unflinching into the appalling eyes that bred madness, and their glance softened, for now at the very end Edmond had come to a curious realization. As his arc dropped toward oblivion, an understanding came to him. He saw finally that it was not Vanny's body alone he loved, but her self-effacement, her loyalty, her adoration, and the many little illusions called character. These were what Sarah, who stood mind to mind with him, had not, nor could ever have, since her heredity forbade it. Thus finally did Edmond confess to himself that he loved Vanny, and thus did he gaze into her simple human eyes, and tell her so. Her answer was only, "Living without you will be tasteless, Edmond, but not so bitter now."

"I must do what I may to sweeten it, Vanny, who have brought to it all the bitterness it holds."

So he took her chin in his serpentine grasp and up-tilted her head, fixing her gaze with his own of burning intensity. Her eyes widened, turned cold and glassy as she surrendered her mind to his keeping for the while; Edmond probed her mentality until it was as if each of his long fingers rested upon some center in her brain, as if he could play upon these as upon an organ's keys. He murmured softly the while:

"Listen to me, Desired One, now on the eve of our dissolution listen and yield you to these things that I command."

She answered tonelessly, "I do yield."

"Then I will that after my departing you shall think never on the manner of it, nor ever return to the place of it, but be content knowing that I go the way of my own devising."

"This I yield."

"I command that your adoration and the love in which you hold me be erased from your memory, so that you think of me no more, nor ever recall this time with regret."

Still tonelessly she murmured, "This I cannot yield."

"For what reason?"

"Because there is a natural law of my being that forbids it."

For a moment Edmond's minds dissociated, considering separately this statement. "Even Vanny's simplicity eludes me at the end." And his other self replied, "Doubtless there are facts entirely beyond the domain of reason, so that some sorts of knowledge by their very nature remain forever unattainable. Of this degree are mind and life."

He returned his thoughts to Vanny, fusing his twin minds again into a unity.

"Then I will have it thus: That if you cannot forget me, you remember me as a being out of very long ago, so that my reality is dim. That you think of me not as your appointed mate, but as a symbol, an aspiration, and a dream, as a mysterious and not-to-be-satisfied longing, but not ever as a Being made of flesh and mind, who loved you and was loved."

"This too I yield," she said.

"Then I send you now to Paul, whom you will love as well as may be. You will love him for his love of you, since you are now the stronger. Out of his simplicity and his ignorance you will love him; he will be the child you lead and the man you inspire. I give not you to Paul, but Paul to you; out of his fleshly vigor you shall love him."

"I yield this too, Edmond," she said.

A moment more he held her passive gaze, while the false vitality of the drug ebbed out of him. He drooped wearily, then raised his hand from her chin, brushing the finger-tips across her wide, unwinking eyes. "Enough," he said, and her eyes suddenly softened and smiled sadly into his own. He tipped two pellets from the vial he carried, swallowed them.

"Edmond," said Vanny, watching him, "does that hold the way?"

"No, dear. This is the means of our farewell, to which we go at once."

Chapter 24
Night on Olympus

After the farewell, which occurred in a human and quite traditional fashion, Edmond sent Vanny to Paul. "Go now," he commanded, and she departed, a little unsteadily but with glowing eyes and an after-sense of ecstasy. She wondered dimly why she left Edmond with so little reluctance; he seemed to her already dead like a memory once poignant out of a distant and half-forgotten past. Yet for a moment her heart wrenched with pain and she kissed him, but his eyes caught hers, and the fire that was burning her died out. Of the happenings during her trance nothing remained in her conscious memory save a sort of vacuity, a feeling of lack or loss. She was unhappy, but not acutely so; if there were pangs, they were quite buried for the present under a sort of lethargy. She moved automatically to follow the course that had been graven very deeply on her mind; below at the curb she entered the gray car that waited there. Nor was she surprised to find Eblis curled on the seat; the great cat mewed and stretched in welcome as she sank wearily to her place at the wheel, and its ebon presence seemed evidence to her mind that she was indeed slipping back into the old life.

Edmond watched her departure with a regret less keen than it might have been had not his lassitude been sweeping back. His drug had been lessening steadily in its potency; the effect of his last dose was vanishing already, and he could feel nothing very passionately. There still remained, however, certain things to be done; he fingered the little vial of alkaloid, and poured the contents into his hand. Half a dozen white pellets rolled in his palm, and suddenly he raised his hand and swallowed them all. A few moments, and the stimulant functioned; he dragged himself erect and moved over to the desk.

He wrote. "I, Edmond Hall, being of sound mind, do hereby devise and bequeath—" He smiled his old ironic smile.

"To my dear friend Alfred Stein the entire contents of my laboratory, together with all designs, books, notes and equipment thereof—"

"The entire remainder and residue of my estate to be divided equally between my beloved wife Evanne and—" he grinned again—"my sister, Sarah Maddox."

"I appoint as joint executors of my estate Alfred Stein of Northwestern University"—he paused for a moment, still with his Satanic smile—"and Paul Varney—"

He left the satiric document on the open desk, and proceeded to his laboratory. Here he removed the accumulators from the atomblaster, dropping them into a jar of nitric acid. The heavy brown fumes set him coughing, and he picked up another tiny vial and departed.

"Alfred would doubtless succeed in destroying himself with this terrific mechanism," he reflected. "I have left him enough to study over, and enough hints of greater things to occupy his life-time."

Back in his chair before the fire, he looked at the vial he held, shaking the tiny purple ovoids it contained.

"Eggs of nothingness," he reflected, "out of which I am to hatch oblivion." He spilled several into his palm, where they rolled with an obscene fungoid shining.

"A billion billion centuries, perhaps," he reflected, "before Chance or the more obscure laws that govern it, shall re-assemble the particular molecules that I call Myself, yet this will seem no longer than from this night until tomorrow. Certainly obliteration is a wonderful thing, and the one conqueror of Time." His other self responded, "Since in eternity all things that can happen must happen, I depart with assurance; all this will be again, and perhaps in happier fashion. I render my payment therefore without regret."

He raised his hand to his lips, and at the moment he became aware of a presence before him. Sarah stood there, or her image made real to his senses. She was watching him with a little glint of regret in her eyes, and a touch of hopelessness about her mouth. He paused, returning her gaze coldly.

"Paul comes," she said. "He comes to kill you."

Edmond's lips twisted again into their thin smile.

"I had thought my accounts were balanced," he said. "However, perhaps I still owe Paul that satisfaction."

"You are a fool, Edmond. You have traded all glory and the very delights of the gods—for what?"

"For a philosophy and a dream, and a bright little gem of truth, Sarah. Not one of you has more."

"You are a fool, Edmond, and I wonder that your passing grieves me in the least, for all reason denies that it should."

"The more fool reason, then," said Edmond. But his cold eyes softened a moment. "I am sorry, Sarah. Believe me when I say I do not forget you."

Sarah's own eyes turned cold, her hopeless mouth became grim. "I leave you to your fool's devices," said she, and vanished.

Edmond thought silently of her warning of Paul. After a moment he rose, a little more weakly now, and proceeded again to his laboratory. He lifted a revolver from the table drawer, and fitted thereto a silencer. Was it the same calibre as Paul's? What matter, since there would be no inquest? Then he deliberately fired the weapon into a towel bundled in the corner; thereafter he removed the silencer and dropped the gun into his pocket. The towel and the bullet it contained he tossed into the jar of nitric acid, where it too disintegrated under the evil brown fumes. Edmond returned to his chair before the fire; he watched the low dying flames and occupied his minds with strange thoughts. He waited.

Then came the sound of a key in the lock—Paul's key, given long ago, he knew, by Vanny. He smiled at the grim irony of the thing, for it amused him to perceive with what bitter humor his god Chance worked his will—that Vanny who loved him should give to Paul who hated him the means of his destruction. And now there moved a shadow in the hall.

Through the library door came Paul, a bleak and desolate figure with staring eyes. He moved into the dim fire-glow; there was a blue glint along the barrel of a revolver he held. He stood before Edmond, and the superman himself, accustomed as he had become to living in a white glare of hatred, was startled by the hate in Paul's eyes.

"I am going to kill you," said Paul in a strained and husky voice as he raised his weapon. Edmond stared at him with cold inhuman eyes, through which for a moment looked both minds. The superman was probably the belligerent opposing mind, building up a mastery, like a man staring down a wild beast. "Lion tamer," jeered a part of his brain.

"I am going to kill you," croaked Paul, and his eyes shifted. He could not look at the emaciated white demon before him, whose eyes now flamed with a fierce intentness. Paul's face was pale and moist with the dread that once again he was about to be defeated. "Where's Vanny?" he muttered. Edmond's thin smile twisted his lips; his opponent's wavering had given him victory, and he held Paul's will.

"She waits for you at your apartment," he replied.

"That's a lie, you sneering devil!"

"I have never lied, finding no need," said Edmond quietly. His lethargy was returning as the drug's power waned, and he felt weakness growing within him. He probed the tortured eyes into which he gazed. "This hysterical fool will drop his gun and run from the scene of his crime," he reflected, "in the best tradition of the stage and the mystery novel. Two weapons here would be highly undesirable." He thrust his glance more fiercely into Paul's eyes.

"Listen to me, Paul. When you leave here, drop your gun into your pocket. Drop your gun into your pocket, and return at once to Vanny. Say nothing to her; I seal your lips upon this night forever."

Edmond read assent in the mad eyes he faced. Paul's gyrating brain might never recall the words, but somewhere in his subconsciousness the command was registered, imperative and compelling.

Edmond drew that which he had prepared from his pocket, clasping his incredible fingers tightly about it. He held his helpless opponent a moment longer in his fiery gaze.

"For what evil I have done you, I render now full recompense," he said, and dropped his eyes.

Silence.

Edmond raised his eyes, and saw Paul's pallid face with sickness and indecision written there, and he saw the weapon wavering and irresolute. He noted too that a familiar misty glory danced behind Paul, and that Homo's expression seemed almost one of welcome. "So at my nadir as at the zenith I still follow my fancy," he mused and smiled his old ironic smile. A command flamed in his eyes; and Paul's hand steadied, as a rush of rage overpowered him. Still smiling, Edmond dropped his eyes again, and the gun crashed.

It was not until he saw the morning papers that Paul realized that Edmond had held in his hand a revolver with one empty cartridge.

Stories

The Brink of Infinity

One would hardly choose the life of an assistant professor of mathematics at an Eastern University as an adventurous one. Professors in general are reputed to drone out in a quiet, scholarly existence, and an instructor of mathematics might seem the driest and least lively of men, since his subject is perhaps the most desiccated. And yet—even the lifeless science of figures has had its dreamers—Clerk, Maxwell, Lobachewski, Einstein and the rest. The latter, the great Albert Einstein himself who is forging the only chain that ever tied a philosophers' dream to experimental science, is pounding his links of tenuous mathematical symbols, shadowy as thought, but unbreakable.

And don't forget that "Alice in Wonderland" was written by a dreamer who happened also to be a mathematician. Not that I class myself with them; I'm practical enough to leave fantasies alone. Teaching is my business.

At least, teaching is my main business. I do a little statistical work for industrial corporations when the occasion presents itself—in fact, you'll find my name in the classified section: Abner Aarons, Statistician and Consulting Mathematician. I eke out my professional salary, and I do at times strike something interesting. Of course, in the main such work consists of graphing trends of consumption for manufacturers, or population increases for public utilities.

And occasionally some up-and-coming advertising agency will consult me on how many sardine cans would be needed to fill the Panama Canal, or some such material to use as catchy advertising copy. Not exactly exciting work, but it helps financially.

Thus I was not particularly surprised that July morning to receive a call. The university had been closed for some weeks; the summer session was about to open, without however, the benefit of my presence. I was taking a vacation, leaving in two or three days for a Vermont village I knew, where the brook trout cared not a bit whether a prizefighter, president, or professor was on the hither end

185

of the line. And I was going alone; three-quarters of the year before a classroom full of the tadpoles called college students had thoroughly wearied me of any further desire for human companionship; my social instincts were temporarily in abeyance.

Nevertheless, I'm not unthrifty enough to disregard an opportunity to turn an honest penny, and the call was far from unwelcome. Even the modest holiday I planned can bite deeply enough into the financial foundation of an assistant professor's pittance. And the work sounded like one of these fairly lucrative and rather simple propositions.

"This is Court Strawn," the telephone announced. "I'm an experimental chemist, and I've completed a rather long series of experiments. I want them tabulated and the results analyzed; do you do that sort of work?"

I did, and acknowledged as much.

"It will be necessary for you to call here for your data," the voice continued. Strangely unctuous, that voice. "It is impossible for me to leave." There followed an address on West Seventieth Street.

Well, I had called for data before. Generally the stuff was delivered or mailed to me, but his request wasn't extraordinary, I agreed, and added that I'd be over shortly. No use delaying my vacation if I could help it.

I took the subway. Taxis are a needless luxury to a professor, and a car of my own was an unrealized ambition. It wasn't long before I entered one of the nondescript brown houses that still survive west of the Avenue. Strawn let me in, and I perceived the reason for his request. The man was horribly crippled; his whole left side was warped like a gnarled oak, and he was hard put to hobble about the house. For the rest—stringy dark hair, and little tense eyes.

He greeted me pleasantly enough, and I entered a small library, while my host bobbled over to a littered desk, seating himself facing me. The deep-set eyes looked me over, and he chuckled.

"Are you a good mathematician, Dr. Aarons?" he asked. There was more than a hint of a sneer in his voice.

"My work has been satisfactory," I answered, somewhat nettled. "I've been doing statistical work for several years."

He waved a shrivelled left band.

"Of course—of course! I don't doubt your practical ability. Are you, however, well versed in the more abstract branches—the theory of numbers, for instance, or the hyper-spatial mathematics?"

I was feeling rather irritated. There was something about the man—"I don't see that any of this is necessary in statistical analysis of experimental results," I said. "If you'll give me your data, I'll be going."

He chuckled again, seemingly hugely amused.

"As a matter of fact, Dr. Aarons," he said smirking, "the experiment isn't completed yet. Indeed, to tell the truth, it is just beginning."

"What!" I was really angry. "If this is your idea of a joke—" I started to rise, thoroughly aroused.

"Just a moment," said Strawn coolly. He levelled a very effective-looking blue-barrelled automatic at me. I sat down again open-mouthed; I confess to a feeling of panic at the sight of the cripple's beady little eyes peering along the ugly weapon.

"Common politeness dictates that you at least hear me out, Dr. Aarons." I didn't like the oily smoothness of his voice, but what was I to do?

"As I was saying, the experiment is just beginning. As a matter of fact, you are the experiment!"

"Eh?" I said, wondering again if the whole thing might not be a joke of some sort.

"You're a mathematician, aren't you?" Strawn continued. "Well, that makes you fair game for me. A mathematician, my good friend, is no more to me than something to be hunted down. And I'm doing it!"

The man was crazy! The realization dawned on me as I strove to hold myself calm. Best to reason with him, I thought.

"But why?" I asked. "We are a harmless lot."

His eyes blazed up with a fierce light.

"Harmless, eh, harmless! Well, it was one of your colleagues that did—this!" He indicated his withered leg with his withered arm. "He did this with his lying calculations!" He leaned forward confidentially. "Listen to me, Dr. Aarons. I am a chemist, or was once. I used to work with explosives, and was pretty good, too. And then one of you damned calculators figured out a formula for me! A misplaced decimal point—bah! You're all fair game to me!"

He paused, and the sneer came back to his lips. "That's simple justice, now, isn't it?"

Well, you can imagine how thoroughly horrified I was, sitting there facing a homicidal maniac with a loaded gun in his hand. Humour him! I'd heard that was the best treatment. Use persuasion, reason!

"Now, Mr. Strawn," I said, "you're certainly entitled to justice. Yes, you certainly are! But surely, Mr. Strawn, you are not serving the ends of justice by venting your anger on me! Surely that isn't justice."

He laughed wildly and continued. "A very specious argument, Dr. Aarons. You are simply unfortunate in that your name is the first in the classified section of the directory. Had your colleague given me a chance—any slightest chance to save my body from this that you see, I might be forgiving. But I trusted that fool's calculations!" He twisted his face again into that bitter leer. "As it is, I am giving you far more of a chance than I had. If, as you claim, you are a good mathematician, you shall have your opportunity to escape. I have no quarrel with the real students of figures, but only"—his leer became a very sinister scowl—"only with the dullards, the fakes and the blunderers. Yes, you'll have your chance!" The grin returned to his lips, but his eyes behind the blue automatic never wavered.

I saw no other alternative but to continue the ghastly farce. Certainly open opposition to any of his suggestions might only inflame the maniac to violence, so I merely questioned. "And what is the proposition, Mr. Strawn?"

The scowl became a sneer again.

"A very fair one, sir. A very fair proposition, indeed." He chuckled.

"I should like to hear it," I said, hoping for an interruption of some sort.

"You shall. It is just this: You are a mathematician, and you say, a good one. Very well. We shall put your claim to the test. I am thinking of a mathematical quantity, a numerical expression, if you prefer. You have ten questions to discover it. If you do so you are free as far as I am concerned. But if you fail"—his scowl reappeared—"well, if you fail I shall recognize you as one of the tribe of blunderers against whom I war, and the outcome will not be pleasant!"

Well! It was several moments before I found my voice, and began to babble protests. "But, Mr. Strawn! That's an utter impossibility! The range of numbers is infinite; how can I identify one with ten questions? Give me a fair test, man! This one offers not a chance in a million! In a billion!"

He silenced me with a wave of the blue barrel of his weapon.

"Remember, Dr. Aarons, I did not say it was a number. I said a numerical expression, which is a vastly wider field. I am giving you this hint without deducting a question; you must appreciate my magnanimity!" He laughed. "The rules of our little game are as follows: You may ask me any questions except the direct question, 'What is the expression?' I am bound to answer you in full and to the best of my knowledge any question except the direct inquiry. You may ask me as many questions at a time as you wish up to your limit of ten, but in any event I will answer not less than two per day. That should give you sufficient time for reflection"—again that horrible chuckle—"and my time too is limited."

"But, Mr. Strawn," I argued, "that may keep me here five days. Don't you know that by tomorrow my wife will have the police searching for me?"

A glint of anger flashed in the mad eyes. "You are not being fair, Dr. Aarons! I know you are not married! I checked up on you before you came here. I know you will not be missed. Do not attempt to lie to me; rather help me serve the ends of justice! You should be more than willing to prove your worth to survive as one of the true mathematicians." He rose suddenly. "And now, sir, you will please precede me through the door and up those stairs!"

Nothing to do but obey! The stubby gun in his hand was enough authority, at least to an unadventurous soul like myself. I rose and stalked out of the room at his direction, up the stairs and through a door he indicated. Beyond was a windowless little cell ventilated by a skylight, and the first glance revealed that this was barred. A piece of furniture of the type known as a day-bed, a straight chair, a deep overstuffed chair, and a desk made up the furnishings.

"Here," said the self-appointed host, "is your student's cell. On the desk is a carafe of water, and, as you see, an unabridged dictionary. That is the only reference allowed in our little game." He glanced at his watch. "It is ten minutes to four. By four tomorrow you must have asked me two questions, and have them well thought out! The ten minutes over are a gift from me, lest you doubt my generosity!" He moved toward the door. "I will see that your meals are on time," he added. "My best wishes, Dr. Aarons."

The door clicked shut and I at once commenced a survey of the room. The skylight was hopeless, and the door even more so; I was securely and ingloriously imprisoned. I spent perhaps half an hour in painstaking and fruitless inspection, but the room had been well designed or adapted to its purpose; the massive door was barred on the outside, the skylight was guarded by a heavy iron grating, and the walls offered no slightest hope. Abner Aarons was most certainly a prisoner!

My mind turned to Strawn's insane game. Perhaps I could solve his mad mystery; at least, I could keep him from violence for five days, and something might occur in the interim, I found cigars on the desk, and, forcing myself to a degree of calm, I lit one and sat down to think.

Certainly there was no use in getting at his lunatic concept from a quantitative angle, I could waste all ten questions too easily by asking, "Is it greater or less than a million? Is it greater or less than a thousand? Is it greater of less than a hundred?" Impossible to pin the thing by that sort of elimination when it might be a negative number, a fraction or a decimal, or even an imaginary number like the square root of minus one—or, for that matter, any possible combination of these. And that reflection gave me my impulse for the first question; by the time my cigar had been consumed to a tattered stub I had formulated my initial inquiry. Nor had I very long to wait; it was just past six when the door opened.

"Stand away from the door, Dr. Aarons," came the voice of my host. I complied perforce; the madman entered, pushing before him a tea caddy bearing a really respectable meal, complete from bouillon to a bottle of wine. He propelled the cart with his withered left band; the right brandished the evil automatic.

"I trust you have used your time well," he sneered.

"At least I have my first question," I responded.

"Good, Dr. Aarons! Very good! Let us hear it."

"Well," I continued, "among numbers, expressions of quantity, mathematicians recognize two broad distinctions—two fields in which every possible numerical expression may be classified. These two classifications are known as real numbers on the one band, including every number both positive and negative, all fractions, decimals, and multiples of these numbers, and on the other hand the class of imaginary numbers, which include all products of operations on the quantity called 'c,' otherwise expressed as the square root of minus one."

"Of course, Dr. Aarons. That is elementary!"

"Now then—is this quantity of yours real or imaginary?"

He beamed with a sinister satisfaction.

"A very fair question, sir! Very fair! And the answer—may it assist you—is that it is either!"

A light seemed to burst in my brain! Any student of numbers knows that only one figure is both real and imaginary, the one that marks the point of intersection between the real and imaginary number graphs. "I've got it!" The phrase kept running through my mind like a crazy drumbeat! With an effort I kept an appearance of calm.

"Mr. Strawn," I said, "is the quantity you have in mind zero?"

He laughed—a nasty, superior laugh that rasped in my cars.

"It is not, Dr. Aarons! I know as well as you that zero is both a real and imaginary number! Let me call your attention to my answer: I did not say that my concept was both real and imaginary; I said it was either!" He was backing toward the door. "Let me further remind you that you have eight guesses remaining, since I am forced to consider this premature shot in the dark as one chance! Good evening!"

He was gone; I heard the bar outside the door settle into its socket with a thump. I stood in the throes of despair, and cast scarcely a glance at the rather sumptuous repast he had served me, but slumped back into my chair.

It seemed hours before my thoughts were coherent again; actually I never knew the interval, since I did not glance at my watch. However, sooner or later I recovered enough to pour a tumbler of wine and eat a bit of the roast beef; the bouillon was hopelessly cold. And then I settled down to the consideration of my third question.

From Strawn's several hints in the wording of his terms and the answers to my first and second queries, I tabulated what information

I could glean. He had specifically designated a numerical expression; that eliminated the x's and y's of algebraic usage. The quantity was either real or imaginary and was not zero; well, the square of any imaginary is a real number. If the quantity contained more than one figure, or if an exponent was used, then I felt sure his expression was merely the square of an imaginary; one could consider such a quantity either real or imaginary. A means of determining this by a single question occurred to me. I scribbled a few symbols on a sheet of paper, and then, feeling a sudden and thorough exhaustion, I threw myself on the daybed and slept. I dreamed Strawn was pushing me into a nightmarish sea of grinning mathematical monsters.

The creaking of the door aroused me. Sunbeams illuminated the skylight; I had slept out the night. Strawn entered balancing a tray on his left arm, holding the ever-present weapon in his free band. He placed a half dozen covered dishes on the tea-cart, removing the remains of the evening meal to his tray.

"A poor appetite, Dr. Aarons," he commented. "You should not permit your anxiety to serve the ends of justice to upset you!" He chuckled with enjoyment of his sarcasm. "No questions yet? No matter; you have until four tomorrow for your next two."

"I have a question," I said, more thoroughly awakened. I rose and spread the sheet of paper on the desk.

"A numerical quantity, Mr. Strawn, can be expressed as an operation on numbers. Thus, instead of writing the numeral '4' one may prefer to express it as a product, such as '2 x 2,' or as a sum, as '3 + 1,' or as a quotient, as '8 ÷ 2' or as a remainder, as '5 - 1.' Or even in other ways—as a square, such as 2^2 or as a root $\sqrt{16}$ or $\sqrt[3]{64}$. All different methods of expressing the single quantity '4.' Now here I have written out the various mathematical symbols of operations; my question is this: Which if any of these symbols is used in the expression you have in mind?"

"Very neatly put, Dr. Aarons! You have succeeded in combining several questions in one." He took the paper from me, spreading it on the desk before him. "This symbol, sir, is the one used." He indicated the first one in my list—the subtraction sign, a simple dash!

And my hopes, to use the triviality of a pun, were dashed as well! For that sign eliminated my carefully thought-out theory of a product or square of imaginaries to form a real number. You can't change imaginary to real by addition or subtraction; it takes multiplication, squaring or division to perform that mathematical magic! Once more I was thoroughly at sea, and for a long time I was unable to marshal my thoughts.

And so the hours dragged into days with the tantalizing slow swiftness that tortures the condemned in a prison death house. I seemed checkmated at every turn; curious paradoxical answers defeated my questions.

My fourth query, "Are there any imaginaries in your quantity?" elicited a cool, definite "No." My fifth, "How many digits are used in this expression?" brought forth an equally definite "Two."

Now there you are! What two digits connected by a minus sign can you name whose remainder is either real and imaginary? "An impossibility," I thought. "This maniac's merely torturing me!" And yet—somehow Strawn's madness seemed too ingenious, too clever, for such an answer. He was sincere in his perverted search for justice. I'd have sworn to that.

On my sixth question, I had an inspiration! By the terms of our game, Strawn was to answer any question save the direct one, "What is this expression?" I saw a way out! On his next appearance I met him with feverish excitement, barely waiting for his entrance to begin my query.

"Mr. Strawn! Here is a question you are bound by your own rules to answer. Suppose we place an equal sign after your quantity, what number or numbers will complete the equation: What is the quantity equal to?"

Why was the fiend laughing? Could he squirm out of that poser?

"Very clever, Dr. Aarons. A very clever question. And the answer is—anything!"

I suppose I shouted. "Anything! Anything! Then you're a fraud, and your game's a damnable trickery. There's no such expression!"

"But there is, Doctor! A good mathematician could find it!" And he departed, still laughing.

I spent a sleepless night. Hour after hour I sat at that hateful desk, checking my scraps of information, thinking, trying to remember fragments of all-but-forgotten theories. And I found solutions! Not one, but several. Lord, how I sweated over them! With four questions—two days—left to me, the solution of the problem began to loom very close. The things dinned in my brain; my judgment counselled me to proceed slowly, to check my progress with another question, but my nature was rebelling against the incessant strain. "Stake it all on your last four questions! Ask them all at once, and end this agony one way or the other!"

I thought I saw the answer. Oh, the fiendish, insane cleverness of the man! He had pointed to the minus sign on my list, deliberately misled me, for all the time the symbol had meant the bar of a fraction. Do you see? The two symbols are identical—just a simple dash—but one use means subtraction and the other division! "1 - 1" means zero, but "1 ÷ 1" means one! And by division his problem could be solved. For there is a quantity that means literally anything, real number or imaginary, and that quantity is "0 ÷ 0"! Yes, zero divided by zero. You'd think offhand that the answer'd be zero, or perhaps one, but it isn't, not necessarily. Look at it like this: take the equation "2 x 3 = 6." See? That's another way of saying that two goes into six three times. Now take "0 x 6 = 0." Perfectly correct, isn't it? Well, in that equation *zero goes into zero six times!* Or "0 ÷ 0 = 6"! And so on for any number, real or imaginary—zero divided by zero equals anything!

And that's what I figured the fiend had done. Pointed to the minus sign when he meant the bar of a fraction, or division!

He came in grinning at dawn.

"Are your questions ready, Dr. Aarons? I believe you have four remaining."

I looked at him. "Mr. Strawn, is your concept zero divided by zero?"

He grinned. "No, sir, it is not!"

I wasn't disheartened. There was just one other symbol I had been thinking of that would meet the requirement—one other possibility. My eighth question followed. "Then is it infinity divided by infinity?"

The grin widened. "It is not, Dr. Aarons."

I was a little panicky then! The end loomed awfully near! There was one way to find out if the thing was fraudulent or not; I used my ninth question:

"Mr. Strawn, when you designated the dash as the mathematical symbol used in your expression, did you mean it as the bar of a fraction or as the sign of subtraction?"

"As the subtraction sign, Dr. Aarons. You have one more question. Will you wait until tomorrow to ask it?"

The fiend was grinning in huge enjoyment. Thoroughly confident, he was, in the intricacies of his insane game. I hesitated in a torture of frenzied indecision. The appalling prospect of another agonized night of doubts decided me.

"I'll ask it now, Mr. Strawn!"

It had to be right! There weren't any other possibilities; I'd exhausted all of them in hour after hour of miserable conjecture!

"Is the expression—the one you're thinking of—infinity minus infinity?"

It was! I knew it by the madman's glare of amazed disappointment.

"The devil must have told you!" he shrieked. I think there were flecks of froth on his lips. He lowered the gun in his hand as I edged toward the door; he made no move to stop me, but stood in a sort of desolate silence, until I gained the top of the stairway. Then—

"Wait a minute!" he screamed. "You'll tell them! Wait just a minute, Dr. Aarons!"

I was down the stairs in two leaps, and tugging at the door. Strawn came after me, his gun levelled. I heard it crash as the door opened and I slipped out into a welcome daylight.

Yes, I reported him. The police got him as he was slipping away and dragged him before an alienist. Crazy, but his story was true; he *had* been mangled in an experimental laboratory explosion.

* * *

Oh, the problem? Don't you see? Infinity is the greatest expression of number possible—a number greater than any conceivable. Figure it out like this:

The mathematician's symbol for infinity is a tipsy eight—so: ∞.

Well, take the question, $\infty + 6 = \infty$. That's true, because you can't add anything to infinity that will make it any greater than it is. See? It's the greatest possible number already. Well then, just by transposition, $\infty - \infty = 6$. And so on; the same system applies to any conceivable number, real or imaginary.

There you are! Infinity minus itself may equal any quantity, absolutely any number, real or imaginary, from zero to infinity. No, there was nothing wrong with Court Strawn's mathematics.

The Circle of Zero

If there were a mountain a thousand miles high, and every thousand years a bird flew over it, just brushing the peak with the tip of its wing, in the course of inconceivable eons the mountain would be worn away. Yet all those ages would not be one second to the length of eternity...

I don't know what philosophical mind penned the foregoing, but the words keep recurring to me since last I saw old Aurore de Néant, erstwhile professor of psychology at Tulane. When, back in '24, I took that course in Morbid Psychology from him, I think the only reason for taking it at all was that I needed an eleven o'clock on Tuesdays and Thursdays to round out a lazy program.

I was gay Jack Anders, twenty-two years old, and the reason seemed sufficient. At least, I'm sure that dark and lovely Yvonne de Néant had nothing to do with it; she was but a child of sixteen.

Old de Néant liked me, Lord knows why, for I was a poor enough student. Perhaps it was because I never, to his knowledge, punned on his name. Aurore de Néant translates to Dawn of Nothingness, you see; you can imagine what students did to such a name. 'Rising Zero'—'Empty Morning'—those were two of the milder sobriquets.

That was in '24. Five years later I was a bond salesman in New York, and Professor Aurore de Néant was fired. I learned about it when he called me up; I had drifted quite out of touch with university days.

He was a thrifty sort. He had saved a comfortable sum, and had moved to New York, and that's when I started seeing Yvonne again, now darkly beautiful as a Tanagra figurine. I was doing pretty well, and was piling up a surplus against the day when Yvonne and I...

At least, that was the situation in August, 1929. In October of the same year, I was as clean as a gnawed bone and old de Néant had but little more meat. I was young, and could afford to laugh;

196

be was old, and he turned bitter. And indeed, Yvonne and I did little enough laughing when we thought of our own future; but we didn't brood like the professor.

I remember the evening he broached the subject of the Circle of Zero. It was a rainy, blustering fall night, and his beard waggled in the dim lamplight like a wisp of gray mist. Yvonne and I had been staying in evenings of late; shows cost money, and I felt that she appreciated my talking to her father, and—after all—he retired early.

She was sitting on the davenport at his side when he suddenly stabbed a gnarled finger at me and snapped, 'Happiness depends on money!'

I was startled. 'Well, it helps,' I agreed.

His pale blue eyes glittered. 'We must recover ours!' he rasped.

'How?'

'I know how. Yes, I know how!' He grinned thinly. 'They think I'm mad. You think I'm mad; even Yvonne thinks so.'

The girl said softly, reproachfully, 'Father!'

'But I'm not,' he continued. 'You and Yvonne, and all the fools holding chairs at universities—yes! But not me.

'I will be, all right, if conditions don't get better soon,' I murmured. I was used to the old man's outbursts.

'They will be better for us,' he said, calming. 'Money! We will do anything for money, won't we, Anders?'

'Anything honest.'

'Yes, anything honest. Time is honest, isn't it? An honest cheat, because it takes everything human and turns it into dust.' He peered at my puzzled face. 'I will explain,' he said, 'how we can cheat time.'

'Cheat?'

'Yes. Listen, Jack. Have you ever stood in a strange place and felt a sense of having been there before? Have you ever taken a trip and sensed that sometime, somehow, you had done exactly the same thing—when you know you hadn't?'

'Of course. Everyone has. A memory of the present, Bergson calls-'

'Bergson is a fool! Philosophy without science. Listen to me.' He leaned forward. 'Did you ever hear of the Law of Chance?'

I laughed. 'My business is stocks and bonds. I ought to know of it.'

'Ah,' he said, 'but not enough of it. Suppose I have a barrel with a million trillion white grains of sand in it, and one black grain. You stand and draw a single grain, one after the other, look at it, and throw it back into the barrel. What are the odds against drawing the black grain?'

'A million trillion to one, on each draw.'

'And if you draw half of the million trillion grains?'

'Then the odds are even.'

'So!' he said. 'In other words, if you draw long enough, even though you return each grain to the barrel and draw again, some day you will draw the black one—if you try long enough!'

'Yes,' I said.

'Suppose now you tried for eternity?'

'Eh?'

'Don't you see Jack? In eternity the Law of Chance functions perfectly. In eternity, sooner or later, every possible combination of things and events must happen. Must happen, if it's a possible combination. I say, therefore, that in eternity, *whatever can happen will happen!*' His blue eyes blazed in pale fire.

I was a trifle dazed. 'I guess you're right,' I muttered.

'Right! Of course I'm right. Mathematics is infallible, Now do you see the conclusion?'

'Why—that sooner or later everything will happen.'

'Bah! It is true that there is eternity in the future; we cannot imagine ending. But Flammarion, before he died, pointed out that there is also an eternity in the past. Since in eternity everything possible must happen, it follows that everything must already have happened!'

I gasped. 'Wait a minute! I don't see-'

'Stupidity!' he hissed. 'It is but to say with Einstein that not only space is curved, but time, to say that after untold eons of millenniums, the same things repeat themselves because they must! The Law of Chance says they must, given time enough. The past and the future are the same thing, because everything that will happen must already have happened. Can't you follow so simple a chain of logic?'

'Why—yes. But where does it lead?'

'To our money! To our money!'

'What?'

'Listen. Do not interrupt. In the past, all possible combinations of atoms and circumstances must have occurred.' He paused, then stabbed that bony finger of his at me. 'Jack Anders, you are a possible combination of atoms and circumstances! Possible because you exist at this moment!'

'You mean—that I have happened before?'

He sneered. 'How apt you are! Yes, you have happened before, and will again.'

'Transmigration!' I gulped. 'That's unscientific!'

'Indeed?' He frowned as if in effort to gather his thoughts. 'The poet Robert Burns was buried under an apple tree. When, years after his death, he was to be removed to rest among the great men of Westminster Abbey, do you know what they found? Do you know?'—shouting.

'I'm sorry, but I don't.'

'They found a root! A root with a bulge for a head, branch roots for arms and legs, and little rootlets for fingers and toes. The apple tree had eaten Bobby Burns—but who had eaten the apples?'

'Who—what?'

'Exactly. Who and what? The substance that had been Burns was in the bodies of Scotch countrymen and children, in the bodies of caterpillars who had eaten the leaves and become butterflies and been eaten by birds, in the wood of the tree. Where is Bobby Burns? Transmigration, I tell you! Isn't that transmigration?'

'Yes—but not what you meant about me. His body may be living, but in a thousand different forms.'

'Ah! And when some day, eons and eternities in the future, the Laws of Chance form another nebula that will cool to another sun and another earth, is there not the same chance that those scattered atoms may reassemble another Bobby Burns?'

'But what a chance! Trillions and trillions to one!'

'But eternity, Jack! In eternity that one chance out of all those trillions must happen—must happen!'

I was floored. I stared at Yvonne's pale and lovely features, then at the glistening old eyes of Aurore de Néant.

'You win,' I said with a long sigh. 'But what of it? This is still nineteen twenty-nine, and our money's still sunk in a very sick securities market.'

'Money!' he groaned. 'Don't you see? That memory we started from—that sense of having done a thing before—that's a memory out of the infinitely dead past—or, which is the same, the infinitely remote future. If only—if only one could remember clearly! But I have a way.' His voice rose suddenly to a shrill scream. 'Yes, I have a way.'

Wild eyes glared at me. I said, 'A way to remember our former incarnations?' One had to humor the old professor. 'To remember—the future?'

'Yes—like incarnation!' His voice crackled wildly. 'Re-incarnatione which is Latin for 'by the thing in the carnation', but it wasn't a carnation—it was an apple tree. The carnation is *dianthus carophyllus*, which proves that the Hottentots plant carnations on the graves of their ancestors, whence the expression 'nipped in the bud.' If carnations grow on apple trees-'

'Father!' cut in Yvonne sharply. 'You're tired!' Her voice softened. 'Come. You're going to bed.'

'Yes,' he cackled. 'To a bed of carnations.'

Some evenings later, Aurore de Néant reverted to the same topic. He was clear enough as to where he had left off.

'So in this millennially dead past,' he began suddenly, 'there was a year nineteen twenty-nine, and two fools named Anders and de Néant, who invested their money in what are sarcastically called securities. There was a clown's panic, and their money vanished.' He leered fantastically at me. 'Wouldn't it be nice if they could remember what happened in, say, the months from December, nineteen twenty-nine, to June, nineteen thirty—next year?' His voice was suddenly whining. 'They could get their money back then!'

I humored him. 'If they could remember.'

'They can!' he blazed. 'They can!'

'How?'

His voice dropped to a confidential softness. 'Hypnotism! You studied Morbid Psychology under me, didn't you, Jack? Yes—I remember.'

'But, hypnotism' I objected. 'Every psychiatrist uses that in his treatments, and no one has remembered a previous incarnation, or anything like it.'

'No. They're fools, these doctors and psychiatrists. Listen—do you remember the three stages of the hypnotic state, as you learned them?'

'Yes. Somnambulism, lethargy, catalepsy.'

'Right. In the first, the subject speaks, answers questions. In the second, he sleeps deeply. In the third, catalepsy, he is rigid, stiff, so that he can be laid across two chairs, sat on—all that nonsense.'

'I remember. What of it?'

He grinned bleakly. 'In the first stage the subject remembers everything that ever happened during his life. His subconscious mind is dominant, and that never forgets. Correct?'

'So we were taught.'

He leaned tensely forward. 'In the second stage, lethargy, my theory is that he remembers everything that happened in his other lives! He remembers the future!'

'Huh? Why doesn't someone do it, then?'

'He remembers while he sleeps; he forgets when he wakes. That's why. But I believe that with proper training he can learn to remember.'

'And you're going to try?'

'Not I. I know too little of finance. I wouldn't know how to interpret my memories.'

'Who, then?'

'You!' He jabbed that long finger against me.

I was thoroughly startled. 'Me? Oh, no! Not a chance of it!'

'Jack,' he said querulously, 'didn't you study hypnotism in my course? Didn't you learn how harmless it is? You know what tommyrot the idea is of one mind dominating another. You know the subject really hypnotizes himself, and that no one can hypnotize an unwilling person. Then what are you afraid of?'

I—well, I didn't know what to answer. 'I'm not afraid,' I said grimly. 'I just don't like it.'

'You're afraid!'

'I'm not!'

'You are!' He was growing excited.

It was at that moment that Yvonne's footsteps sounded in the hall. His eyes glittered; he looked at me with a sinister hint of cunning. 'I dislike cowards,' he whispered. His voice rose. 'So does Yvonne!'

She entered, perceiving his excitement. 'Oh!' she frowned. 'Why do you have to take these theories so to heart, father?'

'Theories?' he screeched. 'Yes! I have a theory that when you walk you stand still and the sidewalk moves back. No—then the sidewalk would split if two people walked toward each other—or maybe it's elastic. Of course it's elastic! That's why the last mile is the longest; it's been stretched!'

Yvonne got him to bed.

He talked me into it. I don't know how much was due to my own credulity and how much to Yvonne's solemn dark eyes. I half-believed the professor by the time he'd spent another evening in argument, but I think the clincher was his veiled, threat to forbid Yvonne my company. She'd have obeyed him if it killed her; she was from New Orleans too, you see, and of Creole blood.

I won't describe that troublesome course of training. One has to develop the hypnotic habit; it's like any other habit, and must be formed slowly. Contrary to the popular opinion, morons and people of low intelligence can't ever do it. It takes real concentration; the whole knack of it is in the ability to concentrate one's attention—and I don't mean the hypnotist, either.

I mean the subject. The hypnotist hasn't a thing to do with it except to furnish the necessary suggestion by murmuring, 'Sleep—sleep —sleep—sleep.' And even that isn't necessary, once you learn the trick of it.

I spent half an hour or more, nearly every evening, learning that trick. It was tedious, and a dozen times I became thoroughly disgusted and swore to have no more to do with the farce. But always, after the half-hour's humoring of de Néant, there was Yvonne, and the boredom vanished. As a sort of reward. I suppose, the old man took to leaving us alone; and we used our time, I'll wager, to better purpose than he used his.

But I began to learn, little by little. Came a time, after three weeks of tedium, when I was able to cast myself into a light somnambulistic state. I remember how the glitter of the cheap stone in Professor de Néant's ring grew until it filled the world, and how his voice, mechanically dull, murmured like the waves of sleep in my ears. I remember everything that transpired during those minutes, even his query, 'Are you sleeping?' and my automatic reply, 'Yes.

By the end of November we had mastered the second state of lethargy, and then—I don't know why, but a sort of enthusiasm for the madness took hold of me. Business was at a standstill; I grew tired of facing customers to whom I had sold bonds at par that were now worth fifty or less—and trying to explain why. After a while I began to drop in on the professor during the afternoon, and we went through the insane routine again and again.

Yvonne comprehended only a part of the bizarre scheme. She was never in the room during our half-hour trials, and knew only vaguely that we were involved in some sort of experiment that was to restore our lost money. I don't suppose she had much faith in it, but she always indulged her father.

It was early in December that I began to remember things. Dim and formless things at first—sensations that utterly eluded the rigidities of words. I tried to express them to de Néant, but it was hopeless.

'A circular feeling,' I'd say. 'No—not exactly—a sense of spiral—not that, either. Roundness—I can't recall it now. It slips away.'

He was jubilant. 'It comes!' he whispered, gray beard a-waggle and pale eyes glittering. 'You begin to remember!'

'But what good is a memory like that?'

'Wait! It will come clearer. Of course not all your memories will be of the sort we can use. They will be scattered. Through all the multifold eternities of the past-future circle you can't have been always Jack Anders, securities salesman. There will be fragmentary memories, recollections of times when your personality was partially existent, when the Laws of Chance had assembled a being who was not quite Jack Anders in some period of the infinite worlds that must have risen and died in the span of eternities. But somewhere too, the same atoms, the same conditions, must have made you. You're the black grain among the trillions of white and with all eternity to draw must have been drawn before—many, many times-'

'Do you suppose,' I asked suddenly, 'that anyone exists twice on the same earth? Reincarnation in the sense of the Hindus?'

He laughed scornfully. 'The age of the earth is somewhere between a thousand million and three thousand million years. What proportion of eternity is that?'

'Why—no proportion at all. Zero.'

'Exactly, and zero represents the chance of the same atoms combining to form the same person twice in one cycle of a planet. But I have shown that trillions, or trillions of trillions of years ago, there must have been another earths another Jack Anders, and'—his voice took on that whining note—'another crash that ruined Jack Anders and old de Néant. That is the time you must remember out of lethargy,'

'Catalepsy!' I said. 'What would one remember in that?'

'God knows.'

'What a mad scheme!' I said suddenly. 'What a crazy pair of fools we are!' The adjectives were a mistake.

'Mad? Crazy?' His voice became a screech. 'Old de Néant is mad, eh? Old Dawn of Nothingness is crazy! You think time doesn't go in a circle, don't you? Do you know what a circle represents? I'll tell you! A circle is the mathematical symbol for zero! Time is zero—time is a circle. I have a theory that the hands of a clock are really the noses because they're on the clock's face, and since time is a circle they go round and round and round and round—'

Yvonne slipped quietly into the room and patted her father's furrowed forehead. She must have been listening.

'Look here,' I said at a later time to de Néant. 'If the past and future are the same thing, then the future's as unchangeable as the past. How, then, can we expect to change it by recovering our money?'

'Change it?' he snorted. 'How do you know we're changing it? How do you know that this same thing wasn't done by that Jack Anders and de Néant back on the other side of eternity? I say it was!'

I subsided, and the weird business went on. My memories—if they were memories—were coming clearer now. Often and often I saw things out of my own immediate past of twenty-seven years, though of course de Néant assured me that these were visions from the past of that other self on the far side of time.

I saw other things too, incidents that I couldn't place in my experience, though I couldn't be quite sure they didn't belong there. I might have forgotten, you see, since they were of no particular importance. I recounted everything dutifully to the old man immediately upon awakening, and sometimes that was difficult, like trying to find words for a half-remembered dream.

There were other memories as well—bizarre, outlandish dreams that had little parallel in human history. These were always vague and sometimes very horrible, and only their inchoate and formless character kept them from being utterly nerve-racking and terrifying.

At one time, I recall, I was gazing through a little crystalline window into a red fog through which moved indescribable faces— not human, not even associable with anything I had ever seen. On another occasion I was wandering, clad in furs, across a cold gray desert, and at my side was a woman who was not quite Yvonne.

I remember calling her Pyroniva, and knowing even that the name meant 'Snowy-fire.' And here and there in the air about us floated queer little bloated fungoid things, bobbing around like potatoes in a water bucket; and once we stood very quiet while a menacing form that was only remotely like the small fungi droned purposefully far overhead, toward some unknown objective.

At still another time I was peering fascinated into a spinning pool of mercury, watching an image therein of two wild, winged figures playing in a roseate glade—not at all human in form, but transcendently beautiful, bright and iridescent.

I felt a strange kinship between these two creatures and myself and Yvonne, but I had no inkling of what they were, nor upon what world, nor at what time in eternity, nor even of what nature was the room that held the spinning pool that pictured them.

Old Aurore de Néant listened carefully to the wild word-pictures I drew.

'Fascinating!' he muttered. 'Glimpses of an infinitely distant future, caught from a ten-fold infinitely remote past. These things you describe are not earthly; it means that somewhere, sometime, men are actually to burst the prison of space and visit other worlds. Some day—'

'If these glimpses aren't simply nightmares,' I said.

'They're not nightmares,' he snapped, 'but they might as well be, for all the value they are to us.' I could see him struggle to calm himself. 'Our money is still gone. We must try, keep trying, for years, for centuries, until we get the black grain of sand, because black sand is a sign of gold-bearing ore—' He paused. 'What am I talking about?' he said querulously.

Well, we kept trying. Interspersed with the wild, all but indescribable visions came others almost rational. The thing became a fascinating game. I was neglecting my business—though that was small loss—to chase dreams with old Professor Aurora de Néant.

I spent evenings, afternoons, and finally mornings, too, lying in the slumber of the lethargic state, or telling the old man what fantastic things I had dreamed—or, as he said, remembered. Reality became dim to me; I was living in an outlandish world of fancy, and only the dark, tragic eyes of Yvonne tugged at me, pulled me back into the daylight world of sanity.

I have mentioned more nearly rational visions. I recall one—a city, but what a city! Sky-piercing, white and beautiful, and the people of it were grave with the wisdom of gods. Pale and lovely people, but solemn, wistful, sad. There was the aura of brilliance and wickedness that hovers about all great cities, that was born, I suppose, in Babylon, and will remain until great cities are no more.

But there was something else, something rather intangible; I don't know exactly what to call it, but perhaps the word decadence is as close as any word we have. As I stood at the base of a colossal structure there was the whir of quiet machinery, but it seemed to me, nevertheless, that the city was dying.

It might have been the moss that grew green on the north walls of the buildings; it might have been the grass that pierced here and there through the cracks of the marble pavements; or it might have been only the grave and sad demeanor of the pale inhabitants. There was something that hinted of a doomed city and a dying race.

A strange thing happened when I tried to describe this particular memory to old de Néant. I stumbled over the details, of course; these visions from the unplumbed depths of eternity were curiously hard to fix between the rigid walls of words. They tended to grow vague, to elude the waking memory. Thus, in this description, I had forgotten the name of the city.

'It was called,' I said hesitatingly, 'Termis or Termolia, or---'

'Termopolis!' hissed de Néant impatiently. 'City of the End!'

I stared amazed. 'That's it! But how did you know?' In the sleep of lethargy, I was sure, one never speaks.

A queer, cunning look flashed in his ale eyes. 'I knew,' he muttered. 'I knew.' He would say no more.

But I think I saw that city once again. It was when I wandered over a brown and treeless plain, not like that cold gray desert, but apparently an arid and barren region of the earth. Dim on the western horizon was the circle of a great cool, reddish sun; it had always been there, I remembered, and knew with some other part of my mind that the vast brake of the tides had at last slowed the earth's rotation to a stop, and day and night no longer chased each other around the planet.

The air was biting cold, and my companions and I—there were half a dozen of us—moved in a huddled group, as if to lend each other warmth from our half-naked bodies. We were all of us thin-legged, skinny creatures, with oddly deep chests and enormous, luminous eyes, and the one nearest me was again a woman who had something of Yvonne in her, but very little. And I was not quite Jack Anders, either; but some remote fragment of me survived in that barbaric brain.

Beyond a hill was the surge of an oily sea. We crept circling about the mound, and suddenly I perceived that sometime in the infinite past that hill had been a city. A few Gargantuan blocks of stone lay crumbling on it, and one lonely fragment of a ruined wall rose gauntly to four or five times a man's height. It was at this spectral remnant that the leader of our miserable crew gestured, then spoke in somber tones—not English words, but I understood.

'The gods,' he said—'the gods who piled stones upon stones are dead, and harm not us who pass the place of their dwelling.'

I knew what that was meant to be. It was an incantation, a ritual; to protect us from the spirits that lurked among the ruins—the ruins, I believe, of a city built by our own ancestors thousands of generations before.

As we passed the wall I looked back at a flicker of movement, and saw something hideously like a black rubber doormat flop itself around the angle of the wall. I drew closer to the woman beside me and we crept on down to the sea for water—yes, water, for with the cessation of the planet's rotation rainfall had vanished also and all life huddled near the edge of the undying sea and learned to drink its bitter brine. I didn't glance again at the hill which had been Termopolis, the City of the End; but I knew that some chance-born fragment of Jack Anders had been—or will be; what difference, if time is a circle—witness of an age close to the day of humanity's doom.

It was early in December that I had the first memory of something that might have been suggestive of success. It was a simple and very sweet memory, just Yvonne and I in a garden that I knew was the inner grounds one of New Orleans' old homes—one of those built, in the Continental fashion, about a court.

We sat on a stone bench beneath the oleanders, and I slipped my arm very tenderly about her and murmured, 'Are you happy, Yvonne?'

She looked at me with those tragic eyes of hers and smiled, and then answered, 'As happy as I have ever been.'

And I kissed her.

That was all, but it was important. It was vastly important, because it was definitely not a memory out of my own personal past. You see, I had never sat beside Yvonne in a garden sweet with oleanders in the Old Town of New Orleans, and I had never kissed her until we met again in New York.

Aurore de Néant was elated when I described this vision.

'You see!' he gloated. 'There is evidence. You have remembered the future! Not your own future, of course, but that of another ghostly Jack Anders, who died trillions and quadrillions of years ago.'

'But it doesn't help us, does it?' I asked.

'Oh, it will come now! You wait. The thing we want will come.'

And it did, within a week. This memory was curiously bright and clear, and familiar in every detail. I remember the day. It was—the eighth of December, 1929, and I had wandered aimlessly about in search of business during the morning. In the grip of that fascination I mentioned I drifted to de Néant's apartment after lunch. Yvonne left us to ourselves, as was her custom, and we began.

This was, as I said, a sharply outlined memory—or dream. I was leaning over my desk in the company's office, that too-seldom-visited office. One of the other salesmen—Summers was his name—was leaning over my shoulder, and we were engaged in the quite customary pastime of scanning the final market reports in the evening 'paper.' The print stood out clear as reality itself; I glanced without surprise at the date-line. It was Thursday, April 27th, 1930—almost five months in the future!

Not that I realized that during the 'vision,' of course, the day was merely the present to me; I was simply looking over the list of the day's trading. Figures—familiar names. Tele-Phone, 210; U. S. Steel, 161; Paramount, 68½.

I jabbed a finger at Steel. 'I bought that at 72,' I said over my shoulder to Summers. 'I sold out everything today. Every stock I own. I'm getting out before there's a secondary crack.'

'Lucky stiff!' he murmured. 'Buy at the December lows and sell out now! Wish I'd had money to do it.' He paused. 'What you gonna do? Stay with the company?'

'No. I've enough to live on. I'm going to stick it in Governments and paid-up insurance annuities, and live on the income. I've had enough of gambling'

'You lucky stiff!' he said again. 'I'm sick of the Street too. Staying in New York?'

'For a while. Just till I get my stuff invested properly. Yvonne and I are going to New Orleans for the winter.' I paused. 'She's had a tough time of it. I'm glad we're where we are.'

'Who wouldn't be?' asked Summers, and then again, 'You lucky stiff.'

De Néant was frantically excited when I described this to him. 'That's it!' he screamed. 'We buy! We buy tomorrow! We sell on the twenty-seventh of May, and then—New Orleans!'

Of course I was nearly equally enthusiastic. 'By heaven!' I said. 'It's worth the risk! We'll do it!' And then a sudden hopeless thought. 'Do it? Do it with what? I have less than a hundred dollars to my name. And you-'

The old man groaned. 'I have nothing,' he said in abrupt gloom. 'Only the annuity we live on. One can't borrow on that.' Again a gleam of hope. 'The banks. We'll borrow from them!'

I had to laugh, though it was a bitter laugh. 'What bank would lend us money on a story like this? They wouldn't lend Rockefeller himself money to play this sick market, not without security. We're sunk, that's all.'

I looked at his pale, worried eyes. 'Sunk,' he echoed dully. Then again that wild gleam. 'Not sunk!' he yelled. 'How can we be? We did do it. You remembered our doing it! We must have found the way!'

I gazed, speechless. Suddenly a queer, mad thought flashed over me. This other Jack Anders, this ghost of quadrillions of centuries past—or future—he too must be watching, or had watched, or yet would watch, me—the Jack Anders of this cycle of eternity. He must be watching as anxiously as I to discover the means. Each of us watching the other; neither of us knowing the answer. The blind leading the blind! I laughed at the irony.

But old de Néant was not laughing. The strangest expression I have ever seen in a man's eyes was in his as he repeated very softly, 'We must have found the way, because it was done. At least you and Yvonne found the way.'

'Then all of us must,' I answered sourly.

'Yes. Oh, yes. Listen to me, Jack. I am an old man, old Aurore de Néant. I am old Dawn of Nothingness, and my mind is cracking. Don't shake your head!' he snapped. 'I am not mad. I am simply misunderstood. None of you understand. Why, I have a theory that trees, grass, and people do not grow taller at all; they grow by pushing the earth away from them, which is why you keep hearing that the world is getting smaller every day. But you don't understand; Yvonne doesn't understand-'

The girl must have been listening. Without my seeing her, she had slipped into the room and put her arms gently about her father's shoulders, while she gazed across at me with anxious eyes.

There was one more vision, irrelevant in a way, yet vitally important in another way. It was the next evening, an early December snowfall was dropping its silent white beyond the windows, and the ill-heated apartment of the de Néants was draughty and chill. I saw Yvonne shiver as she greeted me, and again as she left the room, and I noticed that old de Néant followed her to the door with his thin arms about her, and that he returned with very worried eyes.

'She is New Orleans born,' he murmured. 'This dreadful arctic climate will destroy her. We must find a way at once.'

That vision was a somber one. I stood on a cold, wet, snowy ground; just myself and Yvonne and one who stood beside an open grave. Behind us stretched rows of crosses and white tombstones, but in our corner the place was ragged, untended, unconsecrated. The priest was saying, 'And these are things that only God understands.'

I slipped a comforting arm about Yvonne. She raised her dark, tragic eyes and whispered—'It was yesterday, Jack. Just yesterday that he said to me, 'Next winter you shall spend in New Orleans, Yvonne.' Just yesterday!'

I tried a wretched smile, but I could only stare mournfully at her forlorn face, watching a tear that rolled slowly down her right cheek, hung glistening there a moment, then was joined by another and splashed unregarded on the black bosom of her dress.

That was all, but how could I describe that vision to old de Néant? I tried to evade; he kept insisting

'There wasn't any hint of the way,' I told him. Useless; at last I had to tell anyway.

He was very silent for a full minute. 'Jack,' he said finally, 'do you know when I said that to her about New Orleans? This morning when we watched the snow.'

I didn't know what to do. Suddenly this whole concept of remembering the future seemed mad, insane; in all my memories there had been not a single spark of real proof, not a single hint of prophecy. So I did nothing at all, but simply gazed silently as old Aurore de Néant walked out of the room. And when, two hours later, while Yvonne and I talked, he finished writing a certain letter and then shot himself through the heart—why, that proved nothing either.

So it was the following day that Yvonne and I, his only mourners, followed old Dawn of Nothingness to his suicide's grave. I stood beside her and tried as best I could to console her, and roused from a dark reverie to hear her words: 'Just yesterday that he said to me, 'Next winter you shall spend in New Orleans, Yvonne.' Just yesterday!'

I watched the tear that rolled slowly down her right cheek, hung glistening there a moment, then was joined by another and splashed on the black bosom of her dress.

But it was later, during the evening that the most ironic revelation of all occurred, I was gloomily blaming myself for the weakness of indulging old de Néant in the mad experiment that had led, in a way, to his death. It was as if Yvonne read my thoughts, for she said suddenly, 'He was breaking, Jack. His mind was going. I heard all those strange things he kept murmuring to you.'

'What?'

'I listened, of course, behind the door there. I never left him alone. I heard him whisper the queerest things—faces in a red fog, words about a cold gray desert, the name Pyroniva, the word Termopolis. He leaned over you as you sat with closed eyes, and he whispered, whispered all the time.'

Irony of ironies! It was old de Néant's mad mind that had suggested the visions! He had described them to me as I sat in the sleep of lethargy! Later we found the letter he had written, and again I was deeply moved. The old man had carried a little insurance; just a week before he had borrowed on one of the policies to pay the premiums on it and the others. But the letter—well, he had made me beneficiary of half the amount! And the instructions were:

'You, Jack Anders, will take both your money and Yvonne's and carry out the plan as you know I wish.'

Aurore De Néant had found the way to provide the money, but I couldn't gamble Yvonne's last dollar on the scheme of a disordered mind.

'What will we do?' I asked her. 'Of course the money's all yours. I won't touch it.'

'Mine?' she echoed. 'Why, no. We'll do as he wished. Do you think I'd not respect his last request?'

Well, we did. I took those miserable few thousands and spread it around in that sick December market. You remember what happened, how during the spring the prices skyrocketed as if they were heading back toward 1929, when actually the depression was just gathering breath. I rode that market like a circus performer; I took profits and pyramided them back, and on April 27th, with our money multiplied fifty times, I sold out and watched the market slide back.

Coincidence? Very likely. After all, Aurore de Néant's mind was clear enough most of the time. Other economists predicted that spring rise; perhaps he foresaw it too. Perhaps he staged this whole affair just to trick us into the gamble, one which we'd never have dared otherwise. And then when he saw we were going to fail from lack of money, he took the only means he had of providing it.

Perhaps. That's the rational explanation, and yet—that vision of ruined Termopolis keeps haunting me. I see again the gray cold desert of the floating fungi. I wonder often about the immutable Laws of Chance, and about a ghostly Jack Anders somewhere beyond eternity.

For perhaps he does—did—will exist. Otherwise, how to explain that final vision? What of Yvonne's words beside her father's grave? Could he have foreseen those words and whispered them to me? Possibly. But what, then, of those two tears that hung glistening, merged, and dropped from her cheeks?

What of them?

Graph

"You're on the mend again," said Dr. Felix Kurtius, tossing his black case carelessly on the desk. "Let's see how permanent it is this time!"

Isaac Levinson—mail-order Levinson—rolled down his sleeve and stared sardonically at the doctor.

"Thanks," he growled. "I've heard that before."

"You're feeling better, aren't you?"

The merchandise king nodded reluctantly, staring about his elaborate office.

"Sure," he said. "But for how long? And anyway, why don't you do something? Is this the new medical practice—to let a patient get well by himself? For that I don't need a doctor!"

"I gave you my suggestions," retorted Kurtius. "Three and a half years ago—when you first called me—I told you what to do. Don't blame me because you refuse to follow my advice."

"Vacations!" sneered Levinson. "Rest—change—travel—retire! Could I leave my business with conditions like they were?"

"You certainly could! What's a little more money to you—or a little less?"

"Money—bah! It's my business that needs me."

"Same thing."

"No," said Levinson abruptly. "Not the same thing! My stockholders, my employees, I have obligations to them. The business must be run right, or the one loses money and the other jobs. Could I let some schlemiel make a botch of things while I was telling how the biggest tarpon got away from me. Oser!"

"Just excuses," observed Kurtius. "What you mean is that you didn't want to leave."

"Couldn't is what I said."

"Wouldn't is what you mean."

The doctor gestured at the fittings of his patient's office.

"You don't mean to tell me you're so busy that you haven't time to walk two blocks to my office, do you?—Instead of having me call here to examine you?"

Levinson silently indicated the welter of papers on his desk.

"And that's what you've wedded to!" scoffed Kurtius. "Charts, summaries, statistics." Any clerk could tabulate them for you."

"Charts and statistics," growled Levinson, "are the life-blood of my business."

"And your business is the life-blood of you!"

"Yet you want I should get away from it."

"That's my advice. No man can live year after year on his own blood. You can't; that's the whole trouble with you. That's why medicine or operations are perfectly useless in your case."

"Bah!" Levinson was frowning again. "I have a notion that you doctors recommend the rest cure when you don't know what's wrong. I don't want to rest; I want something that will put me in shape to keep on working. I don't believe it's my business that's doing this to me; for twenty-five years I've lived, eaten, slept, and dreamt this business, and never, until that first time I called you, have I felt an hour's sickness. And now these damned spells—better, worse, better worse—How could it be my business?"

"Well," observed Kurtius, "there's no way of proving it to you. I've told you my diagnosis; that's all I can do. You'll find out sooner or later that I am right."

"I don't believe it." said Levinson stubbornly.

"Well, as I said, there's no way of proving it to you."

"You doctors," continued Levinson, "spend your efforts treating symptoms instead of causes, Because I am tired, I must go somewhere and rest; because I can't sleep, I must get out somewhere and exercise; because I have no appetite, I must go away from my business! Why don't you find why I am tired, and can't sleep or eat? I should run my business like that and in a year I'd be broke—machullah!"

"Didn't you ever hear of functional disorders?" Queried Kurtius mildly.

"Am I the doctor or you?"

"Functional disorders are those where there's nothing the matter with the patient—that is organically. Nothing wrong except in the mind or nervous system."

"Hah! Imaginary sickness I've got."

"It's not imaginary. Functional troubles are just as real as organic ones, and sometimes a damn sight harder to treat—Especially," he added, "if the patient won't cooperate."

"And you think my business is doing that?"

"Just as I told you."

"Bah! For more than twenty years I have had no trouble. And why do I get better and then worse again? You should make a study of your cases."

"Do you think I don't?" snapped Kurtius. "I can give you this case history by heart. Why, look here! Here's something you ought to be able to understand!"

He reached toward his black bag, noting that the catch had opened, spilling a stethoscope and a paper or two on the littered desk. He seized a paper and spread it out before his patient. "What's that?" grunted Levinson.

"Graph of your metabolism," replied the doctor. "Make a study of my cases, eh! Here's your chart month by month for three and a half years."

Levinson scanned the irregular black lines. Suddenly he narrowed his eyes, leaned closer. A moment more and he burst into a snickering laugh.

"What's the matter?" queried Kurtius impatiently. "The chart!" chuckled Levinson. "Hee-hee! It's a graph of our sales I was looking at before you came! Case-record, huh?"

Kurtius glanced at the paper, frowned perplexedly, and suddenly gave vent to a shout of laughter. "Ho!" He roared, slapping the desk. "Funny! Oh, Lord!"

"What's that funny?" asked his patient. "The graph! The sales-chart!" bellowed the doctor. "Your business doesn't affect you, eh? Look!"

He pulled another bit of paper from his bag, spread it beside the first.

"Here's your metabolism! Look it over!"

Peak for Peak, valley for valley, the two graphs were identical!

The Worlds of If

I stopped on the way to the Staten Island Airport to call up, and that was a mistake, doubtless, since I had a chance of making it otherwise. But the office was affable. "We'll hold the ship five minutes for you," the clerk said. "That's the best we can do."

So I rushed back to my taxi and we spun off to the third level and sped across the Staten Bridge like a comet treading a steel rainbow. I had to be in Moscow by evening, by eight o'clock in fact, for the opening of bids on the Ural Tunnel. The Government required the personal presence of an agent of each bidder, but the firm should have known better than to send me, Dixon Wells, even though the N. J. Wells Corporation is, so to speak, my father. I have a—well, an undeserved reputation for being late to everything; something always comes up to prevent me from getting anywhere on time. It's never my fault; this time it was a chance encounter with my old physics professor, Haskel van Manderpootz. I couldn't very well just say hello and good-bye to him; I'd been a favorite of his back in the college days of 2014.

I missed the airliner, of course. I was still on the Staten Bridge when I heard the roar of the catapult and the Soviet rocket Baikal hummed over us like a tracer bullet with a long tail of flame.

We got the contract anyway; the firm wired our man in Beirut and he flew up to Moscow, but it didn't help my reputation. However, I felt a great deal better when I saw the evening papers; the Baikal, flying at the north edge of the eastbound lane to avoid a storm, had locked wings with a British fruitship and all but a hundred of her five hundred passengers were lost. I had almost become "the late Mr. Wells" in a grimmer sense.

I'd made an engagement for the following week with old van Manderpootz. It seems he'd transferred to N.Y.U. as head of the department of Newer Physics—that is, of Relativity. He deserved it; the old chap was a genius if ever there was one, and even now, eight years out of college, I remember more from his course than from half a dozen in calculus, steam and gas, mechanics, and other hazards on the path to an engineer's education. So on Tuesday night I dropped in an hour or so late, to tell the truth, since I'd forgotten about the engagement until mid-evening.

He was reading in a room as disorderly as ever. "Humph!" he granted. "Time changes everything but habit, I see. You were a good student, Dick, but I seem to recall that you always arrived in class toward the middle of the lectures."

"I had a course in East Hall just before," I explained. "I couldn't seem to make it in time."

"Well, it's time you learned to be on time," he growled. Then his eyes twinkled. "Time!" he ejaculated. "The most fascinating word in the language. Here we've used it five times (there goes the sixth time—and the seventh!) in the first minute of conversation; each of us understands the other, yet science is just beginning to learn its meaning, Science? I mean that I am beginning to learn."

I sat down. "You and science are synonymous," I grinned. "Aren't you one of the world's outstanding physicists?"

"One of them!" he snorted. "One of them! And who are the others?"

"Oh, Corveille and Hastings and Shrimski—"

"Bah! Would you mention them in the same breath with the name of van Manderpootz? A pack of jackals, eating the crumbs of ideas that drop from my feast of thoughts! Had you gone back into the last century, now—had you mentioned Einstein and de Sitter—there, perhaps, are names worthy to rank with (or just below) van Manderpootz!"

I grinned again in amusement. "Einstein was considered pretty good, wasn't he?" I remarked. "After all, he was the first to tie time and space to the laboratory. Before him they were just philosophical concepts."

"He didn't!" rasped the professor. "Perhaps, in a dim, primitive fashion, he showed the way, but I—I, van Manderpootz—am the first to seize time, drag it into my laboratory, and perform an experiment on it."

"Indeed? And what sort of experiment?"

"What experiment, other than simple measurement, is it possible to perform?" he snapped.

"Why—I don't know. To travel in it?"

"Exactly."

"Like these time-machines that are so popular in the current magazines? To go into the future or the past?"

"Bah! Many bahs! The future or the past—pfui! It needs no van Manderpootz to see the fallacy in that. Einstein showed us that much."

"How? It's conceivable, isn't it?"

"Conceivable? And you, Dixon Wells, studied under van Manderpootz!" He grew red with emotion, then grimly calm. "Listen to me. You know how time varies with the speed of a system—Einstein's relativity."

"Yes."

"Very well. Now suppose then that the great engineer Dixon Wells invents a machine capable of traveling very fast, enormously fast, nine-tenths as fast as light. Do you follow? Good. You then fuel this miracle ship for a little jaunt of a half-million miles, which, since mass (and with it inertia) increases according to the Einstein formula with increasing speed, takes all the fuel in the world. But you solve that. You use atomic energy. Then, since at nine-tenths light-speed, your ship weighs about as much as the sun, you disintegrate North America to give you sufficient motive power. You start off at that speed, a hundred and sixty-eight thousand miles per second, and you travel for two hundred and four thousand miles. The acceleration has now crushed you to death, but you have penetrated the future." He paused, grinning sardonically. "Haven't you?"

"Yes."

"And how far?"

I hesitated.

"Use your Einstein formula!" he screeched. "How far? I'll tell you. One second!" He grinned triumphantly. "That's how possible it is to travel into the future. And as for the past—in the first place, you'd have to exceed light-speed, which immediately entails the use of more than an infinite number of horsepowers. We'll assume that the great engineer Dixon Wells solves that little problem too, even though the energy output of the whole universe is not an infinite number of horsepowers. Then he applies this more than infinite power to travel at two hundred and four thousand miles per second for ten seconds. He has then penetrated the past. How far?"

Again I hesitated.

"I'll tell you. One second!" He glared at me. "Now all you have to do is to design such a machine, and then van Manderpootz; will admit the possibility of traveling into the future—for a limited number of seconds. As for the past, I have just explained that all the energy in the universe is insufficient for that."

"But," I stammered, "you just said that you—"

"I did not say anything about traveling into either future or past, which I have just demonstrated to you to be impossible—a practical impossibility in the one case and an absolute one in the other."

"Then how do you travel in time?"

"Not even van Manderpootz can perform the impossible," said the professor, now faintly jovial. He tapped a thick pad of typewriter paper on the table beside him. "See, Dick, this is the world, the universe." He swept a finger down it. "It is long in time, and"—sweeping his hand across it—"it is broad in space, but"—now jabbing his finger against its center—"it is very thin in the fourth dimension. Van Manderpootz takes always the shortest, the most logical course. I do not travel along time, into past or future. No. Me, I travel across time, sideways!"

I gulped. "Sideways into time! What's there?"

"What would naturally be there?" he snorted. "Ahead is the future; behind is the past. Those are real, the worlds of past and future. What worlds are neither past nor future, but contemporary and yet—extemporal—existing, as it were, in time parallel to our time?"

I shook my head.

"Idiot!" he snapped. "The conditional worlds, of course! The worlds of 'if.' Ahead are the worlds to be; behind are the worlds that were; to either side are the worlds that might have been—the worlds of if!"

"Eh?" I was puzzled. "Do you mean that you can see what will happen if I do such and such?"

"No!" he snorted. "My machine does not reveal the past nor predict the future. It will show, as I told you, the conditional worlds. You might express it, by 'if I had done such and such, so and so would have happened.' The worlds of the subjunctive mode."

"Now how the devil does it do that?"

"Simple, for van Manderpootz! I use polarized light, polarized not in the horizontal or vertical planes, but in the direction of the fourth dimension—an easy matter. One uses Iceland spar under colossal pressure, that is all. And since the worlds are very thin in the direction of the fourth dimension, the thickness of a single light wave, though it be but millionths of an inch, is sufficient. A considerable improvement over time-traveling in past or future, with its impossible velocities and ridiculous distances!"

"But—are those—worlds of if—real?"

"Real? What is real? They are real, perhaps, in the sense that two is a real number as opposed to $\sqrt{-2}$, which is imaginary. They are the worlds that would have been if—Do you see?"

I nodded. "Dimly. You could see, for instance, what New York would have been like if England had won the Revolution instead of the Colonies."

"That's the principle, true enough, but you couldn't see that on the machine. Part of it, you see, is a Horsten psychomat (stolen from one of my ideas, by the way) and you, the user, become part of the device. Your own mind is necessary to furnish the background. For instance, if George Washington could have used the mechanism after the signing of peace, he could have seen what you suggest. We can't. You can't even see what would have happened if I hadn't invented the thing, but I can. Do you understand?"

"Of course. You mean the background has to rest in the past experiences of the user."

"You're growing brilliant," he scoffed. "Yes. The device will show ten hours of what would have happened *if*—condensed, of course, as in a movie, to half an hour's actual time."

"Say, that sounds interesting!"

"You'd like to see it? Is there anything you'd like to find out? Any choice you'd alter?"

"I'll say—a thousand of 'em. I'd like to know what would have happened if I'd sold out my stocks in 2009 instead of '10. I was a millionaire in my own right then, but I was a little—well, a little late in liquidating."

"As usual," remarked van Manderpootz. "Let's go over to the laboratory then."

The professor's quarters were but a block from the campus. He ushered me into the Physics Building, and thence into his own re-search laboratory, much like the one I had visited during my courses under him. The device—he called it his "subjunctivisor," since it operated in hypothetical worlds—occupied the entire center table. Most of it was merely a Horsten psychomat, but glittering crystalline and glassy was the prism of Iceland spar, the polarizing agent that was the heart of the instrument.

Van Manderpootz pointed to the headpiece. "Put it on," he said, and I sat staring at the screen of the psychomat. I suppose everyone is familiar with the Horsten psychomat; it was as much a fad a few years ago as the ouija board a century back. Yet it isn't just a toy; sometimes, much as the ouija board, it's a real aid to memory. A maze of vague and colored shadows is caused to drift slowly across the screen, and one watches them, meanwhile visualizing whatever scene or circumstances he is trying to remember. He turns a knob that alters the arrangement of lights and shadows, and when, by chance, the design corresponds to his mental picture—presto! There is his scene re-created under his eyes. Of course his own mind adds the details. All the screen actually shows are these tinted blobs of light and shadow, but the thing can be amazingly real. I've seen occasions when I could have sworn the psychomat showed pictures almost as sharp and detailed as reality itself; the illusion is sometimes as startling as that.

Van Manderpootz switched on the light, and the play of shadows began. "Now recall the circumstances of, say, a half-year after the market crash. Turn the knob until the picture clears, then stop. At that point I direct the light of the subjunctivisor upon the screen, and you have nothing to do but watch."

I did as directed. Momentary pictures formed and vanished. The inchoate sounds of the device hummed like distant voices, but with-out the added suggestion of the picture, they meant nothing. My own face flashed and dissolved and then, finally, I had it. There was a picture of myself sitting in an ill-defined room; that was all. I re-leased the knob and gestured.

A click followed. The light dimmed, then brightened. The pic-ture cleared, and amazingly, another figure emerged, a woman, I recognized her; it, was Whimsy White, erstwhile star of television and premiere actress of the "Vision Varieties of '09." She was changed on that picture, but I recognized her.

I'll say I did! I'd been trailing her all through the boom years of '07 to '10, trying to marry her, while old N. J. raved and ranted and threatened to leave everything to the Society for Rehabilitation of the Gobi Desert. I think those threats were what kept her from accepting me, but after I took my own money and ran it up to a couple of million in that crazy market of '08 and '09, she softened.

Temporarily, that is. When the crash of the spring of '10 came and bounced me back on my father and into the firm of N. J. Wells, her favor dropped a dozen points to the market's one. In February we were engaged, in April—we were hardly speaking. In May they sold me out. I'd been late again.

And now, there she was on the psychomat screen, obviously plumping out, and not nearly so pretty as memory had pictured her. She was staring at me with an expression of enmity, and I was glaring back. The buzzes became voices.

"You nit-wit!" she snapped. "You can't bury me out here. I want to go back to New York, where there's a little life. I'm bored with you and your golf."

"And I'm bored with you and your whole dizzy crowd."

"At least they're alive. You're a walking corpse! Just because you were lucky enough to gamble yourself into the money, you think you're a tin god."

"Well, I don't think you're Cleopatra! Those friends of yours—they trail after you because you give parties and spend money—my money."

"Better than spending it to knock a white walnut along a mountainside!"

"Indeed? You ought to try it, Marie." (That was her real name.) "It might help your figure—though I doubt if anything could!"

She glared in rage and—well, that was a painful half-hour. I won't give all the details, but I was glad when the screen dissolved into meaningless colored clouds.

"Whew!" I said, staring at van Manderpootz, who had been reading.

"You liked it?"

"Liked it! Say, I guess I was lucky to be cleaned out. I won't regret it from now on."

"That," said the professor grandly, "is van Manderpootz's great contribution to human happiness. 'Of all sad words of tongue or pen, the saddest are these: It might have been!' True no longer, my friend Dick. Van Manderpootz has shown that the proper reading is, 'It might have been—worse!'"

It was very late when I returned home, and as a result, very late when I rose, and equally late when I got to the office. My father was unnecessarily worked up about it, but he exaggerated when he said I'd never been on time. He forgets the occasions when he's awakened me and dragged me down with him. Nor was it necessary to refer so sarcastically to my missing the *Baikal*; I reminded him of the wrecking of the liner, and he responded very heartlessly that if I'd been aboard, the rocket would have been late, and so would have missed colliding with the British fruitship. It was likewise superfluous for him to mention that when he and I had tried to snatch a few weeks of golfing in the mountains, even the spring had been late. I had nothing to do with that.

"Dixon," he concluded, "you have no conception whatever of time. None whatever."

The conversation with van Manderpootz recurred to me. I was impelled to ask, "And have you, sir?"

"I have," he said grimly. "I most assuredly have. Time," he said oracularly "is money."

You can't argue with a viewpoint like that.

But those aspersions of his rankled, especially that about the *Baikal*. Tardy I might be, but it was hardly conceivable that my presence aboard the rocket could have averted the catastrophe. It irritated me; in a way, it made me responsible for the deaths of those unrescued hundreds among the passengers and crew, and I didn't like the thought.

Of course, if they'd waited an extra five minutes for me, or if I'd been on time and they'd left on schedule instead of five minutes late, or if—*if*!

If! The word called up van Manderpootz and his subjunctivisor—the worlds of "if," the weird, unreal worlds that existed beside reality, neither past nor future, but contemporary, yet extemporal.

Somewhere among their ghostly infinities existed one that repre-sented the world that would have been had I made the liner. I had only to call up Hasket van Manderpootz, make an appointment, and then—find out.

Yet it wasn't an easy decision. Suppose—just suppose that I found myself responsible—not legally responsible, certainly; there'd be no question of criminal negligence, or anything of that sort—not even morally responsible, because I couldn't pos-sibly have anticipated that my presence or absence could weigh so heavily in the scales of life and death, nor could I have known in which direction the scales would tip. Just—responsible; that was all. Yet I hated to find out.

I hated equally not finding out. Uncertainty has its pangs too, quite as painful as those of remorse. It might be less nerveracking to know myself responsible than to wonder, to waste thoughts in vain doubts and futile reproaches. So I seized the visiphone, dialed the number of the University and at length gazed on the broad, humorous, intelligent features of van Manderpootz, dragged from a morning lecture by my call.

I was all but prompt for the appointment the following evening, and might actually have been on time but for an unreasonable traffic officer who insisted on booking me for speeding. At any rate, van Manderpootz was impressed.

"Well!" he rumbled. "I almost missed you, Dixon. I was just go-ing over to the club, since I didn't expect you for an hour. You're only ten minutes late."

I ignored this. "Professor, I want to use your—uh—your sub-junctivisor."

"Eh? Oh, yes. You're lucky, then. I was about to dismantle it."

"Dismantle it! Why?"

"It has served its purpose. It has given birth to an idea far more important than itself. I shall need the space it occupies."

"But what is the idea, if it's not too presumptuous of me to ask?"

"It is not too presumptuous. You and the world which awaits it so eagerly may both know, but you bear it from the lips of the author. It is nothing less than the autobiography of van Mander-pootz!" He paused impressively.

I gaped. "Your autobiography?"

"Yes. The world, though perhaps unaware, is crying for it. I shall detail my life, my work. I shall reveal myself as the man responsible for the three years' duration of the Pacific War of 2004."

"You?"

"None other. Had I not been a loyal Netherlands subject at that time, and therefore neutral, the forces of Asia would have been crushed in three months instead of three years. The subjunctivisor tells me so; I would have invented a calculator to forecast the chances of every engagement; van Manderpootz would have removed the hit or miss element in the conduct of war." He frowned solemnly. "There is my idea. The autobiography of van Manderpootz. What do you think of it?"

I recovered my thoughts. "It's—uh—it's colossal!" I said vehemently. "I'll buy a copy myself. Several copies. I'll send 'em to my friends."

"I," said van Manderpootz expansively, "shall autograph your copy for you. It will be priceless. I shall write in some fitting phrase, perhaps something like *Magnificus sed non superbus. Great but not proud!*" That well described van Manderpootz, who despite his greatness is simple, modest, and unassuming. Don't you agree?"

"Perfectly! A very apt description of you. But—couldn't I see your subjunctivisor before it's dismantled to make way for the greater work?"

"Ah! You wish to find out something?"

"Yes, professor. Do you remember the *Baikal* disaster of a week or two ago? I was to have taken that liner to Moscow. I just missed it." I related the circumstances.

"Humph!" he grunted. "You wish to discover what would have happened had you caught it, eh? Well, I see several possibilities. Among the world of 'if' is the one that would have been real if you had been on time, the one that depended on the vessel waiting for your actual arrival, and the one that hung on your arriving within the five minutes they actually waited. In which are you interested?"

"Oh—the last one." That seemed the likeliest. After all, it was too much to expect that Dixon Wells could ever be on time, and as to the second possibility—well, they hadn't waited for me, and that in a way removed the weight of responsibility.

"Come on," rumbled van Manderpootz. I followed him across to the Physics Building and into his littered laboratory. The device still stood on the table and I took my place before it, staring at the screen of the Horsten psychomat. The clouds wavered and shifted as I sought to impress my memories on their suggestive shapes, to read into them some, picture of that vanished morning.

Then I had it. I made out the vista from the Staten Bridge, and was speeding across the giant span toward the airport. I waved a signal to van Manderpootz, the thing clicked, and the subjunctivisor was on.

The grassless clay of the field appeared. It is a curious thing about the psychomat that you see only through the eyes of your image on the screen. It lends a strange reality to the working of the toy; I suppose a sort of self-hypnosis is partly responsible.

I was rushing over the ground toward the glittering, silverwinged projectile that was the *Baikal*. A glowering officer waved me on, and I dashed up the slant of the gangplank and into the ship; the port dropped and I heard a long "Whew!" of relief.

"Sit down!" barked the officer, gesturing toward an unoccupied seat. I fell into it; the ship quivered under the thrust of the catapult, grated harshly into motion, and then was flung bodily into the air. The blasts roared instantly, then settled to a more muffled throbbing, and I watched Staten Island drop down and slide back beneath me. The giant rocket was under way.

"Whew!" I breathed again. "Made it!" I caught an amused glance from my right. I was in an aisle seat; there was no one to my left, so I turned to the eyes that had flashed, glanced, and froze staring.

It was a girl. Perhaps she wasn't actually as lovely as she looked to me; after all, I was seeing her through the half-visionary screen of a psychomat. I've told myself since that she couldn't have been as pretty as she seemed, that it was due to my own imagination filling in the details. I don't know; I remember only that I stared at curiously lovely silver-blue eyes and velvety brown hair, and a small amused mouth, and an impudent nose. I kept staring until she flushed.

"I'm sorry," I said quickly. "I—was startled."

There's a friendly atmosphere aboard a trans-oceanic rocket. The passengers are forced into a crowded infirmary for anywhere from seven to twelve hours, and there isn't much room for moving about. Generally, one strikes up an acquaintance with his neighbors; introductions aren't at all necessary, and the custom is simply to speak to anybody you choose—something like an all-day trip on the railroad trains of the last century, I suppose. You make friends for the duration of the journey, and then, nine times out of ten, you never hear of your traveling companions again.

The girl smiled. "Are you the individual responsible for the delay in starting?"

I admitted it. "I seem to be chronically late. Even watches lose time as soon as I wear them."

She laughed. "Your responsibilities can't be very heavy."

Well, they weren't of course, though it's surprising how many clubs, caddies, and chorus girls have depended on me at various times for appreciable portions of their incomes. But somehow I didn't feel like mentioning those things to the silvery-eyed girl.

We talked. Her name, it developed, was Joanna Caldwell, and she was going as far as Paris. She was an artist, or hoped to be one day, and of course there is no place in the world that can supply both training and inspiration, like Paris. So it was there she was bound for a year of study, and despite her demurely humorous lips and laughing eyes, I could see that the business was of vast importance to her. I gathered that she had worked hard for the year in Paris, had scraped and saved for three years as fashion illustrator for some woman's magazine, though she couldn't have been many months over twenty-one. Her painting meant a great deal to her, and I could understand it. I'd felt that way about polo once.

So you see, we were sympathetic spirits from the beginning. I knew that she liked me, and it was obvious that she didn't connect Dixon Wells with the N. J. Wells Corporation. And as for me—well, after that first glance into her cool silver eyes, I simply didn't care to look anywhere else. The hours seemed to drip away like minutes while I watched her.

You know how those things go. Suddenly I was calling her Joanna and she was calling me Dick, and it seemed as if we'd been doing just that all our lives. I'd decided to stop over in Paris on my way back from Moscow, and I'd secured her promise to let me see her. She was different, I tell you; she was nothing like the calculating Whimsy White, and still less like the dancing, simpering, giddy youngsters one meets around at social affairs. She was just Joanna, cool and humorous, yet sympathetic and serious, and as pretty as a Majolica figurine.

We could scarcely realize it when the steward passed along to take orders for luncheon. Four hours out? It seemed like forty minutes. And we had a pleasant feeling of intimacy in the discovery that both of us liked lobster salad and detested oysters. It was another bond; I told her whimsically that it was an omen, nor did she object to considering it so.

Afterwards we walked along the narrow aisle to the glassed-in observation room up forward. It was almost too crowded for entry, but we didn't mind that at all, as it forced us to sit very close together. We stayed long after both of us had begun to notice the stuffiness of the air.

It was just after we had returned to our seats that the catastrophe occurred. There was no warning save a sudden lurch, the result, I suppose, of the pilot's futile last-minute attempt to swerve—just that and then a grinding crash and a terrible sensation of spinning, and after that a chorus of shrieks that were like the sounds of a battle.

It was battle. Five hundred people were picking themselves up from the floor, were trampling each other, milling around, being cast helplessly down as the great rocket-plane, its left wing but a broken stub, circled downward toward the Atlantic.

The shouts of officers sounded and a loudspeaker blared. "Be calm," it kept repeating, and then, "There has been a collision. We have contacted a surface ship. There is no danger—There is no danger—"

I struggled up from the debris of shattered seats. Joanna was gone. Just as I found her crumpled between the rows, the ship struck the water with a jar that set everything crashing again. The speaker blared, "Put on the cork belts under the seats. The life-belts are under the seats."

I dragged a belt loose and snapped it around Joanna, then donned one myself. The crowd was surging forward now, and the tail end of the ship began to drop. There was water behind us, sloshing in the darkness as the lights went out. An officer came sliding by, stooped, and fastened a belt about an unconscious woman ahead of us. "You all right?" he yelled, and passed on without waiting for an answer.

The speaker must have been cut on to a battery circuit. "And get as far away as possible," it ordered suddenly. "Jump from the forward port and get as far away as possible. A ship is standing by. You will be picked up. Jump from the—" It went dead again.

I got Joanna untangled from the wreckage. She was pale; her silvery eyes were closed. I started dragging her slowly and painfully toward the forward port, and the slant of the floor increased until it was like the slide of a ski-jump. The officer passed again. "Can you handle her?" he asked, and again dashed away.

I was getting there. The crowd around the port looked smaller, or was it simply huddling closer? Then suddenly, a wail of fear and despair went up, and there was a roar of water. The observation room walls had given. I saw the green surge of waves, and a billowing deluge rushed down upon us. I had been late again.

That was all. I raised shocked and frightened eyes from the subjunctivisor to face van Manderpootz, who was scribbling on the edge of the table.

"Well?" he asked.

I shuddered. "Horrible!" I murmured. "We—I guess we wouldn't have been among the survivors."

"We, eh? We?" His eyes twinkled.

I did not enlighten him.

I thanked him, bade him good-night and went dolorously home.

* * *

Even my father noticed something queer about me. The day I got to the office only five minutes late, he called me in for some anxious questioning as to my health. I couldn't tell him anything, of course. How could I explain that I'd been late once too often, and had fallen in love with a girl two weeks after she was dead?

The thought drove me nearly crazy. Joanna! Joanna with her silvery eyes now lay somewhere at the bottom of the Atlantic. I went around half dazed, scarcely speaking. One night I actually lacked the energy to go home and sat smoking in my father's big overstuffed chair in his private office until I finally dozed off. The next morning, when old N. J. entered and found me there before him, he turned pale as paper, staggered, and gasped, "My heart!" It took a lot of explaining to convince him that I wasn't early at the office but just very late going home.

At last I felt that I couldn't stand it. I had to do something—anything at all. I thought finally of the subjunctivisor. I could see—yes, I could see what would have transpired if the ship hadn't been wrecked! I could trace out that weird, unreal romance hidden somewhere in the worlds of "if." I could, perhaps, wring a somber, vicarious joy from the things that might have been. I could see Joanna once more!

It was late afternoon when I rushed over to van Manderpootz's quarters. He wasn't there; I encountered him finally in the hall of the Physics Building.

"Dick!" he exclaimed. "Are you sick?"

"Sick? No, not physically. Professor, I've got to use your subjunctivisor again. I've got to!"

"Eh? Oh—that toy. You're too late, Dick. I've dismantled it. I have a better use for the space."

I gave a miserable groan and was tempted to damn the autobiography of the great van Manderpootz. A gleam of sympathy showed in his eyes, and he took my arm, dragging me into the little office adjoining his laboratory.

"Tell me," he commanded.

I did. I guess I made the tragedy plain enough, for his heavy brows knit in a frown of pity. "Not even van Manderpootz can bring back the dead," he murmured. "I'm sorry, Dick. Take your mind from the affair. Even were my subjunctivisor available, I wouldn't permit you to use it. That would be but to turn the knife in the wound." He paused. "Find something else to occupy your mind. Do as van Manderpootz does. Find forgetfulness in work."

"Yes," I responded dully. "But who'd want to read my autobiography? That's all right for you."

"Autobiography? Oh! I remember. No, I have abandoned that. History itself will record the life and works of van Manderpootz. Now I am engaged in a far grander project."

"Indeed?" I was utterly, gloomily disinterested.

"Yes. Gogli has been here, Gogli the sculptor. He is to make a bust of me. What better legacy can I leave to the world than a bust of van Manderpootz, sculptured from life? Perhaps I shall present it to the city, perhaps to the university. I would have given it to the Royal Society if they had been a little more receptive, if they—if—if!" The last in a shout.

"Huh?"

"*If!*" cried van Manderpootz. "What you saw in the subjunctivisor was what would have happened if you had caught the ship!"

"I know that."

"But something quite different might really have happened! Don't you see? She—she—Where are those old newspapers?"

He was pawing through a pile of them. He flourished one finally. "Here! Here are the survivors!"

Like letters of flame, Joanna Caldwell's name leaped out at me. There was even a little paragraph about it, as I saw once my reeling brain permitted me to read:

At least a score of survivors owe their lives to the bravery of twenty-eight-year-old Navigator Orris Hope, who patrolled both aisles during the panic, lacing lifebelts on the injured and helpless, and carrying many to the port. He remained on the sinking liner until the last, finally fighting his way to the surface through the broken walls of the observation room. Among those who owe their lives to the young officer are: Patrick Owensby, New York City; Mrs. Campbell Warren, Boston; Miss Joanna Caldwell, New York City—

I suppose my shout of joy was heard over in the Administration Building, blocks away. I didn't care; if van Manderpootz hadn't been armored in stubby whiskers, I'd have kissed him. Perhaps I did anyway; I can't be sure of my actions during those chaotic minutes in the professor's tiny office.

At last I calmed. "I can look her up!" I gloated. "She must have landed with the other survivors, and they were all on that British tramp freighter the *Osgood*, that docked here last week. She must be in New York—and if she's gone over to Paris, I'll find out and follow her!"

Well, it's a queer ending. She was in New York, but—you see, Dixon Wells had, so to speak, known Joanna Caldwell by means of the professor's subjunctivisor, but Joanna had never known Dixon Wells. What the ending might have been if—if—But it wasn't; she had married Orris Hope, the young officer who had rescued her. I was late again.

The Ideal

"This," said the Franciscan, "is my Automaton, who at the proper time will speak, answer whatsoever question I may ask, and reveal all secret knowledge to me." He smiled as he laid his hand affectionately on the iron skull that topped the pedestal.

The youth gazed open-mouthed, first at the head and then at the Friar. "But it's iron!" he whispered. "The head is iron, good father."

"Iron without, skill within, my son," said Roger Bacon. "It will speak, at the proper time and in its own manner, for so have I made it. A clever man can twist the devil's arts to God's ends, thereby cheating the fiend—Sst! There sounds vespers! Plena gratia, ave Virgo."

But it did not speak. Long hours, long weeks, the doctor mirabilis watched his creation, but iron lips were silent and the iron eyes dull, and no voice but the great man's own sounded in his monkish cell, nor was there ever an answer to all the questions that he asked—until one day when he sat surveying his work, composing a letter to Duns Scotus in distant Cologne—one day—

"Time is!" said the image, and smiled benignly.

The Friar looked up. "Time is, indeed," he echoed. "Time it is that you give utterance, and to some assertion less obvious than that time is. For of course time is, else there were nothing at all. Without time—"

"Time was!" rumbled the image, still smiling, but sternly, at the statue of Draco.

"Indeed time was," said the monk, "Time was, is, and will be, for time is that medium in which events occur. Matter exists in space, but events—

The image smiled no longer. "Time is past!" it roared in tones deep as the cathedral bell outside, and burst into ten thousand pieces.

"There," said old Haskel van Manderpootz, shutting the book, "is my classical authority in this experiment. This story, overlaid as it is with medieval myth and legend proves that Roger Bacon himself attempted the experiment and failed." He shook a long finger at me. "Yet do not get the impression, Dixon, that Friar Bacon was not a great man. He was—extremely great, in fact; he lighted the torch that his namesake Francis Bacon took up four centuries later, and that now van Manderpootz rekindles."

I stared in silence.

"Indeed," resumed the Professor, "Roger Bacon might almost be called a thirteenth-century van Manderpootz, or van Manderpootz a twenty-first-century Roger Bacon. His *Opus Majus, Opus Minor,* and *Opus Tertium*—"

"What," I interrupted impatiently, "has all this to do with—that?" I indicated the clumsy metal robot standing in the corner of the laboratory.

"Don't interrupt!" snapped van Manderpootz.

At this point I fell out of my chair. The mass of metal had ejaculated something like "*A-a-gh-rasp!*" and had lunged a single pace toward the window, arms upraised. "What the devil!" I sputtered as the thing dropped its arms and returned stolidly to its place.

"A car must have passed in the alley," said van Manderpootz indifferently. "Now as I was saying, Roger Bacon—"

I ceased to listen. When van Manderpootz is determined to finish a statement, interruptions are worse than futile. As an ex-student of his, I know. So I permitted my thoughts to drift to certain personal problems of my own, particularly Tips Alva, who was the most pressing problem of the moment. Yes, I mean Tips Alva the 'vision dancer, the little blonde imp who entertains on the Yerba Mate hour for that Brazilian company. Chorus girls, dancers, and television stars are a weakness of mine; maybe it indicates that there's a latent artistic soul in me. Maybe.

I'm Dixon Wells, you know, scion of the N. J. Wells Corporation, Engineers Extraordinary. I'm supposed to be an engineer myself; I say supposed, because in the seven years since my graduation, my father hasn't given me much opportunity to prove it. He has a strong sense of the value of time, and I'm cursed with the unenviable quality of being late to anything and for everything. He even asserts that the occasional designs I submit are late Jacobean, but that isn't fair. They're Post-Romanesque.

Old N. J. also objects to my penchant for ladies of the stage and 'vision screen, and periodically threatens to cut my allowance, though that's supposed to be a salary. It's inconvenient to be so dependent, and sometimes I regret that unfortunate market crash of 2009 that wiped out my own money, although it did keep me from marrying Whimsy White, and van Manderpootz, through his subjunctivisor, succeeded in proving that that would have been a catastrophe. But it turned out nearly as much of a disaster anyway, as far as my feelings were concerned. It took me months to forget Joanna Caldwell and her silvery eyes. Just another instance when I was a little late.

Van Manderpootz himself is my old Physics Professor, head of the Department of Newer Physics at N. Y. U., and a genius, but a bit eccentric. Judge for yourself.

"And that's the thesis," he said suddenly, interrupting my thoughts.

"Eh? Oh, of course. But what's that grinning robot got to do with it?"

He purpled. "I've just told you!" he roared. "Idiot! Imbecile! To dream while van Manderpootz talks! Get out! Get out!"

I got. It was late anyway, so late that I overslept more than usual in the morning, and suffered more than the usual lecture on promptness from my father at the office.

Van Manderpootz had forgotten his anger by the next time I dropped in for an evening. The robot still stood in the corner near the window, and I lost no time asking its purpose.

"It's just a toy I had some of the students construct," he explained. "There's a screen of photoelectric cells behind the right eye, so connected that when a certain pattern is thrown on them, it activates the mechanism. The thing's plugged into the light-circuit, but it really ought to run on gasoline."

"Why?"

"Well, the pattern it's set for is the shape of an automobile. See here." He picked up a card from his desk, and cut in the outlines of a streamlined car like those of that year. "Since only one eye is used," he continued, "the thing can't tell the difference between a full-sized vehicle at a distance and this small outline nearby. It has no sense of perspective."

He held the bit of cardboard before the eye of the mechanism. Instantly came its roar of "A-a-gh-rasp!" and it leaped forward a single pace, arms upraised. Van Manderpootz withdrew the card, and again the thing relapsed stolidly into its place.

"What the devil!" I exclaimed. "What's it for?"

"Does van Manderpootz ever do work without reason back of it? I use it as a demonstration in my seminar."

"To demonstrate what?"

"The power of reason," said van Manderpootz solemnly.

"How? And why ought it to work on gasoline instead of electric power?"

"One question at a time, Dixon. You have missed the grandeur of van Manderpootz's concept. See here, this creature, imperfect as it is, represents the predatory machine. It is the mechanical parallel of the tiger, lurking in its jungle to leap on living prey. This monster's jungle is the city; its prey is the unwary machine that follows the trails called streets. Understand?"

"No."

"Well, picture this automaton, not as it is, but as van Manderpootz could make it if he wished. It lurks gigantic in the shadows of buildings; it creeps stealthily through dark alleys; it skulks on deserted streets, with its gasoline engine purring quietly. Then—an unsuspecting automobile flashes its image on the screen behind its eyes. It leaps. It seizes its prey, swinging it in steel arms to its steel jaws. Through the metal throat of its victim crash steel teeth; the blood of its prey—the gasoline, that is—is drained into its stomach, or its gas-tank. With renewed strength it flings away the husk and prowls on to seek other prey. It is the machine-carnivore, the tiger of mechanics."

I suppose I stared dumbly. It occurred to me suddenly that the brain of the great van Manderpootz was cracking. "What the—?" I gasped.

"That," he said blandly, "is but a concept. I have many another use for the toy. I can prove anything with it, anything I wish."

"You can? Then prove something."

"Name your proposition, Dixon."

I hesitated, nonplussed.

"Come!" he said impatiently. "Look here; I will prove that anarchy is the ideal government, or that Heaven and Hell are the same place, or that—"

"Prove that!" I said. "About Heaven and Hell."

"Easily. First we will endow my robot with intelligence. I add a mechanical memory by means of the old Cushman delayed valve; I add a mathematical sense with any of the calculating machines; I give it a voice and a vocabulary with the magnetic-impulse wire phonograph. Now the point I make is this: Granted an intelligent machine, does it not follow that every other machine constructed like it must have the identical qualities? Would not each robot given the same insides have exactly the same character?"

"No!" I snapped. "Human beings can't make two machines exactly alike. There'd be tiny differences; one would react quicker than others, or one would prefer Fox Airsplitters as prey, while another reacted most vigorously to Carnecars. In other words, they'd have—individuality!" I grinned in triumph.

"My point exactly," observed van Manderpootz. "You admit, then, that this individuality is the result of imperfect workmanship. If our means of manufacture were perfect, all robots would be identical, and this *individuality* would not exist. Is that true?"

"I—suppose so."

"Then I argue that our own individuality is due to our falling short of perfection. All of us—even van Manderpootz—are individuals only because we are not perfect. Were we perfect, each of us would be exactly like everyone else. True?"

"Uh—yes."

"But Heaven, by definition, is a place where all is perfect. Therefore, in Heaven everybody is exactly like everybody else; and *therefore*, everybody is thoroughly and completely bored. There is no torture like boredom, Dixon, and—Well, have I proved my point?"

I was floored. "But-about anarchy, then?" I stammered.

"Simple. Very simple for van Manderpootz. See here; with a perfect nation—that is, one whose individuals are all exactly alike, which I have just proved to constitute perfection—with a perfect nation, I repeat, laws and government are utterly superfluous. If everybody reacts to stimuli in the same way, laws are quite useless, obviously. If, for instance, a certain event occurred that might lead to a declaration of war, why, everybody in such a nation would vote for war at the same instant. Therefore government is unnecessary, and therefore anarchy is the ideal government, since it is the proper government for a perfect race." He paused. "I shall now prove that anarchy is not the ideal government—"

"Never mind!" I begged. "Who am I to argue with van Mander-pootz? But is that the whole purpose of this dizzy robot? Just a basis for logic?" The mechanism replied with its usual rasp as it leaped toward some vagrant car beyond the window.

"Isn't that enough?" growled van Manderpootz. "However"—his voice dropped—"I have even a greater destiny in mind. My boy, van Manderpootz has solved the riddle of the universe!" He paused impressively. "Well, why don't you say something?"

"Uh!" I gasped. "It's—uh-marvelous!"

"Not for van Manderpootz," he said modestly.

"But-what is it?"

"Eh—oh!" He frowned. "Well, I'll tell you, Dixon. You won't understand, but I'll tell you." He coughed. "As far back as the early twentieth century," he resumed, "Einstein proved that energy is particular. Matter is also particular, and now van Manderpootz adds that space and time are discrete!" He glared at me.

"Energy and matter are particular," I murmured, "and space and time are discrete! How very moral of them!"

"Imbecile!" he blazed. "To pun on the words of van Mander-pootz! You know very well that I mean particular and discrete in the physical sense. Matter is composed of particles, therefore it is particular. The particles of matter are called electrons, protons, and neutrons, and those of energy, quanta. I now add two others, the particles of space I call spations, those of time, chronons."

"And what in the devil," I asked, "are particles of space and time?"

"Just what I said!" snapped van Manderpootz. "Exactly as the particles of matter are the smallest pieces of matter that can exist, just as there is no such thing as a half of an electron, or for that matter, half a quantum, so the chronon is the smallest possible fragment of time, and the spation the smallest possible bit of space. Neither time nor space is continuous; each is composed of these infinitely tiny fragments."

"Well, how long is a chronon in time? How big is a spation in space?"

"Van Manderpootz has even measured that. A chronon is the length of time it takes one quantum of energy to push one electron from one electronic orbit to the next. There can obviously be no shorter interval of time, since an electron is the smallest unit of matter and the quantum the smallest unit of energy. And a spation is the exact volume of a proton. Since nothing smaller exists, that is obviously the smallest unit of space."

"Well, look here," I argued. "Then what's in between these particles of space and time? If time moves, as you say, in jerks of one chronon each, what's between the jerks?"

"Ah!" said the great van Manderpootz. "Now we come to the heart of the matter. In between the particles of space and time, must obviously be something that is neither space, time, matter, nor energy. A hundred years ago Shapley anticipated van Manderpootz in a vague way when he announced his cosmo-plasma, the great underlying matrix in which time and space and the universe are embedded. Now van Manderpootz announces the ultimate unit, the universal particle, the focus in which matter, energy, time, and space meet, the unit from which electrons, protons, neutrons, quanta, spations, and chronons are all constructed. The riddle of the universe is solved by what I have chosen to name the cosmon." His blue eyes bored into me.

"Magnificent!" I said feebly, knowing that some such word was expected. "But what good is it?"

"What good is it?" he roared. "It provides—or will provide, once I work out a few details—the means of turning energy into time, or space into matter, or time into space, or—" He sputtered into silence. "Fool!" he muttered. "To think that you studied under the tutelage of van Manderpootz. I blush; I actually blush!"

One couldn't have told it if he were blushing. His face was always rubicund enough. "Colossal!" I said hastily. "What a mind!"

That mollified him. "But that's not all," he proceeded. "'Van Manderpootz never stops short of perfection. I now announce the unit particle of thought—the psychon!"

This was a little too much. I simply stared.

"Well may you be dumbfounded," said van Manderpootz. "I presume you are aware, by hearsay at least, of the existence of thought. The psychon, the unit of thought, is one electron plus one proton, which are bound so as to form one neutron, embedded in one cosmon, occupying a volume of one spation, driven by one quantum for a period of one chronon. Very obvious; very simple."

"Oh, very!" I echoed. "Even I can see that that equals one psychon."

He beamed. "Excellent! Excellent!"

"And what," I asked, "will you do with the psychons?"

"Ah," he rumbled. "Now we go even past the heart of the matter, and return to Isaak here." He jammed a thumb toward the robot. "Here I will create Roger Bacon's mechanical head. In the skull of this clumsy creature will rest such intelligence as not even van Manderpootz—I should say, as only van Manderpootz—can conceive. It remains merely to construct my idealizator."

"Your idealizator?"

"Of course. Have I not just proven that thoughts are as real as matter, energy, time, or space? Have I not just demonstrated that one can be transformed, through the cosmon, into any other? My idealizator is the means of transforming psychons to quanta, just as, for instance, a Crookes tube or X-ray tube transforms matter to electrons. I will make your thoughts visible! And not your thoughts as they are in that numb brain of yours, but in ideal form. Do you see? The psychons of your mind are the same as those from any other mind, just as all electrons are identical, whether from gold or iron. Yes! Your psychons"—his voice quavered—"are identical with those from the mind of van Manderpootz!" He paused, shaken.

"Actually?" I gasped.

"Actually. Fewer in number, of course, but identical. Therefore, my idealizator shows your thought released from the impress of your personality. It shows it—ideal!"

Well, I was late to the office again.

A week later I thought of van Manderpootz. Tips was on tour somewhere, and I didn't dare take anyone else out because I'd tried it once before and she'd heard about it. So, with nothing to do, I finally dropped around to the professor's quarters, found him missing, and eventually located him in his laboratory at the Physics Building. He was puttering around the table that had once held that damned subjunctivisor of his, but now it supported an indescribable mess of tubes and tangled wires, and as its most striking feature, a circular plane mirror etched with a grating of delicately scratched lines.

"Good evening, Dixon," he rumbled.

I echoed his greeting. "What's that?" I asked.

"My idealizator. A rough model, much too clumsy to fit into Isaak's iron skull. I'm just finishing it to try it out." He turned glittering blue eyes on me. "How fortunate that you're here. It will save the world a terrible risk."

"A risk?"

"Yes. It is obvious that too long an exposure to the device will extract too many psychons, and leave the subject's mind in a sort of moronic condition. I was about to accept the risk, but I see now that it would be woefully unfair to the world to endanger the mind of van Manderpootz. But you are at hand, and will do very well."

"Oh, no I won't!"

"Come, come!" he said, frowning. "The danger is negligible. In fact, I doubt whether the device will be able to extract any psychons from your mind. At any rate, you will be perfectly safe for a period of at least half an hour. I, with a vastly more productive mind, could doubtless stand the strain indefinitely, but my responsibility to the world is too great to chance it until I have tested the machine on someone else. You should be proud of the honor."

"Well, I'm not!" But my protest was feeble, and after all, despite his overbearing mannerisms, I knew van Manderpootz liked me, and I was positive he would not have exposed me to any real danger. In the end I found myself seated before the table facing the etched mirror.

"Put your face against the barrel," said van Manderpootz, indicating a stovepipe-like tube. "That's merely to cut off extraneous sights, so that you can see only the mirror. Go ahead, I tell you! It's no more than the barrel of a telescope or microscope."

I complied. "Now what?" I asked.

"What do you see?"

"My own face in the mirror."

"Of course. Now I start the reflector rotating." There was a faint whir, and the mirror was spinning smoothly, still with only a slightly blurred image of myself. "Listen, now," continued van Manderpootz. "Here is what you are to do. You will think of a generic noun. 'House,' for instance. If you think of house, you will see, not an individual house, but your ideal house, the house of all your dreams and desires. If you think of a horse, you will see what your mind conceives as the perfect horse, such a horse as dream and longing create. Do you understand? Have you chosen a topic?"

"Yes." After all, I was only twenty-eight; the noun I had chosen was—girl.

"Good," said the professor. "I turn on the current."

There was a blue radiance behind the mirror. My own face still stared back at me from the spinning surface, but something was forming behind it, building up, growing. I blinked; when I focused my eyes again, it was—she was—there.

Lord! I can't begin to describe her. I don't even know if I saw her clearly the first time. It was like looking into another world and seeing the embodiment of all longings, dreams, aspirations, and ideals. It was so poignant a sensation that it crossed the borderline into pain. It was—well, exquisite torture or agonized delight. It was at once unbearable and irresistible.

But I gazed. I had to. There was a haunting familiarity about the impossibly beautiful features. I had seen the face—somewhere—sometime. In dreams? No; I realized suddenly what was the source of that familiarity. This was no living woman, but a synthesis. Her nose was the tiny, impudent one of Whimsy White at her loveliest moment; her lips were the perfect bow of Tips Alva; her silvery eyes and dusky velvet hair were those of Joan Caldwell. But the aggregate, the sum total, the face in the mirror—that was none of these; it was a face impossibly, incredibly, outrageously beautiful.

Only her face and throat were visible, and the features, were cool, expressionless, and still as a carving. I wondered suddenly if she could smile, and with the thought, she did. If she had been beautiful before, now her beauty flamed to such a pitch that it was—well, insolent; it was an affront to be so lovely; it was insulting. I felt a wild surge of anger that the image before me should flaunt such beauty, and yet be—*non-existent!* It was deception, cheating, fraud, a promise that could never be fulfilled.

Anger died in the depths of that fascination. I wondered what the rest of her was like, and instantly she moved gracefully back until her full figure was visible. I must be a prude at heart, for she wasn't wearing the usual cuirass-and-shorts of that year, but an iridescent four-paneled costume that all but concealed her dainty knees. But her form was slim and erect as a column of cigarette

242

smoke in still air, and I knew that she could dance like a fragment of mist on water. And with that thought she did move, dropping in a low curtsy, and looking up with the faintest possible flush crimsoning the curve of her throat. Yes, I must be a prude at heart; despite Tips Alva and Whimsey White and the rest, my ideal was modest.

It was unbelievable that the mirror was simply giving back my thoughts. She seemed as real as myself, and—after all—I guess she was. As real as myself, no more, no less, because she was part of my own mind. And at this point I realized that van Manderpootz was shaking me and bellowing, "Your time's up. Come out of it! Your half-hour's up!"

"O-o-o-o-o-oh!" I groaned.

"How do you feel?" he snapped.

"Feel? All right-physically." I looked up.

Concern flickered in his blue eyes. "What's the cube root of 4913?" he crackled sharply.

I've always been quick at figures. "It's—uh—17," I returned dully. "Why the devil—?"

"You're all right mentally," he announced. "Now—why were you sitting there like a dummy for half an hour? My idealizator must have worked, as is only natural for a van Manderpootz creation, but what were you thinking of?"

"I thought—I thought of 'girl'," I groaned.

He snorted. "Hah! You would, you idiot! 'House' or 'horse', wasn't good enough; you had to pick something with emotional connotations. Well, you can start right in forgetting her, because she doesn't exist."

I couldn't give up hope as easily as that. "But can't you—can't you—" I didn't even know what I meant to ask.

"Van Manderpootz," he announced, "is a mathematician, not a magician. Do you expect me to materialize an ideal for you?" When I had no reply but a groan, he continued. "Now I think it safe enough to try the device myself. I shall take—let's see—the thought 'man.' I shall see what the superman looks like, since the ideal of van Manderpootz can be nothing less than superman." He seated himself. "Turn that switch," he said. "Now!"

I did. The tubes glowed into low blue light. I watched dully, disinterestedly; nothing held any attraction for me after that image of the ideal.

"Huh!" said van Manderpootz suddenly. "Turn it on, I say! I see nothing but my own reflection."

I stared, then burst into a hollow laugh. The mirror was spinning; the banks of tubes were glowing; the device was operating.

Van Manderpootz raised his face, a little redder than usual. I laughed half hysterically. "After all," he said huffily, "one might have a lower ideal of man than van Manderpootz. I see nothing nearly so humorous as your situation."

The laughter died. I went miserably home, spent half the remainder of the night in morose contemplation, smoked nearly two packs of cigarettes, and didn't get to the office at all the next day.

Tips Alva got back to town for a weekend broadcast, but I didn't even bother to see her, just phoned her and told her I was sick. I guess my face lent credibility to the story, for she was duly sympathetic, and her face in the phone screen was quite anxious. Even at that, I couldn't keep my eyes away from her lips because, except for a bit too lustrous make-up, they were the lips of the ideal. But they weren't enough; they just weren't enough.

Old N. J. began to worry again. I couldn't sleep late of mornings any more, and after missing that one day, I kept getting down earlier and earlier until one morning I was only ten minutes late. He called me in at once.

"Look here, Dixon," he said. "Have you been to a doctor recently?"

"I'm not sick," I said listlessly.

"Then for Heaven's sake, marry the girl! I don't care what chorus she kicks in, marry her and act like a human being again."

"I can't."

"Oh. She's already married, eh?"

Well, I couldn't tell him she didn't exist. I couldn't say I was in love with a vision, a dream, an ideal. He thought I was a little crazy, anyway, so I just muttered "Yeah," and didn't argue when he said gruffly: "Then you'll get over it. Take a vacation. Take two vacations. You might as well for all the good you are around here."

I didn't leave New York; I lacked the energy. I just mooned around the city for a while, avoiding my friends, and dreaming of the impossible beauty of the face in the mirror. And by and by the longing to see that vision of perfection once more began to become overpowering. I don't suppose anyone except me can understand the lure of that memory; the face, you see, had been my ideal, my concept of perfection. One sees beautiful woman here and there in the world; one falls in love—but always, no matter how great their beauty or how deep one's love, they fall short in some degree of the secret vision of the ideal. But not the mirrored face; she was my ideal, and therefore, whatever imperfections she might have had in the minds of others, in my eyes she had none. None, that is, save the terrible one of being only an ideal, and therefore unattainable—but that is a fault inherent in all perfection.

It was a matter of days before I yielded. Common sense told me it was futile, even foolhardy, to gaze again on the vision of perfect desirability. I fought against the hunger, but I fought hopelessly, and was not at all surprised to find myself one evening rapping on van Manderpootz's door in the University Club. He wasn't there; I'd been hoping he wouldn't be, since it gave me an excuse to seek him in his laboratory in the Physics Building to which I would have dragged him anyway.

There I found him, writing some sort of notations on the table that held the idealizator. "Hello, Dixon," he said. "Did it ever occur to you that the ideal university cannot exist? Naturally not, since it must be composed of perfect students and perfect educators, in which case the former could have nothing to learn and the latter, therefore, nothing to teach."

What interest had I in the perfect university and its inability to exist? My whole being was desolate over the nonexistence of another ideal. "Professor," I said tensely, "may I use that—that thing of yours again? I want to—uh—see something."

My voice must have disclosed the situation, for van Manderpootz looked up sharply. "So!" he snapped. "So you disregarded my advice! Forget her, I said. Forget her because she doesn't exist."

"But—I can't! Once more, Professor—only once more!"

He shrugged, but his blue, metallic eyes were a little softer than usual. After all, for some inconceivable reason, he likes me. "Well, Dixon," he said, "you're of age and supposed to be of mature intelligence. I tell you that this is a very stupid request, and van Manderpootz always knows what he's talking about. If you want to stupefy yourself with the, opium of impossible dreams, go ahead. This is the last chance you'll have, for tomorrow the idealizator of van Manderpootz goes into the Bacon head of Isaak there. I shall shift the oscillators so that the psychons, instead of becoming light quanta, emerge as an electron flow—a current which will actuate Isaak's vocal apparatus and come out as speech." He paused musingly. "Van Manderpootz will bear the voice of the ideal. Of course Isaak can return only what psychons he receives from the brain of the operator, but just as the image in the mirror, the thoughts will have lost their human impress, and the words will be those of an ideal." he perceived that I wasn't listening, I suppose. "Go ahead, imbeciles!" he grunted.

I did. The glory that I hungered after flamed slowly into being, incredible in loveliness, and somehow, unbelievably, even more beautiful than on that other occasion. I know why now; long afterwards, van Manderpootz explained that the very fact that I had seen an ideal once before had altered my ideal, raised it to a higher level. With that face among my memories, my concept of perfection was different than it had been.

So I gazed and hungered. Readily and instantly the being in the mirror responded to my thoughts with smile and movement. When I thought of love, her eyes blazed with such tenderness that it seemed as if—I, Dixon Wells—were part of those pairs who had made the great romances of the world, Heloise and Abelard, Tristram and Isolde, Aucassin and Nicolette. It was like the thrust of a dagger to feel van Manderpootz shaking me, to hear his gruff voice calling, "Out of it! Out of it! Time's up."

I groaned and dropped my face on my hands. The Professor had been right, of course; this insane repetition had only intensified an unfulfillable longing, and had made a bad mess ten times as bad. Then I heard him muttering behind me. "Strange!" he murmured. "In fact, fantastic. Oedipus—Oedipus of the magazine covers and billboards."

I looked dully around. He was standing behind me, squinting, apparently, into the spinning mirror beyond the end of the black tube. "Hub?" I grunted wearily.

"That face," he said. "Very queer. You must have seen her features on a hundred magazines, on a thousand billboards, on count-less 'vision broadcasts. The oedipus complex in a curious form."

"Eh? Could you see her?"

"Of course!" he grunted. "Didn't I say a dozen times that the psychons are transmuted to perfectly ordinary quanta of visible light? If you could see her, why not I?"

"But—what about billboards and all?"

"That face," said the professor slowly. "It's somewhat idealized, of course, and certain details are wrong. Her eyes aren't that pallid silver-blue you imagined; they're green, sea-green, emerald-colored."

"What the devil," I asked hoarsely, "are you talking about?"

"About the face in the mirror. It happens to be, Dixon, a close approximation of the features of de Lisle d'Agrion, the Dragon Fly!"

"You mean—she's real? She exists? She lives? She—"

"Wait a moment, Dixon. She's real enough, but in accordance with your habit, you're a little late. About twenty-five years too late, I should say. She must now be somewhere in the fifties—let's see-fifty-three, I think. But during your very early childhood, you must have seen her face pictured everywhere, de Lisle d'Agrion, the Dragon Fly."

I could only gulp. That blow was devastating.

"You see," continued van Manderpootz, "one's ideals are implanted very early. That's why you continually fall in love with girls who possess one or another feature that reminds you of her, her hair, her nose, her mouth, her eyes. Very simple, but rather curious."

"Curious!" I blazed. "Curious, you say! Every time I look into one of your damned contraptions I find myself in love with a myth! A girl who's dead, or married, or unreal, or turned into an old woman! Curious, eh? Damned funny, isn't it?"

"Just a moment," said the professor placidly. "It happens, Dixon, that she has a daughter. What's more, Denise resembles her mother. And what's more, she's arriving in New York next week to study American letters at the University here. She writes, you see."

That was too much for immediate comprehension. "How—how do you know?" I gasped.

It was one of the few times I have seen the colossal blandness of van Manderpootz ruffled. He reddened a trifle, and said slowly, "It also happens, Dixon, that many years ago in Amsterdam, Haskel van

Manderpootz and de Lisle d'Agrion were—very friendly—more than friendly, I might say, but for the fact that two such powerful personalities as the Dragon Fly and van Manderpootz were always at odds." He frowned. "I was almost her second husband. She's had seven, I believe; Denise is the daughter of her third."

"Why—why is she coming here?"

"Because," he said with dignity, "van Manderpootz is here. I am still a friend of de Lisle's." He turned and bent over the complex device on the table. "Hand me that wrench," he ordered. "Tonight I dismantle this, and tomorrow start reconstructing it for Isaak's head."

But when, the following week, I rushed eagerly back to van Manderpootz's laboratory, the idealizator was still in place. The professor greeted me with a humorous twist to what was visible of his bearded mouth. "Yes, it's still here," he said, gesturing at the device. "I've decided to build an entirely new one for Isaak, and besides, this one has afforded me considerable amusement. Furthermore, in the words of Oscar Wilde, who am I to tamper with a work of genius. After all, the mechanism is the product of the great van Manderpootz."

He was deliberately tantalizing me. He knew that I hadn't come to hear him discourse on Isaak, or even on the incomparable van Manderpootz. Then he smiled and softened, and turned to the little inner office adjacent, the room where Isaak stood in metal austerity. "Denise!" he called. "Come here."

I don't know exactly what I expected, but I do know that the breath left me as the girl entered. She wasn't exactly my image of the ideal, of course; she was perhaps the merest trifle slimmer, and her eyes—well, they must have been much like those of de Lisle d'Agrion, for they were the clearest emerald I've ever seen. They were impudently direct eyes, and I could imagine why van Manderpootz and the Dragon Fly might have been forever quarreling; that was easy to imagine, looking into the eyes of the Dragon Fly's daughter.

Nor was Denise, apparently, quite as femininely modest as my image of perfection. She wore the extremely unconcealing costume of the day, which covered, I suppose, about as much of her as one of the one-piece swimming suits of the middle years of the twentieth century. She gave an impression, not so much of fleeting grace as of litheness and supple strength, an air of independence, frankness, and—I say it again—impudence.

"Well!" she said coolly as van Manderpootz presented me. "So you're the scion of the N. J. Wells Corporation. Every now and then your escapades enliven the Paris Sunday supplements. Wasn't it you who snared a million dollars in the market so you could ask Whimsy White?"

I rushed. "That was greatly exaggerated," I said hastily, "and anyway I lost it before we—uh—before I—"

"Not before you made somewhat of a fool of yourself, I believe," she finished sweetly.

Well, that's the sort she was. If she hadn't been so infernally lovely, if she hadn't looked so much like the face in the mirror, I'd have flared up, said "Pleased to have met you," and never have seen her again. But I couldn't get angry, not when she had the dusky hair, the perfect lips, the saucy nose of the being who to me was ideal.

So I did see her again, and several times again. In fact, I suppose I occupied most of her time between the few literary courses she was taking, and little by little I began to see that in other respects besides the physical she was not so far from my ideal. Beneath her impudence was honesty, and frankness, and, despite herself, sweetness, so that even allowing for the head-start I'd had, I fell in love pretty hastily. And what's more, I knew she was beginning to reciprocate.

That was the situation when I called for her one noon and took her over to van Manderpootz's laboratory. We were to lunch with him at the University Club, but we found him occupied in directing some experiment in the big laboratory beyond his personal one, untangling some sort of mess that his staff had blundered into. So Denise and I wandered back into the smaller room, perfectly content to be alone together. I simply could rot feel hungry in her presence; just talking to her was enough of a substitute for food.

"I'm going to be a good writer," she was saying musingly. "Some day, Dick, I'm going to be famous."

Well, everyone knows how correct that prediction was. I agreed with her instantly.

She smiled. "You're nice, Dick," she said. "Very nice."

"Very?"

"Very!" she said emphatically. Then her green eyes strayed over to the table that held the idealizator. "What crack-brained contraption of Uncle Haskel's is that?" she asked.

I explained, rather inaccurately, I'm afraid, but no ordinary engineer can follow the ramifications of a van Manderpootz conception. Nevertheless, Denise caught the gist of it and her eyes glowed emerald fire.

"It's fascinating!" she exclaimed. She rose and moved over to the table. "I'm going to try it."

"Not without the professor, you won't! It might be dangerous."

That was the wrong thing to say. The green eyes glowed brighter as she cast me a whimsical glance. "But I am," she said. "Dick, I'm going to—see my ideal man!" She laughed softly.

I was panicky. Suppose her ideal turned out tall and dark and powerful, instead of short and sandy-haired and a bit-well, chubby, as I am. "No!" I said vehemently. "I won't let you!"

She laughed again. I suppose she read my consternation, for she said softly, "Don't be silly, Dick." She sat down, placed her face against the opening of the barrel, and commanded, "Turn it on."

I couldn't refuse her. I set the mirror whirling, then switched on the bank of tubes. Then immediately I stepped behind her, squinting into what was visible of the flashing mirror, where a face was forming, slowly-vaguely.

I thrilled. Surely the hair of the image was sandy. I even fancied now that I could trace a resemblance to my own features. Perhaps Denise sensed something similar, for she suddenly withdrew her eyes from the tube and looked up with a faintly embarrassed flush, a thing most unusual for her.

"Ideals are dull!" she said. "I want a real thrill. Do you know what I'm going to see? I'm going to visualize ideal horror. That's what I'll do. I'm going to see absolute horror!"

"Oh, no you're not!" I gasped. "That's a terribly dangerous idea." Off in the other room I heard the voice of van Manderpootz: "Dixon!"

"Dangerous—bosh!" Denise retorted. "I'm a writer, Dick. All this means to me is material. It's just experience, and I want it."

Van Manderpootz again. "Dixon! Dixon! Come here." I said, "Listen, Denise. I'll be right back. Don't try anything until I'm here—please!"

I dashed into the big laboratory. Van Manderpootz, was facing a cowed group of assistants, quite apparently in extreme awe of the great man.

"Hah, Dixon!" he rasped. "Tell these fools what an Emmerich valve is, and why it won't operate in a free electronic stream. Let 'em see that even an ordinary engineer knows that much."

Well, an ordinary engineer doesn't, but it happened that I did. Not that I'm particularly exceptional as an engineer, but I did happen to know that because a year or two before I'd done some work on the big tidal turbines up in Maine, where they have to use Emmerich valves to guard against electrical leakage from the tremendous potentials in their condensers. So I started explaining, and van Manderpootz kept interpolating sarcasms about his staff, and when I finally finished, I suppose I'd been in there about half an hour. And then—I remembered Denise!

I left van Manderpootz staring as I rushed back, and sure enough, there was the girl with her face pressed against the barrel, and her hands gripping the table edge. Her features were hidden, of course, but there was something about her strained position, her white knuckles—

"Denise!" I yelled. "Are you all right? Denise!"

She didn't move. I stuck my face in between the mirror and the end of the barrel and peered up the tube at her visage, and what I saw left me all but stunned. Have you ever seen stark, mad, infinite terror on a human face? That was what I saw in Denise's—inexpressible, unbearable horror, worse than the fear of death could ever be. Her green eyes were widened so that the whites showed around them; her perfect lips were contorted, her whole face strained into a mask of sheer terror.

I rushed for the switch, but in passing I caught a single glimpse of–of what showed in the mirror. Incredible! Obscene, terror-laden, horrifying things—there just aren't words for them. There are no words.

Denise didn't move as the tubes darkened. I raised her face from the barrel and when she glimpsed me she moved. She flung herself out of that chair and away, facing me with such mad terror that I halted.

"Denise!" I cried. "It's just Dick. Look, Denise!"

But as I moved toward her, she uttered a choking scream, her eyes dulled, her knees gave, and she fainted. Whatever she had seen, it must have been appalling to the uttermost, for Denise was not the sort to faint.

It was a week later that I sat facing van Manderpootz in his little inner office. The grey metal figure of Isaak was missing, and the table that had held the idealizator was empty.

"Yes," said van Manderpootz. "I've dismantled it. One of van Manderpootz's few mistakes was to leave it around where a pair of incompetents like you and Denise could get to it. It seems that I continually overestimate the intelligence of others. I suppose I tend to judge them by the brain of van Manderpootz."

I said nothing. I was thoroughly disheartened and depressed, and whatever the professor said about my lack of intelligence, I felt it justified.

"Hereafter," resumed van Manderpootz, "I shall credit nobody except myself with intelligence, and will doubtless be much more nearly correct." He waved a hand at Isaak's vacant corner. "Not even the Bacon head," he continued. "I've abandoned that project, because, when you come right down to it, what need has the world of a mechanical brain when it already has that of van Manderpootz?"

"Professor," I burst out suddenly, "why won't they let me see Denise? I've been at the hospital every day, and they let me into her room just once—just once, and that, time she went right into a fit of hysterics. Why? Is she-?" I gulped.

"She's recovering nicely, Dixon."

"Then why can't I see her?"

"Well," said van Manderpootz placidly, "it's like this. You see, when you rushed into the laboratory there, you made the mistake of pushing your face in front of the barrel. She saw your features right in the midst of all those horrors she had called up. Do you see? From then on your face was associated in her mind with the whole hell's brew in the mirror. She can't even look at you without seeing all of it again."

"Good—God!" I gasped. "But she'll get over it, won't she? She'll forget that part of it?"

"The young psychiatrist who attends her—a bright chap, by the way, with a number of my own ideas—believes she'll be quite over it in a couple of months. But personally, Dixon, I don't think she'll ever welcome the sight of your face, though I myself have seen uglier visages somewhere or other."

I ignored that. "Lord!" I groaned. "What a mess!" I rose to depart, and then—then I knew what inspiration means! "Listen!" I said, spinning back. "Listen, professor Why can't you get her back here and let her visualize the ideally beautiful? And then stick my face into that" Enthusiasm grew. "It can't fail!" I cried. "At the worst, it'll cancel that other memory. It's marvelous!"

"But as usual," said van Manderpootz, "a little late."

"Late? Why? You can put up your idealizator again. You'd do that much, wouldn't you?"

"Van Manderpootz," he observed, "is the very soul of generosity. I'd do it gladly, but it's still a little late, Dixon. You see, she married the bright young psychiatrist this noon."

Well, I've a date with Tips Alva tonight, and I'm going to be late for it, just as late as I please. And then I'm going to do nothing but stare at her lips all evening.

The Point of View

"I am too modest!" snapped the great Haskel van Manderpootz, pacing irritably about the limited area of his private laboratory, glaring at me the while. "That is the trouble. I undervalue my own achievements, and thereby permit petty imitators like Corveille to influence the committee and win the Morell prize."

"But," I said soothingly, "you've won the Morell physics award half a dozen times, professor. They can't very well give it to you every year."

"Why not, since it is plain that I deserve it?" bristled the professor. "Understand, Dixon, that I do not regret my modesty, even though it permits conceited fools like Corveille, who have infinitely less reason than I for conceit, to win awards that mean nothing save prizes for successful bragging. Bah! To grant an award for research along such obvious lines that I neglected to mention them, thinking that even a Morell judge would appreciate their obviousness! Research on the psychon, eh! Who discovered the psychon? Who but van Manderpootz?"

"Wasn't that what you got last year's award for?" I asked consolingly. "And after all, isn't this modesty, this lack of jealousy on your part, a symbol of greatness of character?"

"True—true!" said the great van Manderpootz, mollified. "Had such an affront been committed against a lesser man than myself, he would doubtless have entered a bitter complaint against the judges. But not I. Anyway, I know from experience that it wouldn't do any good. And besides, despite his greatness, van Manderpootz is as modest and shrinking as a violet." At this point he paused, and his broad red face tried to look violet-like.

I suppressed a smile. I knew the eccentric genius of old from the days when I had been Dixon Wells, undergraduate student of engineering, and had taken a course in Newer Physics (that is, in Relativity) under the famous professor. For some unguessable reason, he had taken a fancy to me, and as a result, I had been involved in several of his experiments since graduation. There was the affair of the subjunctivisor, for instance, and also that of the idealizator; in the first of these episodes I had suffered the indignity of falling in love with a girl two weeks after she was apparently dead, and in the second, the equal or greater indignity of falling in love with a girl who didn't exist, never had existed, and never would exist-in other words, with an ideal. Perhaps I'm a little susceptible to feminine charms, or rather, perhaps I used to be, for since the disaster of the idealizator, I have grimly relegated such follies to the past, much to the disgust of various 'vision entertainers, singers, dancers, and the like.

So of late I had been spending my days very seriously trying wholeheartedly to get to the office on time just once, so that I could refer to it next time my father accused me of never getting anywhere on time. I hadn't succeeded yet, but fortunately the N. J. Wells Corporation was wealthy enough to survive even without the full-time services of Dixon Wells, or should I say even with them? Anyway, I'm sure my father preferred to have me late in the morning after an evening with van Manderpootz than after one with Tips Alva or Whimsy White, or one of the numerous others of the ladies of the 'vision screen. Even in the twenty-first century he retained a lot of old-fashioned ideas.

Van Manderpootz had ceased to remember that he was as modest and shrinking as a violet. "It has just occurred to me," he announced impressively, "that years have character much as humans have. This year, 2015, will be remembered in history as a very stupid year, in which the Morell prize was given to a nincompoop. Last year, on the other hand, was a very intelligent year, a jewel in the crown of civilization. Not only was the Morell prize given to van Manderpootz, but I announced my discrete field theory in that year, and the University unveiled Gogli's statue of me as well." He sighed. "Yes, a very intelligent year! What do you think?"

"It depends on how you look at it," I responded glumly. "I didn't enjoy it so much, what with Joanna Caldwell and Denise d'Agrion, and your infernal experiments. It's all in the point of view."

The professor snorted. "Infernal experiments, eh! Point of view! Of course it's all in the point of view. Even Einstein's simple little synthesis was enough to prove that. If the whole world could adopt an intelligent and admirable point of view—that of van Mander-pootz, for instance—all troubles would be over. If it were possible—" He paused, and an expression of amazed wonder spread over his ruddy face.

"What's the matter?" I asked.

"Matter? I am astonished! The astounding depths of genius awe me. I am overwhelmed with admiration at the incalculable mysteries of a great mind."

"I don't get the drift."

"Dixon," he said impressively, "you have been privileged to look upon an example of the workings of a genius. More than that, you have planted the seed from which perhaps shall grow the towering tree of thought. Incredible as it seems, you, Dixon Wells, have given van Manderpootz an idea! It is thus that genius seizes upon the small, the unimportant, the negligible, and turns it to its own grand purposes. I stand awe-struck!"

"But what—?"

"Wait," said van Manderpootz, still in rapt admiration of the majesty of his own mind. "When the tree bears fruit, you shall see it. Until then, be satisfied that you have played a part in its planting."

It was perhaps a month before I saw van Manderpootz again, but one bright spring evening his broad, rubicund face looked out of the phone-screen at me.

"It's ready," he announced impressively.

"What is?"

The professor looked pained at the thought that I could have forgotten. "The tree has borne fruit," he explained. "If you wish to drop over to my quarters, we'll proceed to the laboratory and try it out. I do not set a time, so that it will be utterly impossible for you to be late."

I ignored that last dig, but had a time been set, I would doubtless have been even later than usual, for it was with some misgivings that I induced myself to go at all. I still remembered the unpleasantness of my last two experiences with the inventions of van Manderpootz. However, at last we were seated in the small laboratory, while out in the larger one the professor's technical assistant, Carter, puttered over some device, and in the far corner his secretary, the plain and unattractive Miss Fitch, transcribed lecture notes, for van Manderpootz abhorred the thought that his golden utterances might be lost to posterity. On the table between the professor and myself lay a curious device, something that looked like a cross between a pair of nose-glasses and a miner's lamp.

"There it is," said van Manderpootz proudly. "There lies my attitudinizor, which may well become an epoch-making device."

"How? What does it do?"

"I will explain. The germ of the idea traces back to that remark of yours about everything depending on the point of view. A very obvious statement, of course, but genius seizes on the obvious and draws from it the obscure. Thus the thoughts of even the simplest mind can suggest to the man of genius his sublime conceptions, as is evident from the fact that I got this idea from you."

"What idea?"

"Be patient. There is much you must understand first. You must realize just bow true is the statement that everything depends on the point of view. Einstein proved that motion, space, and time depend on the particular point of view of the observer, or as he expressed it, on the scale of reference used. I go farther than that, infinitely farther. I propound the theory that the observer is the point of view. I go even beyond that, I maintain that the world itself is merely the point of view!"

"Huh?"

"Look here," proceeded van Manderpootz. "It is obvious that the world I see is entirely different from the one in which you live. It is equally obvious that a strictly religious man occupies a different world than that of a materialist. The fortunate man lives in a happy world; the unfortunate man sees a world of misery. One man is happy with little, another is miserable with much. Each sees the world from his own point of view, which is the same as saying that each lives in his own world. Therefore there are as many worlds as there are points of view.

"But," I objected, "that theory is to disregard reality. Out of all the different points of view, there must be one that is right, and all the rest are wrong."

"One would think so," agreed the professor. "One would think that between the point of view of you, for instance, as contrasted with that of, say van Manderpootz, there would be small doubt as to which was correct. However, early in the twentieth century, Heisenberg enunciated his Principle of Uncertainty, which proved beyond argument that a completely accurate scientific picture of the world is quite impossible, that the law of cause and effect is merely a phase of the law of chance, that no infallible predictions can ever be made, and that what science used to call natural laws arc really only descriptions of the way in which the human mind perceives nature. In other words, the character of the world depends entirely on the mind observing it, or, to return to my earlier statement-the point of view."

"But no one can ever really understand another person's point of view," I said. "It isn't fair to undermine the whole basis of science because you can't be sure that the color we both call red wouldn't look green to you if you could see it through my eyes."

"Ah!" said van Manderpootz triumphantly. "So we come now to my attitudinizor. Suppose that it were possible for me to see through your eyes, or you through mine. Do you see what a boon such an ability would be to humanity? Not only from the standpoint of science, but also because it would obviate all troubles due to mis-understandings. And even more." Shaking his finger, the professor recited oracularly, "'Oh, wad some pow'r the giftie gie us to see oursel's as ithers see us.' Van Manderpootz is that power, Dixon. Through my attitudinizor, one may at last adopt the viewpoint of another. The poet's plaint of more than two centuries ago is an-swered at last."

"How the devil do you see through somebody else's eyes?"

"Very simply. You will recall the idealizator. Now it is obvi-ous that when I peered over your shoulder and perceived in the mirror your conception of the ideal woman, I was, to a certain extent, adopting your point of view. In that case the psychons given off by your mind were converted into quanta of visible light, which could be seen. In the case of my attitudinizor, the proc-ess is exactly reversed. One flashes the beam of this light on the subject whose point of view is desired; the visible light is reflected back with a certain accompaniment of psychons, which are here intensified to a degree which will permit them to be, so to speak, appreciated?"

"Psychons?"

"Have you already forgotten my discovery of the unit particle of thought? Must I explain again how the cosmons, chronons, spations, psychons, and all other particles are interchangeable? And that," he continued abstractedly, "leads to certain interesting speculations. Suppose I were to convert, say, a ton of material protons and electrons into spations—that is, convert matter into space. I calculate that a ton of matter will produce approximately a cubic mile of space. Now the question is, where would we put it, since all the space we have is already occupied by space? Or if I manufactured an hour or two of time? It is obvious that we have no time to fit in an extra couple of hours, since all our time is already accounted for. Doubtless it will take a certain amount of thought for even van Manderpootz to solve these problems, but at the moment I am curious to watch the workings of the attitudinizor. Suppose you put it on, Dixon."

"I? Haven't you tried it out yet?"

"Of course not. In the first place, what has van Manderpootz to gain by studying the viewpoints of other people? The object of the device is to permit people to study nobler viewpoints than their own. And in the second place, I have asked myself whether it is fair to the world for van Manderpootz to be the first to try out a new and possibly untrustworthy device, and I reply, 'No!'"

"But I should try it out, eh? Well, every time I try out any of your inventions I find myself in some kind of trouble. I'd be a fool to go around looking for more difficulty, wouldn't I?"

"I assure you that my viewpoint will be much less apt to get you into trouble than your own," said van Manderpootz with dignity. "There will be no question of your becoming involved in some impossible love affair as long as you stick to that."

Nevertheless, despite the assurance of the great scientist, I was more than a little reluctant to don the device. Yet I was curious, as well; it seemed a fascinating prospect to be able to look at the world through other eyes, as fascinating as visiting a new world–which it was, according to the professor. So after a few moments of hesitation, I picked up the instrument, slipped it over my head so that the eyeglasses were in the proper position, and looked inquiringly at van Manderpootz.

"You must turn it on," he said, reaching over and clicking a switch on the frame. "Now flash the light to my face. That's the way; just center the circle of light on my face. And now what do you see?"

I didn't answer; what I saw was, for the moment, quite indescribable. I was completely dazed and bewildered, and it was only when some involuntary movement of my head at last flashed the light from the professor's face to the table top that a measure of sanity returned, which proves at least that tables do not possess any point of view.

"O-o-o-h!" I gasped.

Van Manderpootz beamed. "Of course you are overwhelmed. One could hardly expect to adopt the view of van Manderpootz without some difficulties of adjustment. A second time will be easier."

I reached up and switched off the light. "A second time will not only be easier, but also impossible," I said crossly. "I'm not going to experience another dizzy spell like that for anybody."

"But of course you will, Dixon. I am certain that the dizziness will be negligible on the second trial. Naturally the unexpected heights affected you, much as if you were to come without warning to the brink of a colossal precipice. But this time you will be prepared, and the effect will be much less."

Well, it was. After a few moments I was able to give my full attention to the phenomena of the attitudinizor, and queer phenomena they were, too. I scarcely know how to describe the sensation of looking at the world through the filter of another's mind. It is almost an indescribable experience, but so, in the ultimate analysis, is any other experience.

What I saw first was a kaleidoscopic array of colors and shapes, but the amazing, astounding, inconceivable thing about the scene was that there was no single color I could recognize! The eyes of van Manderpootz, or perhaps his brain, interpreted color in a fashion utterly alien to the way in which my own functioned, and the resultant spectrum was so bizarre that there is simply no way of describing any single tint in words. To say, as I did to the professor, that his conception of red looked to me like a shade between purple and green conveys absolutely no meaning, and the only way a third person could appreciate the meaning would be to examine my point of view through an attitudinizor while I was examining that of van Manderpootz. Thus he could apprehend my conception of van Manderpootz's reaction to the color red.

And shapes! It took me several minutes to identify the weird, angular, twisted, distorted appearance in the center of the room as the plain laboratory table. The room itself, aside from its queer form, looked smaller, perhaps because van Manderpootz is somewhat larger than I.

But by far the strangest part of his point of view had nothing to do with the outlook upon the physical world, but with the more fundamental elements—with his *attitudes*. Most of his thoughts, on that first occasion, were beyond me, because I had not yet learned to interpret the personal symbolism in which he thought. But I did understand his attitudes. There was Carter, for instance, toiling away out in the large laboratory; I saw at once what a plodding, unintelligent drudge he seemed to van Manderpootz. And there was Miss Fitch; I confess that she had always seemed unattractive to me, but my impression of her was Venus herself beside that of the professor! She hardly seemed human to him and I am sure that he never thought of her as a woman, but merely as a piece of convenient but unimportant laboratory equipment.

At this point I caught a glimpse of myself through the eyes of van Manderpootz. Ouch! Perhaps I'm not a genius, but I'm dead certain that I'm not the grinning ape I appeared to be in his eyes. And perhaps I'm not exactly the handsomest man in the world either, but if I thought I looked like that—! And then, to cap the climax, I apprehended van Manderpootz's conception of himself!

"That's enough!" I yelled. "I won't stay around here just to be insulted. I'm through!"

I tore the attitudinizor from my head and tossed it to the table, feeling suddenly a little foolish at the sight of the grin on the face of the professor.

"That is hardly the spirit which has led science to its great achievements, Dixon," he observed amiably. "Suppose you describe the nature of the insults, and if possible, something about the workings of the attitudinizor as well. After all, that is what you were supposed to be observing."

I flushed, grumbled a little, and complied. Van Manderpootz listened with great interest to my description of the difference in our physical worlds, especially the variations in our perceptions of form and color.

"What a field for an artist!" he ejaculated at last. "Unfortunately, it is a field that must remain forever untapped, because even though an artist examined a thousand viewpoints and learned innumerable new colors, his pigments would continue to impress his audience with the same old colors each of them had always known." He sighed thoughtfully, and then proceeded. "However, the device is apparently quite safe to use. I shall therefore try it briefly, bringing to the investigation a calm, scientific mind which refuses to be troubled by the trifles that seem to bother you."

He donned the attitudinizor, and I must confess that he stood the shock of the first trial somewhat better than I did. After a surprised "Oof!" he settled down to a complacent analysis of my point of view, while I sat somewhat self-consciously under his calm appraisal. Calm, that is, for about three minutes.

Suddenly he leaped to his feet, tearing the device from a face whose normal ruddiness had deepened to a choleric angry color. "Get out!" he roared. "So that's the way van Manderpootz looks to you! Moron! Idiot! Imbecile! Get out!"

It was a week or ten days later that I happened to be passing the University on my way from somewhere to somewhere else, and I fell to wondering whether the professor had yet forgiven me. There was a light in the window of his laboratory over in the Physics Building, so I dropped in, making my way past the desk where Carter labored, and the corner where Miss Fitch sat in dull primness at her endless task of transcribing lecture notes.

Van Manderpootz greeted me cordially enough, but with a curious assumption of melancholy in his manner. "Ah, Dixon," he began, "I am glad to see you. Since our last meeting, I have learned much of the stupidity of the world, and it appears to me now that you are actually one of the more intelligent contemporary minds."

This from van Manderpootz! "Why—thank you," I said.

"It is true. For some days I have sat at the window overlooking the street there, and have observed the viewpoints of the passersby. Would you believe"—his voice lowered—"would you believe that only seven and four-tenths percent are even aware of the existence of van Manderpootz? And doubtless many of the few that are, come from among the students in the neighborhood. I knew that the average level of intelligence was low, but it had not occurred to me that it was as low as that."

"After all," I said consolingly, "you must remember that the achievements of van Manderpootz are such as to attract the attention of the intelligent few rather than of the many."

"A very silly paradox!" be snapped. "On the basis of that theory, since the higher one goes in the scale of intelligence, the fewer individuals one finds, the greatest achievement of all is one that nobody has heard of. By that test you would be greater than van Manderpootz, an obvious *reductio ad absurdum*."

He glared his reproof that I should even have thought of the point, then something in the outer laboratory caught his ever-observant eye.

"Carter!" he roared. "Is that a synobasical interpbasometer in the positronic flow? Fool! What sort of measurements do you expect to make when your measuring instrument itself is part of the experiment? Take it out and start over!"

He rushed away toward the unfortunate technician. I settled idly back in my chair and stared about the small laboratory, whose walls had seen so many marvels. The latest, the attitudinizor, lay carelessly on the table, dropped there by the professor after his analysis of the mass viewpoint of the pedestrians in the street below.

I picked up the device and fell to examining its construction. Of course this was utterly beyond me, for no ordinary engineer can hope to grasp the intricacies of a van Manderpootz concept. So, after a puzzled but admiring survey of its infinitely delicate wires and grids and lenses, I made the obvious move. I put it on.

My first thought was the street, but since the evening was well along, the walk below the window was deserted. Back in my chair again, I sat musing idly when a faint sound that was not the rumbling of the professor's voice attracted my attention. I identified it shortly as the buzzing of a heavy fly, butting its head stupidly against the pane of glass that separated the small laboratory from the large room beyond. I wondered casually what the viewpoint of a fly was like, and ended by flashing the light on the creature.

For some moments I saw nothing other than I had been seeing right along from my own personal point of view, because, as van Manderpootz explained later, the psychons from the miserable brain of a fly are too few to produce any but the vaguest of impressions. But gradually I became aware of a picture, a queer and indescribable scene.

Flies are color-blind. That was my first impression, for the world was a dull panorama of greys and whites and blacks. Flies are extremely nearsighted; when I had finally identified the scene as the interior of the familiar room, I discovered that it seemed enormous to the insect, whose vision did not extend more than six feet, though it did take in almost a complete sphere, so that the creature could see practically in all directions at once. But perhaps the most astonishing thing, though I did not think of it until later, was that the compound eye of the insect, did not convey to it the impression of a vast number of separate pictures, such as the eye produces when a microphotograph is taken through it. The fly sees one picture just as we do; in the same way as our brain rights the upside-down image cast on our retina, the fly's brain reduces the compound image to one. And beyond these impressions were a wild hodgepodge of smell-sensations, and a strange desire to burst through the invisible glass barrier into the brighter light beyond. But I had no time to analyze these sensations, for suddenly there was a flash of something infinitely clearer than the dim cerebrations of a fly.

For half a minute or longer I was unable to guess what that momentary flash had been. I knew that I had seen something incredibly lovely, that I had tapped a viewpoint that looked upon something whose very presence caused ecstacy, but whose viewpoint it was, or what that flicker of beauty had been, were questions beyond my ability to answer.

I slipped off the attitudinizor and sat staring perplexedly at the buzzing fly on the pane of glass. Out in the other room van Manderpootz continued his harangue to the repentant Carter, and off in a corner invisible from my position I could hear the rustle of papers as Miss Fitch transcribed endless notes. I puzzled vainly over the problem of what had happened, and then the solution dawned on me.

The fly must have buzzed between me and one of the occupants of the outer laboratory. I had been following its flight with the faintly visible beam of the attitudinizor's light, and that beam must have flickered momentarily on the head of one of the three beyond the glass. But which? Van Manderpootz himself? It must have been either the professor or Carter, since the secretary was quite beyond range of the light.

It seemed improbable that the cold and brilliant mind of van Manderpootz could be the agency of the sort of emotional ecstasy I had sensed. It must therefore, have been the head of the mild and inoffensive little Carter that the beam had tapped. With a feeling of curiosity I slipped the device back on my own head and sent the beam sweeping dimly into the larger room.

It did not at the time occur to me that such a procedure was quite as discreditable as eavesdropping, or even more dishonorable, if you come right down to it, because it meant the theft of far more personal information than one could ever convey by the spoken word. But all I considered at the moment was my own curiosity; I wanted to learn what sort of viewpoint could produce that strange, instantaneous flash of beauty. If the proceeding was unethical—well, Heaven knows I was punished for it.

So I turned the attitudinizor on Carter. At the moment, be was listening respectfully to van Manderpootz, and I sensed clearly his respect for the great man, a respect that had in it a distinct element of fear. I could hear Carter's impression of the booming voice of the professor, sounding somewhat like the modulated thunder of a god, which was not far from the little man's actual opinion of his master. I perceived Carter's opinion of himself, and his self-picture was an even more mouselike portrayal than my own impression of him. When, for an instant, he glanced my way, I sensed his impression of me, and while I'm sure that Dixon Wells is not the imbecile he appears to van Manderpootz, I'm equally sure that he's not the debonair man of the world be seemed to Carter. All in all, Carter's point of view seemed that of a timid, inoffensive, retiring, servile little man, and I wondered all the more what could have caused that vanished flash of beauty in a mind like his.

There was no trace of it now. His attention was completely taken up by the voice of van Manderpootz, who had passed from a personal appraisal of Carter's stupidity to a general lecture on the fallacies of the unified field theory as presented by his rivals Corveille and Shrimski. Carter was listening with an almost worshipful regard, and I could feel his surges of indignation against the villains who dared to disagree with the authority of van Manderpootz.

I sat there intent on the strange double vision of the attitudinizor, which was in some respects like a Horsten psychomat—that is, one is able to see both through his own eyes and through the eyes of his subject. Thus I could see van Manderpootz and Carter quite clearly, but at the same time I could see or sense what Carter saw and sensed. Thus I perceived suddenly through my own eyes that the professor had ceased talking to Carter, and had turned at the approach of somebody as yet invisible to me, while at the same time, through Carter's eyes, I saw that vision of ecstacy which had flashed for a moment in his mind. I saw—description is utterly impossible, but I saw a woman who, except possibly for the woman of the idealizator screen, was the most beautiful creature I had ever seen.

I say description is impossible. That is the literal truth for her coloring, her expression, her figure, as seen through Carter's eyes, were completely unlike anything expressible by words, was fascinated, I could do nothing but watch, and I felt a wild surge of jealousy as I caught the adoration in the attitude of the humble Carter. She was glorious, magnificent, indescribable. It was with an effort that I untangled myself from the web o fascination enough to catch Carter's thought of her name. "Lisa," he was thinking. "Lisa."

What she said to van Manderpootz was in tones too low for me to hear, and apparently too low for Carter's ears as well else I should have heard her words through the attitudinizor. But both of us heard van Manderpootz's bellow in answer.

"I don't care bow the dictionary pronounces the word!" he roared. "The way van Manderpootz pronounces a word is right!"

The glorious Lisa turned silently and vanished. For a few moments I watched her through Carter's eyes, but as she neared the laboratory door, he turned his attention again to van Manderpootz, and she was lost to my view.

And as I saw the professor close his dissertation and approach me, I slipped the attitudinizor from my head and forced myself to a measure of calm.

"Who is she?" I demanded. "I've got to meet her!"

He looked blankly at me. "Who's who?"

"Lisa! Who's Lisa?"

There was not a flicker in the cool blue eyes of van Mander-pootz. "I don't know any Lisa," be said indifferently.

"But you were just talking to her! Right out there!"

Van Manderpootz stared curiously at me; then little by little a shrewd suspicion seemed to dawn in his broad, intelligent features. "Hah!" he said. "Have you, by any chance, been using the attitu-dinizor?"

I nodded, chill apprehension gripping me.

"And is it also true that you chose to investigate the viewpoint of Carter out there?" At my nod, be stepped to the door that joined the two rooms, and closed it. When he faced me again, it was with features working into lines of amusement that suddenly found utter-ance in booming laughter. "Haw!" he roared. "Do you know who beautiful Lisa is? She's Fitch!"

"Fitch? You're mad! She's glorious, and Fitch is plain and scraw-ny and ugly. Do you think I'm a fool?"'

"You ask an embarrassing question," chuckled the professor. "Listen to me, Dixon. The woman you saw was my secretary, Miss Fitch seen through the eyes of Carter. Don't you understand? The idiot Carter's in love with her!"

I suppose I walked the upper levels half the night, oblivious alike of the narrow strip of stars that showed between the towering walls of twenty-first century New York, and the intermittent war of traf-fic from the freight levels. Certainly this was the worst predicament of all those into which the fiendish contraptions of the great van Manderpootz had thrust me.

In love with a point of view! In love with a woman who had no existence apart from the beglamoured eyes of Carter. It wasn't Lisa Fitch I loved; indeed, I rather hated her angular ugliness. What I had fallen in love with was the way she looked to Carter, for there is nothing in the world quite as beautiful as a lover's conception of his sweetheart.

This predicament was far worse than my former ones. When I had fallen in love with a girl already dead, I could console myself with the thought of what might have been. When I had fallen in love with my own ideal—well, at least she was mine, even if I couldn't have her. But to fall in love with another man's concep-tion! The only way that conception could even continue to exist was for Carter to remain in love with Lisa Fitch, which rather effectually left me outside the picture altogether. She was absolutely unattainable to me, for Heaven knows I didn't want the real Lisa Fitch—"real" meaning, of course, the one who was real to me. I suppose in the end Carter's Lisa Fitch was as real as the skinny scarecrow my eyes saw.

She was unattainable—or was she? Suddenly an echo of a long-forgotten psychology course recurred to me. Attitudes are habits. Viewpoints are attitudes. Therefore viewpoints are habits. And habits can be learned!

There was the solution! All I had to do was to learn, or to acquire by practice, the viewpoint of Carter. What I had to do was literally to put myself in his place, to look at things in his way, to see his viewpoint. For once I learned to do that, I could see in Lisa Fitch the very things he saw, and the vision would become reality to me as well as to him.

I planned carefully. I did not care to face the sarcasm of the great van Manderpootz; therefore I would work in secret. I would visit his laboratory at such times as he had classes or lectures, and I would use the attitudinizor to study the viewpoint of Carter, and to, as it were, practice that viewpoint. Thus I would have the means at hand of testing my progress, for all I had to do was glance at Miss Fitch without the attitudinizor. As soon as I began to perceive in her what Carter saw, I would know that success was imminent.

Those next two weeks were a strange interval of time. I haunted the laboratory of van Manderpootz at odd hours, having learned from the University office what periods he devoted to his courses. When one day I found the attitudinizor missing, I prevailed on Carter to show me where it was kept, and he, influenced doubtless by my friendship for the man he practically worshipped, indicated the place without question. But later I suspect that he began to doubt his wisdom in this, for I know he thought it very strange for me to sit for long periods staring at him; I caught all sorts of puzzled questions in his mind, though as I have said, these were hard for me to decipher until I began to learn Carter's personal system of symbolism by which he thought. But at least one man was pleased—my father, who took my absences from the office and neglect of business as signs of good health and spirits, and congratulated me warmly on the improvement.

But the experiment was beginning to work, I found myself sympathizing with Carter's viewpoint, and little by little the mad world in which he lived was becoming as logical as my own. I learned to recognize colors through his eyes; I learned to understand form and shape; most fundamental of all, I learned his values, his attitudes, his tastes. And these last were a little inconvenient at times, for on the several occasions when I supplemented my daily calls with visits to van Manderpootz in the evening, I found some difficulty in separating my own respectful regard for the great man from Carter's unreasoning worship, with the result that I was on the verge of blurting out the whole thing to him several times. And perhaps it was a guilty conscience, but I kept thinking that the shrewd blue eyes of the professor rested on me with a curiously suspicious expression all evening.

The thing was approaching its culmination. Now and then, when I looked at the angular ugliness of Miss Fitch, I began to catch glimpses of the same miraculous beauty that Carter found in her—glimpses only, but harbingers of success. Each day I arrived at the laboratory with increasing eagerness, for each day brought me nearer to the achievement I sought. That is, my eagerness increased until one day I arrived to find neither Carter nor Miss Fitch present, but van Manderpootz, who should have been delivering a lecture on indeterminism, very much in evidence.

"Uh—hello," I said weakly.

"Ump!" he responded, glaring at me. "So Carter was right, I see. Dixon, the abysmal stupidity of the human race continually astounds me with new evidence of its astronomical depths, but I believe this escapade of yours plumbs the uttermost regions of imbecility."

"M—my escapade?"

"Do you think you can escape the piercing eye of van Manderpootz? As soon as Carter told me you had been here in my absence, my mind leaped nimbly to the truth. But Carter's information was not even necessary, for half an eye was enough to detect the change in your attitude on these last few evening visits. So you've been trying to adopt Carter's viewpoint, eh? No doubt with the idea of ultimately depriving him of the charming Miss Fitch!"

"W—why."

"Listen to me, Dixon. We will disregard the ethics of the thing and look at it from a purely rational viewpoint, if a rational viewpoint is possible to anybody but van Manderpootz. Don't you realize that in order to attain Carter's attitude toward Fitch, you would have to adopt his entire viewpoint? Not," he added tersely, "that I think his point of view is greatly inferior to yours, but I happen to prefer the viewpoint of a donkey to that of a mouse. Your particular brand of stupidity is more agreeable to me than Carter's timid, weak, and subservient nature, and some day you will thank me for this. Was his impression of Fitch worth the sacrifice of your own personality?"

"I—I don't know."

"Well, whether it was or not, van Manderpootz has decided the matter in the wisest way. For it's too late now, Dixon. I have given them both a month's leave and sent them away—on a honeymoon. They left this morning."

LaVergne, TN USA
21 December 2009
167802LV00001B/166/A